Dress 2 Impress
A Jennifer Cloud Novel

JANET LEIGH

ISBN-13: 9781518808753
ISBN-10: 1518808751
Library of Congress Control Number: 2015919023
CreateSpace Independent Publishing Platform
North Charleston, South Carolina

For my two awesome beta readers,
Linda Bryant and Julie Wiebersch.

Prologue

Shoes are like men; you can pass by several pairs, knowing they are not right for you. You can tell by looking at them that the fit will be wrong. Then you see a pair that just catches your eye, and you know you will look fabulous together. The shoes are expensive, but you go for them anyway. In reality, after you wear them one time, they kill your feet; you know you will wear them only on very special occasions.

Then there are the shoes that fit great, go with almost every outfit, and everyone gives you compliments when you wear them. But after wearing them for a while, they leave a small blister, and you decide that these also should be worn for a short time, maybe for a vacation or a wedding.

Finally, there is the shoe that fits like a glove, comfortable. You can wear them anywhere, but they don't always match your outfit. You love these shoes, but sometimes you wish they treated you more like your fancy shoes, making you feel special, sexy. Just when you are ready to throw out the fancy shoes and wear the comfortable ones forever, you notice a small rip in the seam, and you realize your comfortable shoes also have faults. So you just say, "What the hell," and go barefoot.

Chapter 1

Scotland 1602

I was sitting with my forehead resting on my knees, cursing Caiyan for leaving me here alone. My body ached from two days of riding on horseback around the Scottish countryside, looking for our mark. The mud oozed around me, stuck to my tartan skirt, and slipped inside my loafers. The icy rain drizzled down around me, and I wondered how much longer we were going to lie in this pigpen, waiting on our bad guy to appear. *Damn him for leaving me here to wait.*

I moved deeper into my shelter and sighed, reminding myself that I, Jennifer Cloud, had chosen to be part of this. Well, I'd chosen to continue to be part of the WTF, or World Travel Federation. When I was eighteen, I discovered I had the gift of time travel. Apparently, I inherited some special gene that allows me to travel through time. Great-Aint Elma Jean Cloud left me her time machine. The WTF refers to it as my time vessel. I call it a smelly old outhouse that scares the crap out of me every time I travel in it. I smiled at the memory of the argument my parents always had about the word *aint*. My dad is from the backwoods of East Texas, and everyone down there has aints, not aunts, as my East Coast parochial school mom would have corrected.

The friendly and much-wrinkled face of Aint Elma flashed to my mind. The vision of the little old lady with eyes the color of a summer sky, clapping with excitement over my gift, surfaced from my memories. When I met her at the age of nine, I didn't understand what was in store for me. A warm tingle caressed the skin above my heart. I reached up to touch the other gift Aint Elma had left me—her key. A medallion made from moonstone hung from a dainty but inviolable titanium chain around my neck. The unique medallion lay flat on my chest, hidden under the high-necked blouse with the plaid buttons. Carved in the moonstone was a crescent moon surrounded by tiny blue diamonds that sparkled like they had been freshly polished. I could feel a slight hum from the key, almost as if it were alive. In order for my outhouse to take me back in time, I have to wear the key and say a magic word. Sometimes I feel like I fell out of a Disney story.

I pulled the wool coat closer, trying to keep the wind at my back. My hair was secured under an ugly brown toboggan that matched my equally ugly wool coat. But I could feel the tendrils of my blond hair brush against my neck as they made their escape from the cap. One of the rules of the WTF was no hair dye. This rule was just in case I was sent back to a time when hair dye was obsolete. I think that might be the Stone Age, in which case, the locals wouldn't give a hoot what color my hair was as long as they could grab it and drag me to their cave. I put my foot down about going back to the dishwater blond from my childhood and finally compromised on a Marilyn Monroe blond. No highlights, no lowlights. Other rules included no tattoos, no fake fingernails, no body piercings (too late for that one—I had my ears pierced when I was five), and above all no implants. A prior transporter was injured back in time, and the local doctors operated on her, revealing her breast implants. The doctors promptly removed them, and she remained under arrest until the WTF could rescue her and convince the authorities the "water balloons" were not some kind of secret smuggling device. Thankfully, I inherited my mom's slim hips and voluptuous bustline.

The rain was tap-dancing above me on the small troll bridge that provided my shelter. How much longer was I going to wait? I had my limits. Caiyan had disappeared into the twilight, telling me to, "*Wait here, lassie.*" I should have known the important question was "How long?" Instead, I just shook my head and smiled up into his gorgeous green eyes. The thoughts of last night's passion-filled frolic still embedded in my mind clouded my judgment. Caiyan is a defender. He works for the WTF and is sent back in time to capture the bad guys, or what the WTF calls brigands. I am a transporter. The defenders can't haul the bad guys around, so it's up to me to come back and transport any brigands that Caiyan may catch back to headquarters. I am also his backup. Well, at least his backup in training. Since I am new to the WTF, Caiyan had to pull a few strings to allow me to assist him on this mission.

Before I left on this assignment, I was given a history lesson by my boss, Jake, on seventeenth-century Scotland. Jake was my childhood friend, and we had history together. I was as surprised as he was when our paths met again after a long on-again, off-again love affair. He took a job with the CIA, and I discovered how to time travel. Mamma Bea used to say, "Things happen for a reason, sugarplum." Those things keep happening to me like flies drawn to a cow pie. The reasons remain unknown.

Jake speed-tutored me for this trip, even though he didn't want me to travel until I was better trained. He threw all the customs and rituals of the very poor to the upper elite at me like darts at a dartboard. If only I could have unscrewed my head and poured the information in like cake batter, I might have recollection of them. Right now, all the information was a jumbled mess. Maybe Jake was right; I needed more training. The main brigand Caiyan usually followed was a smarmy guy named Rogue. Our mission was to capture him and bring him into custody at the WTF. I had helped capture Rogue on our first adventure together, but sadly, he escaped.

Rogue is after the missing key, allegedly owned by Mary Stuart, the queen of Scots. Although she didn't have the gift—that we can prove—we have a picture of her wearing the key. It was one of the few oils painted of her while Queen Elizabeth I imprisoned her. Although they were cousins, we believe Queen Elizabeth I was in cahoots with Lord Byron Mafuso, a known brigand. Rumors say they were responsible for the death of Mary's second husband, Lord Darnley. Blown up...

Rogue knows she gave the key to her lady's maid for safekeeping before she was beheaded on drummed-up charges of betraying Queen Elizabeth I. The trail is lost there until we get to 1746, when the key appears in a painting around Flora MacDonald's neck.

The MacDonalds are known for having the gift. We assume she used the key to transport Charles Edward Stuart, better known as Bonnie Prince Charlie, to safety during the Scottish rebellion. Rogue has attempted many times to retrieve the key before it gets to Flora.

There is some confusion as to what happens to the key after that, but Caiyan assures me the key is safe, and we need to keep it that way.

⁓

The boggy scent of decaying vegetation rose up from the river bottoms. Huge naked trees hugged the sides of the riverbank and extended their branches like skeletal hands intertwined in prayer. I sighed as a small mud-covered frog leaped over my loafer. Jeez, the inhabitants of the river that ran under the bridge were starting to come after me. What was probably a beautiful babbling brook in the summer had turned into a raging river in November. The water below me swooshed and churned as I watched a tree branch float by at maximum velocity. I pulled tight on my coat and carefully exited my hidey-hole into the cool rain.

"Going somewhere, lassie?" Caiyan asked from above me. He was leaning casually on the railing of the bridge, staring down at me. Water dripped from the brim of his hat and cascaded down the shoulders of his black riding coat.

"How long have you been up there?"

"Only a minute. I rode back toward the village, and I saw Rogue stop at the inn."

"So is he coming?"

"Aye, I think Rogue will come this way after he has rested a bit. It's not an easy journey to cross the Minch by boat this time of year. He is most likely tired and hungry, but he knows he is out of time."

The rain had slowed to a light sprinkle and tickled as it hit my face. I scrunched my nose as I looked up at him. His silhouette was dark against the full moon over his left shoulder. A murky gray sky had hidden the sun all day, and the remaining light was waiting for the night to pull its cover over her.

"We should get under the bridge. It may be an hour or more before he passes here."

I grumbled at the thought but crawled back into the alcove. My feet squished in the mud as I moved over to allow Caiyan room in the space.

"Are ye cold?" He moved closer and drew me into his arms. It is impossible to carry anything with us when we go back in time. Money, food, and weapons are all things we have to acquire once we travel. We have the clothes on our backs and the keys around our necks. The only place items can be smuggled from present day is in our mouths. Before he met me, Caiyan would sneak condoms on his travels, in case he needed to sacrifice his body for the greater good. This random act of kindness would not have met with approval from our superiors. If the boss found out we'd brought an item from the present back in time, he would ground us. This meant our key would be locked up, and we could not lateral travel, which is the best perk about having this gift. I can go anywhere, anytime in the present, in the blink of an eye. I can also carry things in my pockets like money and cell phones. Last weekend I was in Paris buying *macarons* at Ladurée and dining at Le Soufflé.

"What's wrong?" he asked, removing his hat and placing it on the ground next to him.

"Nothing," I said.

"Ye huffed."

"No, I didn't."

"Aye, ye did."

Maybe I did. "I'm tired and cold and wet. Why can't we just go catch Rogue in a dry place?"

"Aye, today is *dreich*. Fetching the bad guys is not always done under sunny skies." I arched an eyebrow at him, and he snuggled in closer to me.

"Did your contact tell you this is the best place to get him before he gets the key?" I asked with a hint of sarcasm.

The last time we had to catch a brigand, Caiyan's contact was his past lover. She looked like she belonged on the cover of a fashion magazine, with a body like Jennifer Lopez and hair like spun silk. I knew that even if there was a contact, he wasn't going to divulge that information. Last time I found out by accident, actually by spying on him, but that's beside the point.

"No contact this time, lass." His face was inches from mine, and his green eyes seemed to glow in the shadows of the troll bridge. "I'm afraid we have to sit and wait this one out," he said, moving closer. He started to run his nose up the inside of my neck. Hot flashes nipped at my jaw and ran straight to my boy howdy. I turned my head and pressed my lips gently to his. A muffled, "Jeez," rumbled from deep inside his throat, and he kissed me hard. I intertwined my fingers through the back of his thick, dark hair. He moved slightly and ran his hand up my thigh and under my skirt. I was working the buttons on his wool coat when the sound of horse hooves beat overhead.

"*Shite!*" He scrambled from under the bridge. I made it out just in time to see Caiyan run up the hill and take a flying leap onto the back of Rogue's unsuspecting horse. The horse reared up and threw both men to the ground. I recognized Rogue from our previous meeting, when I was eighteen and had time traveled by mistake. Our first encounter was from a distance, so I was surprised when he spoke with a strong Russian accent.

"Not this time, McGregor. You are not getting me before I git that key."

"I am afraid so, my friend. Ye cannae have what doesn't belong to ye."

"You are no friend of mine, Scottish bastard." Rogue lunged at Caiyan, grabbing him around the middle. He was shorter than

Caiyan but quite stocky, and his bulk knocked Caiyan off his feet and to the ground. Fists were flying, kilts were ripping, and curses were being yelled out in five languages. One loud crack and Caiyan was knocked out cold. Rogue pushed himself to his feet with a satisfied smile on his face. His knuckles were oozing blood, and he was rubbing his hand. I panicked and ran forward to help Caiyan. Rogue's head snapped up, making me realize he hadn't seen me behind the crest of the hill.

He sneered at me. "What is this?"

I stopped and tried to channel the local accent. "I am a friend of Caiyan's. We just met in the Highlands."

"I think not." He walked toward me, cutting off my path to Caiyan.

"I know who you are, little lady." He pointed a stubby, bloody finger at me. "You are the transporter, and as you can see, I will not be going on a ride with you today. In fact, I am going to make sure you don't take anyone anywhere, ever again!" He closed in on me, and I turned to run, but there was nowhere to go except the river. He caught me at the top of the embankment. Grabbing the collar on the back of my coat, he threw me to the ground. I quickly got to my feet, and we struggled. I was trying to remember the lessons my boss and ex-boyfriend, Jake, had given me on self-defense, but the only thing I could recall was to make it count. I reared back and sent my knee straight up into his groin. He released me, and I fell backward, landing with a hard thud onto my butt. His face paled with shock, and a Russian profanity (I am sure of it) escaped as a whisper from between his lips. He curled into a ball, rolled head over ass down the hill, and plopped into the raging water. I saw his head surface as he went bobbing down the river and out of sight.

As I stood to climb up the knoll and check on Caiyan, my shoes slipped on the muddy surface, and I began sliding down toward the river. My arms flailed in the air, and as I started my descent, a firm hand grabbed around my wrist, pulling me to safety.

"Now where do ye think ye are going, lassie?" Caiyan, thank God. He dragged me to the top of the hill, and we both collapsed, faces to the sky, panting from the physical effort. My adrenaline spike wore off, and the aftershock caused my entire body to shiver. He wrapped his arms around me until I settled.

"Are you hurt?" I asked him, trying to check his face for cuts in the dimming light.

"I think I might have broken a finger or two, but I'm used to the battle scars."

"We didn't get Rogue," I said, thankful that it was now too dark to see the disappointment in his eyes.

"Nay, but he will remember ye fer the next few days while he's icing his manhood." He chuckled and stood up, holding out his uninjured hand to help me to my feet. "We should go. Call your vessel."

"Don't you think we should try to track him? What if he comes back and takes the key?"

"The way that river is moving, I would say he will be lucky if he gets out before he hits the Atlantic Ocean. Besides, we dinnae have much time left."

I agreed with that. We only had about three to five days of the full-moon cycle before we had to return, and we had already spent a day in England and two days on horseback trekking around looking for the smarmy bastard. I didn't want to take any chances of getting stuck in the past because we missed our window of time. We stood in a clearing about thirty feet from the troll bridge, and I summoned my vessel. There was a crack of thunder, and presto, my outhouse appeared about ten feet in front of us. Weathered gray wood stood tall like a soldier waiting for the next assignment. The symbol of my key was carved above the door. A few seconds later, Caiyan's bright-red phone booth materialized next to my vessel.

"Don't you want to ride with me again?" I asked.

"Darlin'," he said, mocking my Texas accent, "I have seen you drive."

"Fine, you go first," I told him.

"Are ye afraid to face the boss man alone?" Caiyan asked, raising a dark eyebrow and crossing his arms over his chest.

"I just want to make sure you aren't going to stay behind for another shot at Rogue."

"I wouldnae dream of having all that fun without ye."

"OK, let's go at the same time."

A wisp of wind blew a stray lock of my hair across my face. Caiyan reached out and tucked it into my cap. His eyes stayed on mine, and I felt the long stare of contemplation piercing the back of my mind.

Caiyan leaned forward and kissed me good-bye. I entered my vessel and watched him enter his. I gave him a finger wave and sat there for a minute, going through the events of the past three days and trying to decide what to tell Jake.

Chapter 2

Three days earlier

We followed Rogue to London, 1602. The WTF is certain Rogue is trying to get the key to Lord Mafuso before Queen Elizabeth kicks the bucket in March of 1603. After that, Mary Stuart's son becomes king and Lord Mafuso loses his head.

Caiyan and I were to land at the estate of Lord Bryant. He was hosting a ball for his niece, Lady Sarah. The estate grounds were quite substantial and offered us cover for landing. After a rocky ride, I landed with a big thump. Our vessel chooses the clothing for our journey, making it impossible to tell we are not from this time. Mine had me in some kind of frilly mess. I had material pushed up against my face, confining me against the back of the outhouse. A large collar of lace ringed my neck and scratched at my face.

I heard Caiyan wrench my vessel door open, and the cool air swept into my outhouse like a winter gale.

"Lass, are ye OK?"

"Get me out of here. I'm suffocating." I gestured to the mounds of silk and lace. "What is all this?"

Caiyan pulled the large hoopskirt down, and I saw his face for the first time since our landing. I gasped. His dark wavy hair was pulled back tight against his head. Long sideburns framed his face, and he had a ponytail. I was certain that when we left, his hair only grazed the neck of his shirt. A fancy handkerchief collar covered his key. Caiyan pulled me out, and I surveyed the outcome of our dress change.

"Looks like we're going to a ball," he said, looking down at his pantaloons. His green velvet evening jacket fit like a glove and only enhanced the color of his eyes.

I, on the other hand, was all hoopskirts, lace, and satin from neck to toes. I had long gloves that stopped at the elbow. My dress had a keyhole bodice that displayed my milky-white cleavage. I felt like a be-jeweled Scarlet O'Hara.

Caiyan's eyes roamed the length of my dress and stopped at the keyhole.

"Ye look perfect."

I felt a steady stream of anxiety start in the pit of my stomach and head straight for my heart. The reality of pretending to be a seventeenth-century lady of the courts gave me chills. Caiyan pulled me to him as our vessels disappeared into the night. He was warm, and his familiar smell of piney woods and cinnamon wrapped around me like an invisible cloak, disguising all my insecurities. He looked down at me and tucked a stray hair behind my ear. My lower half caught fire. I don't know why that simple gesture always made my heart flip. It was the first thing he did when we met—well, after he abducted me—and it still makes me go all gooey inside.

He smiled. "Don't look at me like that, lassie, or we'll have to see what ye have on under that dress."

I rolled my eyes because I was pretty sure I was commando under all this fluff.

The night had begun to make its appearance, and walking in the wooded part of the estate created a challenge for me in my ball gown. Caiyan had to stop and untangle me from the underbrush as we made our way to the edge of the main grounds. Scents of moist soil and fresh-ly trimmed greenery met us as we drew closer to the well-manicured gardens. Torches lit the walkway, several people were scattered about around a large fountain, and bits of conversation floated our way. We stuck close to the shadows until we could ease into the scene without being noticed. Caiyan offered his arm, and I rested my gloved hand in the crook of his elbow. We strolled around the garden, gazing at the full moon like the other guests.

"Is that your real hair?" I asked, tugging on his ponytail.

"Aye, sometimes the vessel gives me hair that fits with the time. The last time I was in 1985, it gave me hair like Dee Snider from Twisted Sister. Ye should have seen me trying to tame that beast."

I couldn't help but laugh at the picture he painted. We rounded a corner and saw a group of men standing next to a statue of a lion. One of the men was flailing his arms in animated conversation, and the others were laughing. The man at the center of the conversation excused himself from the group and walked toward us. As he approached, I could tell by his stature that he was a man of importance, with dark hair that had started to gray at the temples. He wore a black waistcoat, and unlike Caiyan's fuller pantaloons, his trousers were long. He was walking with his head high and shoulders back in spite of his hand-carved cane.

"Let me do the talking, aye?" Caiyan ordered, but he added his Scottish rhetorical gab of a question at the end to make me feel like I had a say in the matter.

"I am Lord Bryant. Have I the pleasure of your names?"

"Yes, I am Lord Caiyan McGregor; this is my sister, Lady Jennifer."

"Sister!" I spat out.

Caiyan raised a brow at me. We had orders to be husband and wife. The WTF thought it was wise to go in as a married couple. They felt we would be more easily accepted into upper society. Lord Richard Bryant III was our contact. He was a known traveler researched by the WTF. He was about sixty years old and had recently passed his key to his grandson, Lord Richard Bryant V.

Lord Bryant winked at me. "On occasion, I too have a sister I take to out-of-town functions."

"My sister is a little weary from our travels," Caiyan said.

Lord Bryant nodded his head in agreement. "How are you here at my party uninvited?"

"If I could have a word in private with you, my lord," Caiyan said as he peeled down the layers of his collar to reveal his key.

"Yes, let's do just that," Lord Bryant agreed, looking around suspiciously as if brigands were hiding in the bushes.

He escorted us to the main house. Guests looked at us questioningly as we passed, and two large men flanked us as we made our way to the main house. Lord Bryant had bodyguards. We entered through a side door and walked down a dark, narrow hall illuminated with candle sconces. Lord Bryant stopped outside a set of double doors, and one of the large men entered first, followed by Lord Bryant. I would call the room a study or office in my time. I overheard Lord Bryant refer to it as the drawing room. Dark wood paneled the walls, and several beautiful tapestries were hung on them like art at the Louvre. A long walnut desk was centered in the room under a two-tier chandelier, and a stone fireplace behind Lord Bryant's desk was lit, warming the room.

Lord Bryant turned as Caiyan and I entered behind him. The two men who had followed us into the house stood at attention outside the door. A male servant appeared and waited for Lord Bryant's command. Lord Bryant offered us something to drink, and Caiyan declined for both of us.

"That will be all." He gave the servant a head nod, and the man exited, closing the door behind him.

He pointed his cane at Caiyan's neck. "Let me see it again."

Caiyan obeyed and removed his lacy collar. The blazing sun etched in his moonstone lay flat against his chest. The diamonds that filled the sun's rays reflected the glow from the fire.

"I have never seen this one. Who are your people?" Lord Bryant examined the key with avid curiosity.

"Clan McGregor, before that Scandinavian, more precisely, Viking."

"Your travel year?" he asked.

"2015," Caiyan responded.

"Good God!" He placed a hand over his heart in disbelief. "What is it like three hundred years from now?"

"Crowded," I answered.

Lord Bryant raised both eyebrows.

"And the women often speak out of turn," Caiyan said, annoyed I was obviously still pouting about the "sister" thing. My inner voice told me to get a grip. I was here on a mission, and if Caiyan thought I should be his sister, then so be it. He had more experience in the field than me. My inner voice tucked her pencil behind her ear, and I wished she would wipe that satisfied smile off her face.

Caiyan nudged me with his elbow, bringing me back from my internal lecture, and I wondered if I had missed a question from Lord Bryant.

Lord Bryant laughed and asked, "How can I help you?"

After the whole out-of-turn thing, I let Caiyan do the explaining. "We are looking for a lady's maid who once served Mary Stuart."

"I know of the key, and I also know Mary didn't have the gift of travel." Lord Bryant put a finger to his lips.

"Aye, a brigand is after that key. We need to find this maiden before he does."

"I do not have anyone in my employ who has served Queen Mary, but some of London's elite are here tonight, and maybe she exists with them." He placed a finger on his chin. "I will introduce you as the son and daughter of my childhood friend."

⌒

*L*ord Bryant escorted us to the ballroom. A string quartet was playing in the corner of the room hidden by a lovely paneled screen, and a large number of people were dancing. The minuet, I think. There was no time for dancing lessons before our mission, so I hoped that Caiyan would keep me off the dance floor. I knew how to do the two-step, but the intricate moves of the seventeenth-century Baroque-style dancing were way out of my league.

As we entered the ballroom, the high-swept ceilings supported by the intricate Greek-inspired columns made me feel as if I had walked into a royal palace.

The women were dressed in a similar fashion to me. A group of ladies were engaged in a conversation to our left. A woman with hair Marie Antoinette would have been envious of immediately greeted Lord Bryant.

"Darling, who do I have the pleasure of meeting?"

"My dear, this is Lord McGregor and his sister Lady Jennifer of the Inverness McGregors." He waved a hand in presentation. "My wife, Lady Eleanor."

Her look of surprise indicated we were not on the guest list. "The son and daughter of a dear childhood friend of mine." He coughed into a balled-up fist. "I wasn't sure they would make the trip," Lord Bryant added.

"How wonderful of you to come all this way."

She offered her hand to Caiyan, and he kissed her gloved fingers. "Lord McGregor, is there a wife at your manor?"

"No, I am afraid I have not found the woman of my dreams."

I stiffened next to him. The last month of incredible sex must have slipped his mind.

"Come, let me introduce you to some of our young ladies."

Caiyan gave me the play-along face, and I gave him a smirk back. I watched as Lady Eleanor escorted him off, and a gaggle of girls swarmed around him.

As I was contemplating several ways to torture him later, I scoped out the situation. There was no sign of Rogue. Most of the attendees were young—sixteen to twenty, I would guess. There was a scatter-ing of people about my age, and then the chaperone age of about thirty-five and older.

Lord Bryant returned with a glass of wine.

"Thank you," I said, taking a sip.

Walking toward me was a nice-looking man with dark hair and a slim build.

"Lord Wadsworth," Lord Bryant greeted. "May I present Lady Jennifer McGregor."

He took my hand and kissed my gloved fingertips. The sound of "Lady McGregor" had a nice ring to it, and my inner voice was doodling it on her notebook. I mentally told her to grow up. At least I thought it was mentally, but then Lord Wadsworth turned to me and asked, "I beg your pardon?"

I was searching for an excuse when the male servant from earlier spoke abruptly behind me, startling me a little. He seemed always to be lurking about. "Lord Bryant, you are needed in the dining hall."

Lord Bryant stared at me for an instant, as if he wasn't sure if he should leave me alone. Finally, he nodded to his servant and left me alone with Lord Wadsworth.

We watched Caiyan waltz with a young woman on the dance floor as if he was born a seventeenth-century lord.

Lord Wadsworth saw me staring at Caiyan.

"He is my brother," I tried to explain.

"Your brother is a very good dancer," he said.

"Yes, he has always been very good at everything."

I might have said this a little too profoundly, because he looked at me.

"Would you care to dance, my lady?"

"I'm sorry, my lord, I am not swift on my feet." I was making an attempt at the verbiage of this time. Jake had me reading historical romance novels and working with a linguistics coach the week before to prepare for this trip. I had the accent down, but the dialect was much more difficult.

"Might I suggest a stroll out on the terrace?"

"Sure," I replied. Anything to get away from watching the debutantes drool over Caiyan.

I handed my glass to a servant standing near the exit, and we walked out onto the terrace.

"The gardens are lovely," I said, moving toward the edge of the veranda for a better view. The full moon cast a beautiful glow over the torch-lit gardens below.

"Not as lovely as you," he said, wrapping an arm around my waist.

I stepped away, causing his arm to drop from my waist. A cool breeze blew across the veranda and caused me to shiver.

"Are you cold?" he asked. "Let's walk closer to the building. It will provide shelter from the night's wind."

A small snicker escaped from me. *The night's wind.* I felt like I was one of the women in distress in the historical romance novels I'd read for research. He escorted me toward a lanai that ran next to the house and had open arches running down one side with stone benches about every third arch for couples to rest. The lanai was not as well lit as the veranda, and I felt Lord Wadsworth getting a bit close for my taste.

As I was about to suggest we go back inside, he pulled me into the shadows and his hand came up to grope my breast. He squeezed as if it was a summer melon, checking if it was ripe enough to be picked.

I gave a yelp in pain and slapped his arm away. "Lord Wadsworth, this is highly inappropriate."

He made a move to kiss me on the mouth.

"Lord Wadsworth, really, you must stop this immediately."

"I know you would like to kiss me," he said, making another go at it.

My huge skirt prevented me from doing my signature move, knee to the balls. I thought about screaming, but that might screw up our mission. My childhood mantra began playing in my head: *I'm spunky and I'm fierce and I'm smarter than most men. Bad guys run and hide 'cuz here comes SuperJen.*

I allowed him to go in for the kiss and bit him hard on the lip.

"You bitch!" he yelled as he pulled away. A drop of blood stained his bottom lip. He reached for a handkerchief and began blotting his lip. "I should strike you for that."

"Get away from me, you pervert." He looked confused at my words.

"Why, Lord Wadsworth, what young lady are you holding hostage out here on the terrace?" a voice asked from behind Lord Wadsworth.

He turned, revealing a woman about my age. She was very petite with a tall blond wig and a tiny waist.

"Lady Sarah. I was just instructing Lady Jennifer about the ways of the court." He waved his hankie at her. "Apparently, she has not been educated."

"Why, Lord Wadsworth, you seem to have bitten your lip. You should go see my mother. She has the perfect remedy to take the swelling down."

"Swelling?" He looked alarmed.

"Why yes, your lip looks about the size of a summer cherry."

He covered his mouth with his hankie and left us immediately.

"When a man asks you to walk on the terrace, it is an invitation for a little frivolous flirtation," the woman told me.

"I didn't know," I said.

"I am Lady Sarah. The niece of Lord Bryant."

"Thanks for saving me," I said. "Hey, aren't you the guest of honor?"

"Yes, my uncle sent me in search of you." She raised her eyebrows at my slang, and my inner self drew a slash under my mistakes column. I felt six feet tall next to her small frame. "He told me you are the daughter of a mate from his youth."

"Yes, from Scotland. My father was the Duke of Hamilton." I held my breath, hoping the title would not prove false. There were so many names to remember and so many heads cut off, I lost count. Jake had given me a bio, but I was supposed to be married to Lord McGregor because my father was a duke. In this time, the fathers usually arranged marriages based on social status. In other words, I was a good catch with a large dowry, so no questions would be asked about why Caiyan and I were wed. I was definitely the daughter of the Duke of Hamilton—or was it Hampton? Jeez.

She put a finger to her lips. "I haven't met the Duke of Hamilton, but I have heard he is a fine man. I didn't realize he had any children."

"Surely they haven't been keeping me a secret. Are you sure?"

"As sure as mayflies eat their young."

"Ewww." I couldn't help it.

She laughed. "Come with me, and I will introduce you to a few distinguished men of the court, and you can tell me all about your brother."

Oh boy.

Chapter 3

L ady Sarah was certainly a draw. Men were fetching us cider and begging for dances, which she fended off with the need to introduce me. I met so many people; my head was beginning to ache from all the names I was trying to remember. As I was talking with the other women, Caiyan would waltz by with a pretty starry-eyed girl gazing up at him. I don't think he ever left the dance floor. As soon as one song would end, another girl would be at his heels for a romp around the ballroom. Another of Sarah's admirers had presented me with a glass of cider. I excused myself from the conversation and found a settee. My feet were killing me, and I was trying to figure out how to sit down in the enormous dress. If I sat down, the hoop was going to bell upward, exposing the ballroom inhabitants to my lack of undergarments. Easy to pee, not to sit. I perched on the edge of a tufted stool and carefully tucked the hoop of my dress under my bottom. This created a sort of balance, and I was able to sit and drink my cider. Lady Sarah came over and sat down beside me with the grace of a professional hoopskirt wearer.

"Tell me about your brother," she said, placing her glass on the tray of a nearby servant.

"What's to tell," I said. "He's an annoying, arrogant man who cannot follow orders." *At least I didn't lie.*

"Is he in line for a dukedom?"

A dukedom? I had no idea what lineage I was supposed to follow. We were to be husband and wife. That way the questions would be directed at Lord McGregor, future Duke of Dumb. Since Caiyan was off gallivanting with the ladies, I had no choice but to deliberately spill my wine all over my dress.

"Oh my, I'm so clumsy," I said, jumping to my feet. Lady Sarah looked up at me, aghast, with her hand over her mouth.

"Accidents do happen," she said. A servant was already dabbing a linen cloth at my dress. Lady Sarah instructed the servant to take me upstairs to find her lady's maid and clean my dress.

I apologized and followed the man into the foyer and up two glorious flights of stairs. Tapestries hung in the alcoves, and the rugs felt as if I was walking on a pillow. He led me down a long hall adorned with gold-framed oil paintings of past Bryants. He stopped at a door and knocked. A short, sturdy woman who reminded me of my aunt Agnes answered the door. The man explained our situation, and she escorted me inside. The room was lavishly decorated. A large fireplace was to my right, and a small fire crackled gently in the hearth, adding warmth to the large room. Beyond an adjoining door, a huge four-poster bed stood in the center, draped with purple velvet.

The maid went to work on the bodice of my dress. After a bit of yanking and pulling, she removed the outer layer of clothing until I was down to the underskirts, corset, and hoop.

I turned around to face her. "My name is Lady Jennifer." I spoke because I felt if I was going to be half-naked in front of her, I should at least be on speaking terms.

She stood staring at me. Her eyes were wide and fearful. She stepped back a pace, and I followed her eyes to my chest. My key was visible. I automatically reached for it.

"Where di' ye git that?" she asked.

"It was a gift," I stuttered. Then a thought crossed my mind. Maybe this maid would know the whereabouts of the maid we were looking for. "Have you ever seen one before?"

She harrumphed at me and changed the subject. "I'm Mrs. Ogilvy. I am sure I can have yer gown cleaned quickly, Lady Jennifer."

I stood patiently on the padded floor as Mrs. Ogilvy brought out an exquisite royal-blue dressing gown. "This will keep ye warm while I clean yer gown." She went to work at the washbasin, scrubbing the dress with a small stone.

"There ye are, good as new." She squeezed out the water and hung the dress near the fire to dry. She told me she would be back shortly to help me dress. I wandered around Lady Sarah's room. Her dressing table held an ivory brush and comb set. A small round mirror lay next to the grooming set. I picked it up and caught a glimpse of myself. A wave of shock hit me as I saw my hair for the first time. I knew it was in some sort of updo, but I didn't realize it was rolled up like two giant strombolis on my forehead. How difficult it must have been for a woman of this time to check her appearance. She relied on her lady's maid or reflections from the looking glass, which was a distorted piece of metal hanging in a gaudy gold frame in the entry hall.

After a short time, the maid returned and began preparing me for the dress. She fluffed my layers of skirt and tightened the pillow behind my butt that made my ass look three times its normal size.

"Have you worked for Lady Sarah a long time?" I asked.

"No, I jest been her lady's maid fer two weeks. My daughter has been her lady's maid fer some time, but she is pregnant with her first bairn, and the doctor wanted her to stay in bed."

"Were you employed before here?" I asked.

The woman stopped what she was doing and gave me a careful study. "Aye, I was handmaiden to Queen Mary Stuart." Her chest puffed as she said the name.

My heart began to pump swiftly. Maybe this WAS the handmaiden?

"You mean, Mary, queen of Scots."

"Aye, 'tis sad she was taken to the stock at such a young age." The woman looked sad as she began tightening the bodice of the dress, and I regretted the large pepperoni pizza Caiyan and I had shared last night.

"Did you stay with her until the end?" I asked.

21

"Nay, she sent me away the day she was to be executed. I cried like a babe because she always treated me with such respect. Like one of her own instead of a servant." She drew in a quick breath, and with one hard yank she tied off the bodice. I knew if I took a deep breath my boobs would pop out the top, and we would have to start the whole process over.

"Now let's have a look at ye." She spun me around to face her. "Ye'll do."

I smiled at her, grateful for the help but unsure of how to approach the topic of the key.

"Mrs. Ogilvy, did the queen ever give you anything of value?"

She took two steps back from me. "What do ye mean?"

"Well, she was the rightful queen of England. I just thought she might have given you something special." I stammered a little. "You know, to remember her by."

"Aye, Queen Mary was a generous one. She gave me enough gold to get home to Inverness and start my family. Ye see, I had my eye on Mr. Ogilvy. He was a blacksmith in my hometown. As soon as I returned, he married me on the spot. Didn't want to let a good thing get away. Ye get me."

I laughed and realized I had seen this woman before. When I was eighteen and I traveled for my very first time to 1568. The year Mary, queen of Scots, escaped Loch Leven and rode through the Scottish countryside. I had seen the runaway queen when I met Caiyan. She was riding with two men and a handmaiden, a much younger Mrs. Ogilvy.

"I been at home raisin' my bairns until my husband died last year. My children are all grown now, and my eldest is married to her second cousin, who was one of the grooms who worked fer Mr. Bryant. They have both moved back to the family home, so they kin raise my first grandchild." She said this with pride and a little sorrow.

"Did Queen Mary ever give you any jewelry like the necklace I wear?" I asked. I knew I had to tread very carefully here. If she had the key, I didn't want to scare her into hiding.

She stood staring at me as if she might have seen a ghost. "Are ye asking me about the key?"

I breathed a sigh of relief. She knew.

"Yes!" I almost knocked her over with my burst of enthusiasm.

She began to unbutton her blouse and opened the neck to show me the key Rogue sought so desperately. It was a pale-blue moonstone engraved with an ocean wave. Tiny blue diamonds formed the crest of the wave. I moved closer to inspect the key.

"It's lovely," I said. "And Queen Mary gave it to you?"

She spoke slowly and with some trepidation about whether to tell me the story.

"It was mine, ye see. I gave it to Queen Mary fer good luck when we were leaving Scotland. My grandmother gave it to me. She told me it was a special key, but she didnae tell me what lock it opened. She said, 'Mary Margaret MacDonald Beaton, this is a key to a precious gift, and it should always remain in our family.'"

The name MacDonald rang a bell. This maid was a MacDonald, and it did indeed need to stay with this family.

"I knew I shoudnae have given it to the queen, but my grandmother told me it was magic, and I knew the queen needed help. I think it was the reason she lived as long as she did. I believe Lord Mafuso was in cahoots with Queen Elizabeth and wanted her executed right away."

"I think you did the right thing, but now more than ever you need to protect that key," I said.

She swiped at a loose hair that had come undone from her cap. "My grandmother told me the time would come when a member of our clan would work the key's magic, and I would know if the person was worthy."

I placed a hand on her arm. She didn't have the gift. "She was right, but there is a bad man looking for you. He wants the key." She started to take it off from around her neck, but I shook my head. "No, you need to give it to one of your grandchildren."

"How will I know?" she asked.

"When the grandchild reaches sixteen years, you will place it around the child's neck. If it begins to glow, the child has the gift." I decided sixteen was a safe age to tell Mrs. Ogilvy. A traveler could actually ly present much earlier than sixteen, but I figured if a sixteen-year-old could get a license to drive in my time, it was good enough for time travel as well. I wasn't sure about the vessel. My luxury mode of transportation was given to me with my key. Maybe Caiyan could shed some light on how to find the vessel for her.

She swallowed hard and nodded her head. "I am leaving fer home tomorrow. Lady Sarah is heading to the country estate and has a maid there. I was merely filling in."

"Good." I thought for a moment. "My brother and I will escort you. I am without a lady's maid, and we will need to go to Scotland tomorrow as well." I was pleased with my plan, but Mrs. Ogilvy looked a little out of sorts.

"My daughter's probably had the bairn by now, and she'll need me to help with the little angel." Her eyes lit up as she spoke of her new grandbaby and the task of returning home.

I returned to the ball as the music ended. I found Caiyan drinking a pint of ale with no less than five ladies dangling on his every word. Up front was Lady Sarah. I frowned. Prying off the ladies who would return home tonight was one thing, but having one staying in the very same house might be a different story.

"Brother," I said as I approached him. He looked up at me with a sheepish grin. "Could I have a word with you?"

"Maybe later, dear sister. As ye can see, I am completely occupied by these lovely ladies." He took a drink of his ale and licked his lips.

"It's about that piece of jewelry you were looking for yesterday." His head snapped up, and his eyes widened with curiosity.

"Oh, is it something rare?" asked one of the ladies.

"Absolutely," he said, disentangling himself from the lady on his left who was trying to ease her way into his lap. "Please excuse me, ladies."

A simultaneous sigh came from the group as he made his way over toward me.

"What in the hell do you think you're doing?" I asked with an artificial smile plastered across my face as the ladies watched our every move.

He gently steered me toward an alcove under the stairs. "I am questioning all the ladies at the ball about their lady's maids."

"Well, you can stop it, because I found her."

He looked at me in disbelief. "Where?"

"She's filling in for Lady Sarah's maid, who is having a baby." I crossed my arms over my chest, causing my breasts to bulge.

"Good work—and I like the dress." He was ogling the amount of cleavage spilling over the top of my neckline.

I crooked a smile at him. "You shouldn't look that way at your sister. People will talk."

His eyes turned hazy. "I think we should meet in my room so ye can fill me in on yer findings, and I can fill ye in—"

"There you are." Lady Sarah appeared, looping her arm through Caiyan's.

"Just having a few words with my sister over a misplaced piece of jewelry."

"Oh, I hope you find it." She smiled a beautiful smile. Many of the girls did not have pretty teeth. Most were stained from wine or poor grooming habits. There were no braces in this age, and overbites were considered a sign of beauty. Sarah had inherited a nice straight set of pearly whites. "What does it look like?"

"It's just an old piece of stone, nothing important." I shrugged.

"I'm sure it will turn up after all the guests have returned home. We always find bits of this and that the valet has to deliver the next day. Keeps him quite busy."

Lord Bryant appeared and explained the ladies would be leaving for the night, but the men would be gathering in the smoking room. He invited Caiyan to join them after he freshened up in his room. The head servant escorted us up two flights of stairs to my room, which was next door to Lady Sarah. She bid me good night with a peck on the cheek. Caiyan, however, got a full kiss right on the mouth. He looked as astonished as I did, and the head servant stood by, clearing his throat as a gentle reminder that this was not the proper way for ladies to act. At least not in this time. He beckoned Caiyan to follow, and Lady Sarah stood in the hallway staring after him.

"Has he offered for anyone?" she asked.

Oh, you betcha. He offers all the time. I sighed. I knew what she was asking. "No."

"How is that possible?" she asked, turning her perky nose toward me. "He's so gallant."

Now there was a word I had never associated with Caiyan. He was sexy, charismatic, and definitely sneaky. Gallant, we would have to wait and see.

I gave her a palms-up and yawned.

"Oh, please forgive me. You must be so tired from your journey." We parted ways, and I entered my room. I peeked out the door again to see if the coast was clear to go hunt down Caiyan, the gallant, before he went downstairs to the smoking room.

"What ye lookin' fer, miss?" came a voice behind me. I jumped three feet and let out a shriek.

"Sorry to give ye a fright, miss." The young girl was obviously here to help me with my dress because there was no way I was getting out of it by myself. She curtsied.

She talked nonstop the entire time she helped me undress. Her name was Daisy, and she was fourteen and excited to be assisting such a fine lady tonight. I looked around to see whom she was referring to, when I decided she meant me. After Daisy stoked the fire and put away my dress, she left me standing in the center of the room in a white see-through shift. No underwear. I climbed into the bed and looked up at the regal ceiling. Daisy came and patted down the thick down bedcovers and then placed a tin pan she had retrieved from the fireplace under my mattress. "That'll keep ye warm, mistress."

She retired for the evening, leaving me in stark silence. The room was not quite as elegant as Lady Sarah's, but it was a nice shade of blue and the bed was goose down. I decided that if Caiyan wanted to talk, he would have to find me, because I was not wandering around this estate barely dressed. Time travel left me exhausted. My plan was to escort Mrs. Ogilvy into Scotland and the safety of her people. I could take her by vessel, but I had never done a lateral travel in the past. I assumed it was probably the same. I just needed to concentrate on an area, and my vessel would do the rest. My mind drifted off into a deep sleep. I was dreaming a hand was running up my thigh and light kisses were being caressed down my neck. Caiyan was whispering into my ear as his hand reached under my gown and massaged my nipple, which was already aroused from his touch. I came slowly back to my senses and realized Caiyan was in the bed with me.

"What are you doing?" I asked with a half smile.

"I'm committing incest with my sister." He kissed me full on the mouth, and the taste of whisky made my bottom lip tingle. As I returned his kisses, he didn't seem like himself. He was not in control. He was whispering things like how beautiful I looked tonight. Well, OK, he had told me that before but never with such emphasis and never without copping a feel.

"We shouldn't be doing this," I said. "Lady Sarah is in the next room. She might hear us."

"I dinnae care if she hears," he said a little too loudly. "I want to make love with my lady. Lady Jennifer, my one true love."

I stopped cold. Did he just say he loved me? My inner voice pursed her lips and explained not really. Yes, he definitely said the L word. My heart began to race—and then it happened. He passed out on top of me. Caiyan was drunk. I had never seen him like this before. Out of control. Uncalculated. Romantic. I rolled him off me, and he lay there all mussed and gorgeous. I cuddled up next to him, enjoying the bond of heat between his intoxicated body and mine. We both drifted off into a deep sleep.

Chapter 4

I sat bolt upright in the bed. Something had awakened me, but I couldn't figure out what until I heard it again. A woman screamed. This time Caiyan sat up, too.

"What was that?" he asked, grabbing the side of his head as if a wasp had stung him.

"Someone screamed," I said. It sounded like it came from Lady Sarah's room. I left the bed and pulled on the blue dressing gown Mrs. Ogilvy had given me earlier.

"I cannae go oot there like this," Caiyan said, still holding his head and trying to put his pants on. His morning arousal stood at attention, making it a difficult task.

"I agree," I said, unable to take my eyes off his imminent problem.

He grimaced and continued pulling on his pants.

I opened the bedroom door and peered out into the hallway.

Lady Sarah was standing in the hallway surrounded by half-dressed servants and her uncle in his dressing robe. She saw me crack my door open and gestured for me to come out. I made my way into the hallway, trying to ignore Caiyan's protest from behind me to wait until he was dressed.

"There was a man in my room," she said. "He was going through my jewelry, and he ran when I screamed."

"Search the house and notify my guards," Lord Bryant command-ed. The servants began to scatter. "I want every square inch checked for this intruder."

One of the servants returned and said, "Lord Bryant, I have to inform you, Lord McGregor is missing, and he hasn't slept in his bed."

All eyes turned to me. "I'm sure my brother was in his bed last night."

Another scream sounded from inside my room.

Everyone rushed inside to find a half-dressed, very hungover Caiyan being held prisoner by Daisy. She had him backed into a cor-ner, pointing a fire poker at his bare chest as if she were Zorro. His hair was long and hung around his shoulders. He looked like he belonged on a Harlequin romance novel cover. His bloodshot eyes scanned the crowd. "Shite."

"What is the meaning of this?" Lady Sarah asked, placing her hands on her hips.

"I can explain," Caiyan stammered. Another first for him. "Lady Jennifer and I—"

Lady Sarah cut him off. "It's obvious you are having relations with your sister. That's disgusting and illegal. I shall report the two of you immediately."

Lord Bryant looked in my direction, as if we were putting his fam-ily in danger. He took his niece by the arm. "I will take care of them, my dear. Go to your chamber and see if anything is missing."

Mrs. Ogilvy began consoling Lady Sarah as they returned to her room.

Lord Bryant instructed us to dress and meet him downstairs in the drawing room.

Caiyan stumbled off to his room, and Daisy helped me get dressed. "I'm sorry, mistress, I didnae know he was yer lover," she said. "I had a second cousin that got on with his sister. They had bairns that were wrong in the head, if ye git my meaning."

"Thanks for the warning, but it's complicated," I said.

"I cannae say that I blame ye. He is a fine-looking man."

Jeez, even incest couldn't mar Caiyan's good looks.

"How did you get into my room?" I asked her.

"The servants' entrance, there." She pointed toward a small door partially hidden by the fabric wall coverings. It was discreetly covered to match the walls. That must have been how the intruder was sneaking about the estate without being noticed. I had a feeling the intruder was our brigand, Rogue. He was obviously looking for the key. Did he think the maid would have given the key to Lady Sarah?

After I washed, peed in a chamber pot (*ick!*), and had my hair done, Daisy helped me with a riding dress. I hoped it didn't belong to Lady Sarah because she probably wasn't too keen on having the incestuous slut wear her clothing. I returned to the study. Caiyan was there already, explaining to Lord Bryant that he assumed the intruder was Rogue, and we needed to take Mrs. Ogilvy to safety immediately. He was freshly shaven, and his long hair was pulled away from his face into a man bun.

The servants reported back, describing a man bearing Rogue's appearance who had escaped over the back wall. Lady Sarah sent one of the chambermaids to report her jewelry was accounted for, but her schedule book was missing. Each night Mrs. Ogilvy updated the book with the next day's affairs for Lady Sarah.

One of the kitchen maids was found tied up in the conservatory. Lord Bryant's valet escorted her into the drawing room. She looked disheveled and frightened as someone brought her a hot drink. She told us she had been questioned by the man about all the maids who worked for Lord Bryant. This meant Rogue knew the location but didn't know which maid. We were one step ahead of him. Lady Sarah's schedule would have shown her lady's maid was leaving for Scotland. If he put two and two together, he would assume Mrs. Ogilvy was the one he was after.

"He will probably try to get her on the way home," Caiyan said.

Lord Bryant nodded in agreement. "You should take her by vessel," he said.

Caiyan and I both agreed it would take too long by horse, but how could we get Mrs. Ogilvy—who obviously knew nothing about time travel—into an outhouse? Lord Bryant had his servants busy getting

Lady Sarah ready for her journey to the country while we walked with Mrs. Ogilvy and Lord Bryant into the back gardens where we had originally landed.

As we came to the clearing in the back of the estate, Lord Bryant took Mrs. Ogilvy's hand in his own. "Now, do not be alarmed at what you will see," he said. "I trust these people, and you will learn the magic of the key so you can pass it down to your family members who possess the gift."

Mrs. Ogilvy looked at him suspiciously. "What gift are ye talkin' about?"

I approached the woman and put my hand on her arm. "Caiyan and I are from the future. We have the ability to travel back in time." I paused for a moment to let it sink in. "We use the key to command a special vessel that takes us back in time, but it can also take us places in the same time much faster than a horse and carriage."

Lord Bryant had guards attending the entrances to the grounds to make sure we were alone. I raised my hand to my throat and placed it on my key. The warm vibrating sensation grew strong. I said one word: "Come." The wind whipped around us, and my outhouse materialized ten feet in front of us. Mrs. Ogilvy fainted.

"I was afraid that might happen," Caiyan said.

"It's always a shock the first time," Lord Bryant said, holding Mrs. Ogilvy's sagging body. We maneuvered her into the outhouse. Lord Bryant reached in and kissed my fingers. "Very exciting to meet you both. I hope our paths will cross again one day."

Caiyan shook his hand and squeezed in on the other side of Mrs. Ogilvy.

I smiled. As a transporter, I can carry up to three people safely. Caiyan, being a defender, is supposed to travel alone. Last month we pushed the limits when I jumped into his vessel to escape the notorious Pancho Villa.

"What?" he asked.

"This is the first time you've ridden with me."

"Well, lass, I didn't want Mrs. Ogilvy coming aboot in the middle of the journey and ye ending up in Timbuktu."

His drunken admissions from the night before gave a small tug on my heart, and a mischievous little smile crept across my face. Even if he didn't remember saying he loved me, I still got to hear him say it.

Caiyan rubbed the back of his neck and squinted at me curiously. "Let's go, lassie."

⌣⟶

*W*e made a smooth landing, and I wondered if it was because Caiyan was riding shotgun. I opened the door to a field of clover. Mrs. Ogilvy started to regain consciousness, and Caiyan helped her outside the vessel. Her eyes went wide when she saw her daughter's cottage at the bottom of an adjacent hill.

"I can't believe mine eyes—there's my daughter's cottage." Caiyan and I gave her some room to get adjusted to the travel. "We're here."

Her daughter lived on a small island called the Isle of Harris, in the Outer Hebrides. These were the western isles off the mainland of Scotland, and the surroundings were breathtaking. The cottage sat at the base of a hill overlooking a small loch. I explained the gift of time travel to her again. She gave me a hesitant nod, but she could not dispute the fact we were in Scotland.

"Rogue may try to steal it from ye again, so be very careful," Caiyan warned. "We have aboot two more days to find him, and then we must return."

She gave us a hug, and we gave her a head start down the hill. She needed time to explain us to her daughter. We would be friends of Lord Bryant who needed a place to stay while traveling. It wasn't exactly a lie.

"What's our next move?" I asked.

"My gut feeling tells me he's going to come after her." Caiyan was sitting on his haunches surveying the area. He reached down, pulled a piece of clover, and handed it to me.

A four-leaf clover. He smiled. Maybe this was our lucky day to catch Rogue.

Mrs. Ogilvy's daughter had married her second cousin, Seamus MacDonald. They were a nice couple, and just as Mrs. Ogilvy said, the new baby had arrived, and she was beautiful. I held the tiny bundle while her mother and Mrs. Ogilvy fussed over a pot of stew. Small dark-red curls sprouted like a cap from her tiny head. I reached in and she grasped my finger. I didn't feel any special tingle, but if it were there, it wouldn't make itself known for some time. Caiyan was sitting on a sofa keeping an eye out the front window. He looked at me, and an uneasy feeling rolled around in my gut. Did I want one of these? Did I want one of these with Caiyan? He raised an eyebrow, and my inner self ran around dousing the flames of my raging hormones.

We hung out at the cottage, helping with the chores. I decided this was not the life I was cut out for because everything had to be done by hand—clothing, cooking, and cleaning. By the end of the day, my back was screaming from scrubbing. These people could really benefit from a vacuum cleaner. It seemed like as soon as I dusted, more dust settled in its place. The cottage was small, and the MacDonalds were sharing a bedroom about the size of my closet back home. Mrs. Ogilvy had the second bedroom (even smaller), Caiyan and I slept on the floor. Mrs. Ogilvy made a nice pallet for me next to the fire. Since it was too cold to sleep in the barn, it was agreed Caiyan would sleep by the door. Mrs. Ogilvy cut her eyes at Caiyan as she bid us good-night. It was a telepathic warning to stay on his side of the room. I couldn't help but giggle at the unspoken threat.

Even with the close quarters, in the middle of the night Caiyan moved his blankets next to mine and pulled me closer to him.

"Mrs. Ogilvy is not going to like you moving over here," I said.

"Mrs. Ogilvy is naught resting her tired body on the cold, drafty floor. The fire burned slowly in the fireplace, and he made love to me on the handwoven rug Mrs. Ogilvy told me had been in her family for centuries.

I wanted to ask him about the previous night. Did he remember the declaration of love he had made? I just couldn't seem to find the right words. *Caiyan, did you mean you loved me the other night?* Or, *Hey, Caiyan, about those words, my true love…*

My inner self clicked her tongue at me and shook her head. Did I love him? I wasn't sure. Everyone had warned me about his wandering ways. There was something keeping me from shouting those three scary words. I decided I just needed more time to make sure Mr. Right wasn't Mr. Right now.

Caiyan and I borrowed the couple's only horse and scouted the outer island in search of Rogue. For the next two days, in order to give the new family a little space, we rode, watched the incoming traffic from the ferry, and stayed close to the cottage. Our time was running out. If Rogue was going to make a move, it would have to be tonight, because it was time to leave. It was dangerous to extend the stay more than three days. Caiyan told me the pain starts when the moon's waning period is over, about five days after the full moon.

"Why doesn't he just pop over like we did?" I asked.

"He doesn't know where she is, and it's dangerous to lateral travel outside of yer own time."

"Dangerous?" I asked, because there was no mention of danger when we were hauling Mrs. Ogilvy across the continent.

"Aye. Some travelers have been known to get lost in time."

"L-lost in time?" I stuttered, not entirely because it was cold outside.

"Are ye cold?" Caiyan immediately became concerned. I assumed it was to change the subject. A light drizzle had begun, and we stopped at a local inn in the village. A man and his wife staffed the inn, and we were their only customers. They served a welcome home-cooked meal and a pint of ale, which I had begun to develop a taste for. Since we had been there the previous day, the owners offered idle talk of the local gossip. The innkeeper's wife had just returned from a trip to the main island for supplies, and she told us there was man on the Isle of Sky asking questions about the MacDonald clan. She said he was on the ferry with her that afternoon, but he looked like a scoundrel, and she didn't give him any information about the MacDonalds.

Caiyan and I finished our meal quickly, barely getting time to thaw out from the cold. We were back on the horse when Caiyan saw a man walking toward the stables. He jerked up on the reins and led our horse out of sight. Caiyan circled around to the main road that led toward the cottage.

"If he comes this way, he will have to go over this bridge," Caiyan said as we came upon a small bridge. He helped me down from the horse and then dismounted.

"Do you think there are any trolls under there?" I asked.

"Only one way to find out." Caiyan knelt down and had a look under the bridge. After he declared it free from trolls, he said, "Wait here, lassie. I'm going to see what he's up to."

"You want me to wait here alone?" I asked.

"I will only be gone for a short time. I think this will be the best place to grab him. I can hide on the other side of the bridge. Ye can't see it from here." He pointed across the small river, and I agreed it would surprise Rogue if Caiyan jumped him from that side.

"What am I supposed to do?"

"Hide under the bridge. It will provide a warm spot until I return. Then we can decide how ye will help me snag this brigand."

I gave him a long kiss, and the lingering effects reflected in his eyes.

"Go on now, lass."

I obeyed, hunkered down in my troll bunker, and waited.

⟮⟶

I returned from my reverie. Well, that was a plan that went haywire thanks to lust and hormones. If I was going to be a good transporter, I was going to have to put my craving for Caiyan at a distance. I sighed and organized my story for the debriefing, leaving out the mishap in the bedroom at Lord Bryant's estate and the fact I was almost fish food. My inner voice gave me the thumbs-up, and I headed back to the WTF for the debriefing and the scolding Jake would give us for not completing our mission.

⟮⟶

Chapter 5

My vessel came to a screeching halt, banging my knee against the door. First on my list is getting a flying lesson, so to speak. No matter how calm I try to remain or how hard I focus, my vessel bounces around like a bobber on a fishing line that just snagged a great white. Ace, my good friend and fellow transporter, travels in a photo booth. It's similar to the kind found at a carnival, where a group of friends would get in, pull the curtain, and in three magic minutes a strip of four photos slides out the front. It is rare that a male becomes a transporter instead of a defender, but that's just how Ace rolls. Ace's vessel sails as smooth as silk, and he pipes in his own music and disco lights.

The WTF has a secret headquarters under the highest level maximum security prison at Gitmo. Twelve landing blocks forming a four-by-three grid are housed in a large underground space similar to an aircraft hangar. I opened the door to my vessel. Jake was standing in a black suit, hands on hips, waiting for me. His dark-brown hair was immaculately groomed into position with some space-age gel. The boy I knew from high school, who could have been Zac Efron's twin, now looked like he should star in an espionage thriller. Caiyan's red phone booth was on the platform to my left, empty. I searched the room, but no Caiyan.

"He's already been debriefed and sent to medical," Jake said as he came forward and assisted me down from the landing platform.

"Already been debriefed?" I asked. I glanced at the TAG Heuer watch Jake wore on his wrist, a gift from his father. I was back exactly three hours from the time I originally left. "How long has he been back?"

"Two hours," Jake said firmly.

"Two hours?" *How did he beat me back by two hours?* Another question in my notebook of things that needed answers.

"Your vessel is empty," he said, pointing at my outhouse.

"Well, since Caiyan is already here, I'm sure you're aware we didn't catch Rogue. But he didn't get the key, either," I added for good measure.

"I'm glad you're safe, but if you insist on being a transporter, you'll need more training." Jake shook his finger at me as if I was five. "I'm not going to authorize more travel for you until I feel you're not a threat to our mission."

"A threat?" I pushed the sleeves of my Donna Karan cashmere sweater up to my elbows and thanked God I was back in my own clothes. "What do you mean threat?" Then it dawned on me. Caiyan told him about my mishap and almost falling into the river. Caiyan had purposely returned earlier than I had so he could tell Jake I needed more training. The little tattletale.

I stepped toward Jake, and he grabbed my wrist.

"Ouch!" His touch caused my arm to ache.

He held my arm up and pushed my sleeve up to my biceps. Dark black bruises tattooed the length of my arm where I had fought against Rogue. An ugly welt was beginning to form around my forearm where Caiyan had grabbed me to prevent my fall.

Jake grimaced. Ever since he found out I'd had "relations," as he put it, with Caiyan, our friendship had been strained. Jake and I had been best friends since fourth grade. I wasn't sure I liked "boss" Jake.

"It's nothing." I jerked my arm free and pulled down my sleeve.

"We need to go down to the debriefing room. General Potts is waiting for your account of what happened." He wrapped an arm around my shoulders, and that warm comfortable feeling enveloped me. His cologne, the same cologne he wore in high school, caught the air, and I could feel my knees weaken just a little.

"I was really worried about you," he said under his breath.

"I know." I smiled up at him. His big, brown puppy-dog eyes that I have loved since fourth grade looked back at me. This was "friend" Jake. He gave my shoulders a squeeze, and we walked casually down the long corridor to my inquisition.

$$\sim$$

*G*eneral Potts stood as we entered the debriefing room. The long mahogany table cut him mid–robust belly, making it seem as if he was only a body propped up on the table like a Beethoven bust. He greeted me with his gravel-laden voice. "Uhm, Miss Cloud, pleasure to see you returned unharmed." He coughed slightly and indicated one of the chairs in the room. "Please have a seat."

"Thanks," I said, returning with a half smile. Better to go in with a smile than to let him see the fear that was brewing up from the bowels of my gut. I chose the seat to his left. The seat on his right was occupied by his secretary, a pretty brunette who winked at Jake and seemed to know his coffee order by heart. Jake and I had made peace since I first started working for the WTF. Our on-again, off-again relationship was interrupted by my intrigue with Caiyan and Jake's inability to commit. Jake set a cup of coffee down in front of me, and I took a casual sip as General Potts returned to his seat. Jake stood to the back, as all good CIA agents do. Caiyan had apparently given his account of the Rogue adventure and left to get his boo-boos treated. The rat.

"Miss Cloud, please explain your account of what happened in Scotland and why you failed to return with the brigand." General Potts clicked his pen a few times and moved the pad of paper around in front of him. I never understood why General Potts had a pad of paper. He never wrote anything down. All accounts of the travel were meticulously entered into the laptop his secretary carried around like a small child. I explained my side of the story, making sure to point out that Caiyan was unconscious and I was going after Rogue myself. It was just a tiny little lie. I mean Caiyan didn't know I wasn't battling it out with Rogue. I was the only one who knew Rogue didn't even see me until I went to help Caiyan. In my mind, SuperJen appeared and went after Rogue with her amazing judo chop.

When I was little, my brother, Eli; my sister, Melody; and I would play superheroes. I would be SuperJen, the amazing hero, and spent the day running around in my bright-green leotard and blue bath-towel cape. Disguised with an old Zorro mask, I would stand on the back of the couch and holler, "I'm spunky and I'm fierce and I'm smarter than most men. Bad guys run and hide 'cuz here comes SuperJen." The mantra is on permanent play cycle when I need a little courage. I could feel the ditty trying to make its way to the front of my mind and immediately squashed it with my subconscious thumb.

There was a lot of huffing from Potts, and Jake chimed in a few times, defending my actions, which made the pretty brunette pound harder on her keyboard. In the end, it was determined I would be placed on a training schedule to make sure I was properly prepared to handle a brigand on my own. I thought it sounded like being grounded, but I realized I needed some training. SuperJen may be great with a judo chop, but normal Jen could only chop lettuce.

After General Potts released me, I walked with Jake to the travel lab. "I need to check in with the monitoring agents, and I thought you might like to say hello," Jake said as he walked to a panel on the wall and used his key fob. The panel slid open, revealing a keypad. Jake punched in a number and then placed his chin on a little stand. A retinal scan was completed, Jake stepped back, and the unit closed. I felt like any second a flying droid was going to come out and give me a full-body probe. A large door appeared to the left of the panel, and just like in *Star Wars*, it slid open without a sound.

The room was set up similar to the *Star Trek Enterprise*, but instead of having windows for Captain Kirk to view the space-time continuum, the travel lab had large projection screens illuminating the walls in front of me. In the center of the room, a trio of leather chairs offered a comfortable resting place for General Potts or any of the other head gurus when they came to watch our shenanigans into the past.

While we're time traveling, we appear as tiny blinking dots on a map. It helps the WTF to know where we are and if there are any brigands close by. Sometimes they can send help back if it looks like we're in trouble. I was watching the screens as we entered, and the dots began to disappear, indicating the time portal was closing, and all the travelers, good and bad, were returning to the present.

To the right of the command station was a semicircular desk where several flat screens flickered. The two men who staffed the travel lab were in front of these screens. Old Albert, whom I often refer to as Father Time, had his head in a huddle with Pickles, one of the defenders from Jamaica. He had been injured in a travel and was now confined to a wheelchair. They were arguing about something on the screen in front of them.

"Hi, guys," I said as we approached them. There was a mumble, but neither man looked in our direction. Jake and I walked over to see what prompted the intense conversation.

"Gentlemen," Jake said, "what seems to be the problem?"

Al's head bobbed up, and his eyes focused behind his thick spectacles as if noticing Jake for the very first time. "We have an ID on the mystery traveler, sir."

"What do you mean?" Jake asked.

Pickles held up a printout of a map, and Jake moved forward to have a look. "Well, tis red dot is de one I'm concerned wit. De September moon cycle, it appeared, and den I track it back to de Everglades and bouncing around Florida."

I peeked over Jake's shoulder at the map. "I thought the WTF was blue and the brigands were black. Who is red?" I asked.

Al gave me a grandfatherly smile. "When we don't know who they are, we make them red. It keeps the level of confusion down until we identify them."

"Where was the final landing?" Jake asked.

"Das de thing," Pickles explained. "When it first appeared on our screen, we tracked it to England, possibly London or very close. De next time it stopped in Louisiana, probably getting some boudin." Pickles chuckled at his own joke.

"It disappeared close to Orlando, Florida," Al said. "It was always moving laterally during travel, but in the October moon cycle it went back in time, to California."

"After dat, de traveler returned to Orlando and blipped around the present world." Pickle's voice elevated with excitement. "Dis moon cycle it was in New York City, and it doesn't look like it's returning dis time, either." He pointed his index finger to his head and made the crazy sign.

"The problem is the brigand looks like he's staying this time, too." Al pointed to the black dot hopping around the screen close to the red dot.

Everyone digested this last bit of information. The moon cycle was closing. If the traveler didn't return soon, he or she would have to wait for the next cycle and endure the painful ramifications of travel lag.

Jake snapped to attention at the mention of the traveler not returning. "Does General Potts know of these circumstances?"

"Yes." Al motioned to the door. "General Potts and Mr. McGregor came in earlier."

Yeah, like two hours earlier. Where was that snitch? My inner voice pulled out her magnifying glass to start looking for clues.

Jake's cell pinged, and I could hear the very sexy voice of my favorite beotch telling Jake he was needed in General Potts's office.

"I'm going to see Jen to her vessel and check with the general. Then I'll be back to help you guys troubleshoot."

Al and Pickles eyed each other as if they were telepathically passing a secret message in the air over my head.

Jake and I left as I gave the guys a wave and promised to come say hi the next time I was in town.

⌐⌐

During our walk back to my vessel, Jake reminded me about General Poopy Potts giving me the third degree and how I was too inexperienced and needed more training—blah, blah, blah. "I'm looking forward to spending more time with you in our training sessions."

I gave him a sideways glance, and his dark-brown eyes tugged on my heart. Jake and I had history. We had grown up together. We had thrown rocks at the bullies, played jokes on my siblings, and spent many afternoons floating around his swimming pool, trying to plan our grown-up lives. I always had that warm, safe, comfy feeling when he pulled me in tight for a hug.

As I was trying to decide how to respond, we reached the atrium where the vessels were docked. Leaning against his phone booth was Caiyan. He was dressed head to toe in black. Diesel jeans, T-shirt, and black Doc Martens. His arms were crossed over his chest, legs crossed at the ankles in an I've-got-better-things-to-do pose. I heard a deep rumble, almost a growl coming from Jake.

"I thought you were dismissed," Jake snarled at Caiyan.

Caiyan pushed away from his vessel and walked toward us. A sly smile tugged at the corners of his mouth. "I had unfinished business, yeah?" He pulled me into his arms and kissed me hard on the mouth. I felt Jake tense beside me. As he released me, I looked from Jake to Caiyan. Jake was well aware of my affair with Caiyan. He didn't have to like it, but it was my choice.

"Take care, Jen. I'll see you on Friday at eighteen hundred hours." Then he turned on his heel and left the room.

"What was that aboot?" Caiyan asked, casually running his hand across my back. His broken finger had been splinted, and he had a Band-Aid across a small gash on his forehead.

"I have to come here for training every weekend. I'm not allowed to travel until I have more training." At this, I turned to stare at him. "I have you to thank for that. Why did you tell them about the problem at the river?" I put my hands on my hips for emphasis and cocked an eyebrow up at the intense green eyes that stared back at me.

"Jen, ye were almost killed. I cannae have that on my conscience. I should have never requested ye to go with me." He straightened up, but his eyes were softening, and my temper simmered down a few degrees. He reached down and took my hand in his. "Jen, I have to go out of town fer business next week, and I may be difficult to reach."

I felt a few warning bells go off inside my head, but I quickly dismissed them as he ran a thumb over the back of my hand.

"I'll probably be pretty busy, too. Jake gave me orders to report to Gitmo every Friday at six p.m. I'm training every weekend until the WTF feels like I'm ready to be out in the field." I scuffed the toe of my shoe against his, and he pulled me into his arms.

"I hope Jake is not training ye personally." He leaned back and cocked a brow at me. "We have several highly qualified military personnel to handle that job. If I didnae have to go overseas for my 'real' job, I would train ye myself."

"As a matter of fact, he's the one who's training me." I took a step back, breaking his embrace.

"I didnae think they would let Jake train ye. I thought a more experienced agent would be brought in to do the job."

"I'm sure Jake knows what he's doing. He has always been very thorough." I didn't mean to put so much emphasis on the word thorough, but I was still a few degrees north of mad. "Is that a problem?"

Caiyan grimaced, and his grip tightened on my fingers. His face hardened a little, making me feel like it was a problem. I wasn't sure if he was concerned I would be spending too much time with Jake or that my training would not be sufficient to meet his standards. But when I looked up into his eyes, the hard emerald green turned soft again. He bent down, pulled me in tight, and kissed me long.

"I'll call ye if I get the chance, yeah?"

Why do Scotsmen always end everything with a question? I thought to myself as I watched Caiyan enter his vessel, and *crack, boom*, he was gone.

Two men in black stood at the entrance to the "cave," as I call it, pretending not to notice my über friendliness with Caiyan. I gave them a finger wave and boarded my vessel for home.

The funny thing about time travel is I can stop at Gitmo, then return to my place, and I have only been gone a couple of hours. The time warp took a little getting used to. After being gone for three days, I would have to remind myself I was really gone for only three hours. I stepped out of my vessel into the cold, dreary November. I thought for a second it wasn't much different from the rain I had left behind in Scotland. Texas really only has two seasons—hot and not so hot. If we're lucky, we may have two weeks of spring before the ninety-degree temperatures of summer begin, ending with triple digits through September. October brings about two weeks when the leaves change colors and fall to the ground as quickly as they can get there.

And I realize my family is here, and it's where I feel grounded. I grew up in a small, tight-knit community outside of Dallas called Sunnyside. My parents recently moved to a retirement community to party and left me with their narrow, two-story townhouse, my cousin Gertie, and a rent payment. My vessel sits in the backyard like a large garden ornament. Since I inherited the outhouse, my backyard has turned into an oasis of beautiful green plants and flowers. My dad scratches his head every time he comes over for a visit because the only thing that grew in the backyard of my childhood was crabgrass.

As I exited the outhouse, bushes of blue moon roses bowed like servants, giving me a path to the house. Behind me, they encircled the base of the outhouse, forming a ring of defense against any trespassers. They are truly the most beautiful roses I have ever seen, and they have the sharpest thorns.

I opened the sliding glass door and hung up my coat on the peg next to the door. I was wearing my favorite Burberry rain boots, and I sat down on a chair in the kitchen to pull them off. I was tugging at my boot when I felt something soft rub the back of my neck. I turned in time to see attack cat balancing on the back of the chair and swatting a clawless paw at me. "Not this time, buddy," I said, standing up and jumping up and down on one leg to pull off the remaining boot. The big gray tabby licked his paw with indifference, possibly plotting his next move. For a cat that doesn't have any front claws, he sure can draw blood.

Gertie walked into the kitchen, stirring a cup of hot chocolate.

"Hey, have you been somewhere exciting?" she asked, wide-eyed and giving attack cat a scratch behind the ears. "Dubai? Paris? Antarctica, maybe?"

"Antarctica is not on my list of exciting places." I moved into the kitchen, avoiding attack cat, and reached up to get a mug to join Gertie in some hot chocolate. "Besides, you know I can't tell you."

"You were with Caiyan, right?"

"Yep."

"Well, you can just skip to the dirty details. I have to live vicariously through you since my love life is on the blink."

"What happened to the new library aide?" Gertie was finishing her bachelor's degree in history at Southern Methodist University, and she worked in the library on campus. She loved to sneak up on college students making out in the stacks and scare the bejeezus out of them.

Gertie rolled her eyes and sighed. "Girlfriend."

"Pretty?"

"Cheerleader."

"Sorry."

"Me too."

On my last adventure back in time, Gertie jumped into my outhouse just as the door slammed shut, and I was rocketed back to 1915. We had a run-in with the notorious Pancho Villa, and Gertie fell madly in love with Caiyan's buddy Brodie, who is also a defender. Brodie, however, lives in Australia and isn't as sweet on Gertie. She has been pining away ever since.

I stirred the marshmallows in my hot chocolate and told Gertie about my crazy training schedule.

"Wow, sounds like Jake wants to keep you busy."

In Jake's defense, I said, "I have a lot to learn." But in reality, I felt the same. "Do you think the training is a ploy by Jake to keep me away from Caiyan?"

"I think he wants to keep you close."

Gertie was on a study binge. She was wearing her pink terry cloth robe, gray Ugg slippers, and her mane of bright-red hair was in pigtails twisted into buns on her head. The Patsy Cline song "Crazy" started to play from Gertie's robe pocket. She set her mug down on the table and dug out her cell phone. She tapped on the screen. "What do you think of him?" she asked, showing me a picture of a guy standing in a bathtub wearing nothing but his tighty-whities.

"Why is he in his underwear?"

"I think he's about to take the Ice Bucket Challenge."

Gertie and I had done the same challenge a month earlier to support ALS. We stood in the backyard as her twin brothers poured a garbage can full of ice water over us from the upstairs balcony. We had worn swimsuits, and her brothers posted it on Facebook. They got over a thousand likes. It was for a good cause, but I would not have posted a picture on social media in my underwear. My inner voice agreed it was fashion suicide, not to mention it repelled women like bug spray.

"Is he a friend of yours?" I asked, trying to focus on the face, not the Fruit of the Looms.

"Not yet. He swiped me on Sweetie Swipe."

I knew Gertie was trying out a few Internet dating sites. She wasn't having much luck finding a nice guy.

"What is that?"

Gertie eyed the picture and pursed her lips together. "It's an app. If you see someone you like, you can swipe right for yes, you would like to meet, or swipe left, for not interested. If both people swipe yes, the phone numbers are exchanged, you can send a text message, and eventually meet for a date."

"Is that safe?"

"I don't know. I haven't tried it yet." She scowled at me as if I was stomping out her last chance to find the man of her dreams.

"I think if you decide to go out with one of these guys you should at least give me his name and the place you're meeting."

"You know this superspy stuff you have going on is getting annoying." She rolled her eyes but finally agreed better safe than sorry. At least if she was abducted, I could interview the bartender at the last sighting. A brigand had captured and held Gertie hostage during my last time travel. She wasn't hurt, but I don't think she wants to be a hostage ever again. Gertie picked up her mug and rinsed it in the sink as she mulled over the picture on her phone.

"Are you considering Captain Underpants?" I asked as I sat down at the table and sipped my drink.

"If I swipe left, he goes away forever." She began chewing on the outside of her thumbnail.

"If you don't want to meet him, why is this is a problem?"

"I have a hard time letting go."

I rolled my eyes, and she pocketed the phone. "Best to make him wait anyhow." She grabbed a copy of the *Historical Tribune* and headed off upstairs. "Gotta study. See ya later." Attack cat followed behind Gertie, flicking his tail with condolences about my man troubles.

Chapter 6

My alarm clock kicked on, waking me from a deep, dreamless sleep. The golden sun streaming in my window caused me to squint as I shut off the Beatles song playing on my alarm clock. There was hope for a bright, sunshiny day, but I had that nagging feeling something was amiss. My stomach grumbled loudly. One of the side effects of time travel is increased hunger. The other is severe fatigue, usually following the second travel back to the present. I slept like a log last night, taking care of the fatigue, but I couldn't put my finger on the uneasiness I felt. I blamed the hunger pains as I dressed for work.

After I lost my job as an assistant purchasing agent at Steve Stone Shoes, I began working for my brother, Eli, at his chiropractic office. I still couldn't believe Mr. Steve Stone was arrested for tax evasion. I loved that job. My favorite part of that job was going downtown to Dallas Market Hall and purchasing shoes for the next season. Steve Stone carried his own brand, but he also carried all the high-end shoes. He gave his employees a sizable discount, and I reciprocated by buying shoes every paycheck. At least I have a nice collection of shoes, and maybe with the extra income from the transporter job I can maintain my shoe fetish. It is less expensive to buy Italian shoes wholesale in Italy than pay retail in America. And now, with my transporter abilities, I can buy shoes wherever I desire. This thought made me smile as I put on my yellow Monday scrubs.

Standing in front of the mirror, I gasped. I could literally stop traffic in the darn things; they were one shade below neon. Mary, the clinic's office manager, decided we should have matching scrubs for each day of the week. Monday is yellow to start the patients off in a good mood. I had to admit I did feel a little more cheery, but the bruises on my arm showed and were turning a nice purple-green color. I retreated to my closet and pulled out a Tory Burch long-sleeve shirt. I layered it under my scrub top, and it hid all my bruises. I added some Betsy Johnson dangling earrings in the shape of small cupcakes. I pulled on my black leather boots and moved the contents of my purse into my Prada tote. I headed downstairs to scrounge up breakfast.

Gertie caught me standing at the open fridge, surveying the contents. Half a jug of milk, three eggs—no time for that—and some lettuce.

"Dang, I need to talk to you, but wait—let me get my sunglasses." She giggled, holding her hand up to shield her eyes from my scrubs. "The reflection off those scrubs is giving me a headache."

I shrugged off Gertie's inner comedian. "Gertie, isn't it your week to go food shopping?"

"I did. I'm on the new shake diet. I can lose up to ten pounds a week just drinking shakes." She pulled open the freezer and showed me her stash of frozen fruits and veggies for shake making. I wouldn't describe Gertie as fat, maybe plump or big boned. She is about five foot five and has cute freckles that cut across her nose. She is always on some kind of diet. I think if she would throw away the Ben and Jerry's she has hiding under the frozen spinach, she would lose the weight. But who am I to judge?

"Don't you think fresh fruits and vegetables would be better?" I asked her cautiously.

"No, I read an article that said frozen is better because they freeze it right away and that preserves the vitamins." She grabbed a bag of frozen kale and dumped it in the blender with some pineapple and a scoop of something from a bag that smelled like garlic. If she didn't lose weight, at least she would keep the vampires away.

"Do you want some?" she asked.

I shook my head and decided I would risk my luck at the fast-food drive-through. I pulled on my white fuzzy North Face jacket and headed out to my car. Gertie followed, making sucking noises as she drank her shake through a straw.

The morning air was crisp, with scents of fall whipping my hair into my face. Thanksgiving was right around the corner, and the trees were shedding their leaves. They would go from dark green to naked in a matter of weeks. When Ace took me to New York on our first lateral travel, I was amazed to see the seasonal change of color on the East Coast. Brilliant colors of rust and orange provided a beautiful background for our walk through Central Park. Children were rolling around in piles of leaves, and couples sat on blankets along the banks of the small lake, enjoying a picnic.

My inner voice tapped her wristwatch, indicating I needed to get a move on or I would be late to work again.

As I passed the outhouse, it stood glorious in the backyard, with lush vegetation wrapping around its outer shell. Yellow and orange flowers sprang up from the small garden surrounding my vessel, and at its base, the blue moon roses had the morning dew weeping from the petals. It was as if my outhouse was giving Mother Nature the finger for the drought-filled summers and the short fall season. I noticed a peculiar vine curling haphazardly around the outhouse. As I moved in for a closer look, I saw four tiny pumpkins clinging to the curly vine. I pulled my jacket around me to block the cool wind as Gertie caught up with me.

"We have pumpkins." I pointed.

"Yeah, I saw that this morning when I let Smokey out for his morning stretch. Cool, huh?"

"I guess we can make our own pumpkin pie this Thanksgiving."

Gertie gave me a look that said, *Why would you want to do that when you can buy one for five bucks at the bakery?*

We turned to walk through the back gate that led to our carport. A large metal awning protected both cars from the elements.

"I was thinking maybe we could have a double date when Caiyan gets back from his business trip," Gertie suggested, holding the gate open for me.

"And who, pray tell, would be your date?" I slid her a sidelong glance, knowing full well she wanted to see Brodie again. "Possibly Captain Underpants?"

"No, I swiped left," she said, looking sullen. "Maybe Caiyan could get a hold of Brodie, and we could go somewhere fun, like Egypt."

"Gert, you know we're not allowed to take people riding around the universe in our vessels."

"It was just an idea." She sulked.

Gertie was still having hurt feelings over the library boy, so I said, "I'll check with Caiyan when he returns, and maybe Brodie will come for a visit."

She perked up at this and gave me a wave as she got into her car.

⌒⟩

*G*ertie hopped in her red BMW 330, revved the engine, gave me a beep, and sped off down the road. When Gertie was sixteen, her mother, my cousin Trish, married Vincent Gambino, also known as Vinnie the fish. Gertie's life went from trailer parks to Park Avenue. She and her two half brothers lived the life of luxury for about a week, and then they were shipped off to boarding schools. I think Gertie still has a few unresolved issues with her stepfather, but the perks of having a rather nice allowance and her shiny red car keep them at bay.

My white Mustang convertible was waiting for me. I peeked out from under the carport at the sun, and a swift breeze had me ducking back in, zipping up my jacket. I was not putting the top down on my car today. Occasionally, November will give us a few days of eighty-degree weather, but not today. I sighed, got into my car, and drove off to work.

I made the loop past my dad's health food/feed store. A person could get all-natural pet food and B vitamins while sipping one of my dad's homemade juices. He claimed all his herbal remedies and juices were an ancient Indian secret. I'm not sure about that, but his carrot juice keeps my skin clear. After my mom and dad moved to an adult community to play golf and become social anthropologists, he cut his hours back at the store. I didn't see his Ford pickup in the employee parking lot behind the store, so I motored out to Highway 80 and headed east. Maroon 5 came on the radio. I cranked it up and sang a duet with Adam Levine. My inner voice agreed—today would be a good day.

Eli had chosen the quaint town of Coffee Creek because it was about thirty miles outside Dallas. The people were small town and very friendly. I pulled into the drive-through at Mickey D's and picked up a caramel latte, two breakfast sandwiches, and a side of hash browns. This transporter thing was going to make me gain weight. My inner self suggested getting some exercise or trying one of Gertie's shakes. Neither sounded very appealing to me. I told her no as I took a bite out of the sandwich.

I made the block around the big red courthouse and whipped into a parking space behind the strip center where my brother's office was located. Ten minutes to nine—I was on time for once. Crumpling the paper of my first breakfast sandwich, I took a sip of my latte as I made my way through the courtyard that separated Eli's office from a vacant space. The humming of saws and the smell of fresh paint flowed through the air. The vacant space next door was getting a new occupant, and it looked like they were putting the finishing touches on it. A large vehicle equipped with a cherry picker was parked in front of the vacant office. The boom of the vehicle was extended, and a man in the cherry picker was installing a sign on the front of the building: "Coffee Creek Medical Spa." The windows were lettered, advertising Botox injections, facelifts, and laser hair removal. Interesting, I thought to myself. My brother is an all-natural health care provider trying to make you live longer using chiropractic and nutrition, and right next door you can have all kinds of poison injected to make you look younger. Choices—isn't that what life is all about?

Upon entering the office, the smell of incense hit me like a brick wall. "Whoa, who's burning the incense?" I asked the gray-haired office manager, Mary, as I passed by her desk.

She had a phone balanced between her neck and shoulder as she clacked away on her keyboard. Looking up, she held up her index finger adorned with a very long red polished fake fingernail. Thanking the person on the other end of the phone, she hung up and said, "Su Le had an early patient this morning."

Well, that explained the smell that radiated around the room. The moxa, a substance Su Le used for burning on the ends of her acupuncture needles, smelled almost like marijuana. Last month we had an influx of teenagers stopping by after school to smell our air. Unfortunately for them, the giddiness they claimed to feel was purely a placebo. Su Le started using incense to mask the scent. Apparently, the smell of eucalyptus is not as inviting to the teens, and they moved on to GameStop.

⸺

I said my hellos to the other staff as I headed back to find my brother, Eli. He was seated at his desk perusing the morning schedule. His dark-black hair had grown out some and was threatening to hide his shirt collar.

"Don't let Mom see that hair touching your collar, or she'll pull out the trimming shears."

He glanced up at me. His blue eyes looked at me through dark-rimmed glasses, and a slow smile stretched across his face. "Well, well, well. Look who's on time today."

"I'm not on time—I'm early."

"You should be careful. The other employees might think you're trying for a raise." He smirked at me and cocked his head to one side. "I like the hair—are you trying for Marilyn Monroe or Miley Cyrus?"

I realized Eli hadn't seen me since I did the bottle-blond dye job. "I was going for more like Mom's color."

He gave a small chuckle. "Well then, you need to go back to your hair gurus and tell them to use Rachel Ray brown."

"Get out. Mom dyed her hair brown?" My mom has been proudly blond her entire life. Only in the past few years has she added some extra blond highlights to give it "*life*," as she would say.

"Yep, saw Mom and Dad on Sunday. You know that day the entire family gets together for lunch after we attend church."

A little guilt flushed my face. "I'm taking some classes." It wasn't a total lie. I was taking Transporting 101 classes with Jake at the WTF starting on Saturday.

He raised his eyebrows. "That's great, Jen, but you should probably tell Mom. You know how she loves getting the family together to try out whatever recipe her clients are cooking up."

Our mother is a cookbook editor for celebrities, and is frequently serving up one of the many dishes waiting for her final approval before going to print.

"What was the feast on Sunday?" I asked.

"Lamb chops with some kind of sticky sauce. I think it had peaches in it." He kissed his fingers and made some Italian gesture. "They were pretty tasty but probably loaded with sugar. Dad rolled his eyes every time he took a bite." My dad is off sugar, gluten, and anything that has an additive or preservative. My Mom force-feeds him anything and everything that contains those things—her way of "testing" her clients' recipes. He's a good sport about it, but I know he runs an extra three miles and does a colon cleanse every Monday to rid his body of "those nasty chemicals."

Eli's eyes returned to the computer screen, and I made a mental note to call my parents.

"Are we busy today?"

"I should say, yes." He turned the screen around so I could see the multicolored lines representing our patients for the day. We scheduled different colors for the type of services the patients were receiving, and the schedule was blinking like a neon sign in Vegas.

"Wow, I better go clock in and get my chiropractic assistant legs on." As I stood to leave, Eli was summoned to treat the first patient.

I stored my purse in my workstation and started up to the front office to see if I could help answer phones, when someone grabbed my wrist from behind. Pain surged through my arm from the pressure on the bruises, and after the intense situation at the WTF, I was a little jumpy. I jerked my arm away, turned with a vehemence I didn't know I possessed, and went into defense mode, fists up, ready to strike out.

Su Le let out a startled yelp and had her hands in karate-chop mode. We both stood staring fiercely at each other. Then recognition set in on my part, and I dropped my warrior hands to my sides.

"I'm sorry, Su Le. You frightened me."

Her normally almond-shaped eyes were bulging with surprise. She relaxed and adjusted her headband back into place on her shiny black bob. "That's OK, Jen. I have an emergency at home. I need to leave."

"OK. You should tell Mary."

"I did tell her, but I have a patient on acupuncture needles, and I need you to take him off."

Normally the thought of seeing a person with fifty needles sticking out would have me running the opposite direction, but Su Le had trained me to remove needles, and I was a fearless member of the WTF, for crying out loud. "Sure, no problem," I responded, hoping Su Le didn't see my lip quiver.

Su Le inserts the needles, dims the lights, turns on her aromatherapy machine, and lets the patient rest for thirty minutes. If she has several patients, she uses two rooms. She will get the patient started, and then Paulina, the other assistant, or I (if absolutely necessary) will follow behind and remove the needles. Su Le gave me her timer and the patient's chart. I looked through the chart, which included a sketch of a body with little red dots showing where all the needles were located for this patient and the number of needles used. I needed to remove twenty-five needles. I thought that wasn't so bad.

I recalled the first time I had helped Su Le remove needles. The patient had at least fifty. It was Mrs. Jones, an elderly lady who was coming in for constipation and leg pain. I entered Mrs. Jones's room, and the soft sounds of waves lapping up on the beach greeted me. Su Le had the relaxation music on low and the aromatherapy on eucalyptus. My nose started running immediately upon entering the room. The tall medical table was motorized for elevation and the back was inclined.

The patient was resting comfortably, head dropped down to her shoulder and needles poking out of her hands, legs, stomach, and almost every surface in between. My stomach felt queasy, and I started summoning my inner superhero. The mantra was on playback in my head, drowning out the relaxation music. I took a deep breath and turned off the aromatherapy machine. I picked up the small metal tray containing cotton balls soaked in alcohol for the needle removal. I reached over to turn off the music, and the room went dead quiet. I looked over at the patient, and she hadn't moved a muscle. In fact, I couldn't see the steady rise and fall of her sleeping chest. Goose bumps started at the top of my head and spread over my body, making the hair on my arms stand at attention. I turned and bumped into the patient's walker. The clatter was loud in the quiet room, but the patient remained still as stone. I flicked on the overhead light. "Uhm, Mrs. Jones," I said from across the room. Nothing. Oh jeez. I prayed silently, *Please don't be dead. Please don't be dead.* I slowly approached the patient and laid a hand on her arm, "Mrs. Jones," I said, giving her a little shake. Her eyes popped open, and she let out a blood-curdling scream. I screamed and jumped away from the patient, knocking her walker into the wall. The small metal tray with the cotton balls went flying and clattered to the floor. Eli and Paulina came running into the room.

"What's wrong?" they asked in unison.

Mrs. Jones looked around, blinking her eyes rapidly, finally fully awake from her deep sleep.

"I just came in to take out the needles," I said, still cowering in the far corner of the room.

Eli came over to the patient and rested his hand on her shoulder. "Mrs. Jones, this is Jennifer. She's going to remove the needles, OK?"

Mrs. Jones looked at me, shrugged her shoulders, and smiled. "Well, she scared the bejeezus out of me and I shat myself, so I'm happy with the results. I didn't think this acupuncture stuff was going to work."

"Jen!" A voice snapped me from my thoughts. Paulina, Eli's assistant, with the cute turned-up nose and cheerful personality, was standing in front of me, hands on hips. "Your timer is beeping."

She pointed at the small square timer I had in my right hand, and sure enough, it was making a beeping noise. Paulina is one of those people who use every body part when engaging in conversation.

"Oh, right. I'm on my way in now."

"That is so awesome!" she exclaimed, waving her hands in the air and giving me a double fist pump. "Because Mr. Crane doesn't like to be left on the needles past the allotted time." She gave me a perky smile, turned, waved, and headed in the direction of the front office. Off to sprinkle some merriment on the next unsuspecting person.

I entered the acupuncture room, and to my surprise, the lights were blazing. The room was devoid of the soft relaxation music and the smell of essential oils. Instead, an aroma of acrid body odor curled around the room, strangling any aromatherapy that lingered. The patient was not lying on the acupuncture table but sitting upright in a chair across the room. He was a large, heavy man. His dark hair was overgrown and unkempt, and he had a scraggly beard that extended past his chin. His beady brown eyes, hidden under a jungle of eyebrows, looked me up and down as I approached him. A black Ozzy Osbourne T-shirt stretched across his protruding belly, hanging on for dear life to his love handles and a pair of faded blue jeans cut off above the knee, exposing his tree-trunk legs.

"Hello, Mr. Crane, I'm Jennifer. I'm going to remove your needles today." I placed my paperwork on the counter to prepare the cotton balls with alcohol.

"You're late," he bellowed. "My timer went off three minutes ago."

"I'm sorry," I apologized, giving him a sweet, comforting smile. His arms and legs were pinned up with needles, but he managed to flick a hand at me. I took that as the carry-on sign and proceeded. I began removing needles from his left arm and tried not to gag at the odor he emitted. His eyes followed my every move.

"So are you from Coffee Creek?" I asked, trying to make conversation while I counted the needles I was removing.

"Don't talk to me; you'll lose count."

I shrugged and got down on my hands and knees to remove the needles from his bulky legs. His skin was covered in small pustules I assumed were some kind of psoriasis. The skin on his legs was taut like an overstuffed sausage. I was sure that when I pulled a needle out, his leg would deflate like a leaking balloon. When I removed the first needle, a drop of blood formed at the small hole, threatening to drip down the patient's leg. I quickly dabbed it with the cotton ball. Each needle had the same response. By the time I got to the second leg, I had gone through six cotton balls. As I was applying pressure to the latest bleeder, I looked up at Mr. Crane. His weight and size seemed to amplify his breathing, and his birdlike eyes stared down at me. A sleazy smile crept across his face, and I followed his gaze to my chest. The gap in my scrub top gave him a perfect view of my cleavage. Since the only bra I had clean today was a fluorescent yellow Victoria's Secret push-up bra, my girls were sitting up perky on their little span-dex shelf, illuminated in the glow from my bra like the sun reflecting off the space shuttle. I felt the color rise into my face, and I adjusted my position to block the view. Mr. Crane licked his lips, and I quickly stood up to start on the arms.

After I finished removing and disposing of the needles, I said, "There you go, Mr. Crane. I'm sorry Su Le had an emergency, but she would like to see you back in"—I consulted the chart—"five days."

"Are you going to be here?"

"I work every day, Monday through Friday," I replied, trying to be as perky as Paulina.

"Good, I'll be here when I get here." He pulled his bulk from the chair and exited the room, leaving his stifling body odor behind.

⁓

*A*fter my encounter with Mr. Crane, I helped Mary in the front office, scheduling patients and calling insurance companies to verify patients' benefits. Elvira, the collections CA who normally calls the insurance companies, was out sick today. I feel like the insur-ance companies breathe a sigh of relief when I call, because Elvira is an ex-guitar-playing truck driver. She is about six feet tall, curses like a sailor, and I'm pretty sure she has more than one tattoo. Eli hired her because she needed a job, and Eli is a sucker for a woman in need, no matter how gruff. She doesn't take no for an answer, which is a good quality when trying to collect money. Eli told me his collections doubled after he hired her. I would hate to see the body count on the patients who refused payment.

My stomach was grumbling, which meant it was time for lunch. The good thing about Coffee Creek is there are at least four good local restaurants within walking distance. Eli came sauntering in, stood behind me, and gave my shoulders a massage rub. One of the many benefits of having a chiropractor for a brother. Mary finished checking out the last patient of the morning, and Eli asked, "Anyone up for the Pitts today?"

The Pitts was a barbeque restaurant located on the opposite side of the square. "Sorry, Dr. Cloud, I have to run errands at lunch today," Mary said. "My husband, God rest his soul, left some loose ends I need to tie up today." Eli and I made the cross sign as all good Catholic children were taught when referring to the dead. Mary's husband had died a few months ago after a long battle with lung cancer. He was Mary's fifth husband and she swore he was the last, but I heard through the grapevine that she was seeing Mr. Covey who owned the hardware store. If Mary came back from lunch with a hammer, I was putting my money on husband number six.

I grabbed my purse and waited while Eli locked the office door. I was glad Paulina also had errands at lunch. She was so bubbly that sometimes my brain needed to take a break from Princess Perky.

Eli and I walked the block to the Pitts. The smell of barbeque met us halfway there, and I floated the rest of the way, not even bothering to window-shop as we passed Baubles and Beads, one of my favorite boutiques. Eli was telling me about our mom's latest client. Our mother's job as a cookbook editor connects her with many well-known clients. She told us every celebrity wants to write some kind of book, and the easiest one to hire a ghost writer for is a cookbook. Like Kris Jenner really wrote her own cookbook. Go figure...

Her newest client has his own cooking show but keeps setting things on fire. She was in Dallas trying to put the final touches on her manuscript for his third cookbook when he asked her to have a taste of the flaming cherries jubilee for inclusion in the book. Mom set the manuscript on the counter and two seconds later, poof! The manuscript and the tips of Mom's fake fingernails were on fire. Eli was very comical relaying the latest mishap to me, and my inner voice was tsking me for not calling my mom. Working with the WTF was going to take some juggling so I wouldn't forget to call my parents.

We entered the small hash house, my Steve Stone leather biker boots with the tough-girl studs and black stacked wooden heels making a clicking sound on the rustic, hand-scraped wood floors. Eli and I walked up to the counter and ordered two barbeque sandwiches, chips, and root beers. Blake Shelton's latest hit played from the antique jukebox in the corner, and I doubted Caiyan would ever eat at a place like this. I wondered if he even liked barbeque. My inner voice agreed that maybe I should get to know him a little better outside the sheets.

"Jen." Eli nudged me with his elbow.

Eli had collected our root beers, and the cashier was trying to hand me a square tile with a number six on it for our order.

"You just put this number in the holder on the table, and we'll bring it right out when it's ready," she said.

I knew the drill. We had eaten here many times, but my mind had wandered off, and Eli looked at me a little concerned. We sat in a booth across the room, and I placed the number in the tall holder in the center of the table. The small place was decorated with pictures of old Western movies, memorabilia from the local high schools, and past events that made Coffee Creek a small friendly town

"You seem a little out of it lately," Eli said, giving me a brotherly stare of concern.

"I've just been busy." I took a pull off my root beer and changed the subject. "What's up with Mr. Crane?"

Eli shrugged. "He's a mess. Diabetes, high cholesterol, weight issues."

"Yeah, I can see that. I felt like he was sneering at me the entire time I removed his needles."

Eli picked up a red crayon and began doodling a tic-tac-toe board on the paper tablecloth. I chose a blue crayon and proceeded to match his Xs with my Os. "Mr. Crane has some pretty deep issues. I tried to get him to try chiropractic because his spine looks worse than a Kansas City twister, but he refused and agreed on the acupuncture."

The server delivered our sandwiches, and Eli beat me in tic-tac-toe.

"Next time I'll send Elvira in with him. He's probably not someone I want you to be with in close quarters."

"He is kind of creepy," I agreed. "But I want to do my job, so if I need to help Su Le, that's OK."

"I'm glad you're trying to work at the CA position. I know you would rather be selling shoes—or at least buying them."

"A girl's gotta do what a girl's gotta do to make a living." I smiled, finished my sandwich, and drew out another tic-tac-toe board. If Eli only knew the half of it.

⟶

*e*li headed back to work, and I stopped off at Baubles and Beads to pick up a little gift for my mom. If she'd dyed her hair brown, she might need a little pick-me-up or an intervention. She was always the first one to object when I wanted to turn my dishwater-blond hair a few shades darker. The shop's door gave a tinkle as I entered, alerting the sales clerk that a new customer had arrived. The scent of hazelnut coffee and vanilla drifted around the store, creating a warmth, as if you were receiving a hug as you entered.

The clerk behind the desk, a woman in her midfifties with a cute red pixie cut, looked up from polishing a silver cuff bracelet. "Hi, Jen. Can I help you today?"

"Just browsing, Helen, but thanks." She nodded and went back to her polishing. Beautiful paintings and tapestries hung on every available wall surface. Tiny chandeliers and large ornate light fixtures dangled from the ceiling, adding sparkle and glam to the historic building. Overstuffed accent chairs adorned with chenille throw pillows were scattered throughout the store, providing an ambiance of comfort. I rummaged through a table display of scarves, but nothing caught my eye. Admiring a few paintings, I made my way to the back where the discounted items were kept. A pair of silver French candlesticks stood on a mahogany credenza. I reached for one, and it was heavier than I had anticipated. These would look really good on Mom's dining table. The price had been marked down twice but was still a little steep for my budget. I never bought her a housewarming gift, so I hefted the pair up to the counter. Helen set the polishing aside and was enthusiastic I was buying instead of browsing. I also found a pair of dangling silver earrings, and while Helen was wrapping the candlesticks in Bubble Wrap, I eyed the cuff bracelet Helen had been polishing earlier. The little voice inside my head hollered, *You are such an impulse shopper—you do not need another bracelet.*

Helen bagged up the candlesticks and said, "It would go really nice with the earrings." She paused as she slid the earrings into a small brown sack to show me how they complemented each other. She was right.

I ignored my inner voice. "I'll take them," I heard myself say as I handed over my credit card. I checked my phone for the time. Damn, I was late for work. The fretting over the bracelet had made me lose track of time. I should have bought the damn thing, fretted later, and then returned it. Now I was going to have to get a lecture from Mary about my punctuality. I thanked Helen and power walked around the square to the clinic. The candlesticks were quite heavy, and as I was looking down, adjusting my bags, a body came hurriedly out of the new plastics center. Wham! We ran smack into each other, and as I looked up, I realized it was Mr. Crane. The hairs stood up on my arms, and I felt my heart rate increase.

"Mr. Crane," I said in no more than a whisper. He stood, his body odor oozing out around him. At that moment I knew exactly what a cootie was, and Mr. Crane had expunged his all over me. We were eye to eye. His massive girth disguised his stature. His beady eyes stared as if he was planning his next meal. A small smile crept into the corner of his mouth. I sidestepped around him and scooted on by, taking refuge in the comfort of Mary's voice telling me I was late as I entered the clinic.

Chapter 7

Friday came faster than expected. The clinic kept me busy and kept my mind off the upcoming "training session" at Gitmo. Thankfully, I didn't see Mr. Crane again. Su Le had a family emergency and had to make a trip to Shanghai. Her acupuncture patients were rescheduled for the following week. I breathed a sigh of relief as I picked up Gertie on Friday afternoon from SMU to catch a bite before I left for training. She came out of the library wearing a red lace long-sleeved top covered by a black leather vest and black cargo pants. Her hair was French braided on one side and circled the back of her head, finishing into a braid with a leather tie on the opposite side.

"Is that the new dress code for library aides?" I asked as she got into my car.

"It's my Katniss Everdeen look." She flipped the visor down to get a view of her look in the mirror. "There's this guy in my History of the Ages class who's really into *The Hunger Games*."

"Does he know you're hunting him?" I joked.

"Not yet, but he asked if I would e-mail him the last lecture notes, so...I'm making progress." She flipped the visor back into position, and we motored off down the street to our favorite French bistro.

Gertie was foregoing her weight-loss shake for a spinach quiche, and I had just taken my first bite of chicken pasta when Gertie asked, "Any word from Caiyan about our double date?"

"No, I haven't heard from him all week," I replied, mouth full of food and thankful my taste buds operated normally. It was scrumptious. "He did say he was out of town on business."

"Dang, don't you think that's weird? Where can you go that you can't call someone for a whole week?"

I knew one place, but there was no way he could travel. The next moon cycle wasn't until mid-December.

"I was hoping we could go somewhere fun," Gertie said. "I'm so bored when you're gone." She made a pouty face, and I couldn't help but laugh because before I started this travel thing, she was never home when I was home. We worked opposite schedules, and she usually hung out with her friends from school. I agreed with her; it was odd I had not heard a word from Caiyan. I rolled the thought around in my head as I finished my pasta. Maybe Jake would have a few answers, but I hated asking him because our past history just made things awkward. He didn't approve of my relationship with Caiyan, the playboy. He would much rather I have a relationship with Jake, the playboy. Jeez, men just made life complicated.

"You're doing that thing with your hair." Gertie pointed her fork at the strand of hair that I was twisting in between my thumb and forefinger. I immediately dropped it. "You always do that when you're worried."

"No, I don't." My inner voice was nodding her head in agreement with Gertie.

"Yep, you do, and if I had a hot piece of meat like Caiyan and he wasn't calling me, I would be worried, too."

"Thanks for your concern, but I'm not worried," I said and blocked the mental picture of my inner voice running around with her pants on fire.

Gertie shrugged. "Just saying."

My phone gave a ping. I retrieved it from my handbag and read the text from Jake: "See you in an hour."

I sighed. "Looks like we got to go." I held my phone up so Gertie could see the text. "The boss man is making sure I won't be late."

Gertie finished her quiche, and we got a couple of sweet teas to go. "If you see Brodie this weekend, tell him I said hey."

I was sure Brodie didn't need any training, but I agreed anyway. As we got into my car, I thought I saw Mr. Crane drive by in an old Cadillac Seville. The car sloped to the driver's side, looking off balance as it drove off down the street.

"What's wrong?" Gertie asked as I slid behind the wheel and buckled my seat belt.

"Did you see the guy in the Caddy that just drove by?"

"No, was he hot?"

I gave Gert an eye roll. "Definitely not." I put the key in the ignition and waited for Gertie to buckle up. As I started to back out, here came the Cadillac again. I slammed on the brakes, throwing Gertie forward and spilling some tea on her lap.

"There!" I pointed as the car went behind us. She snapped her head around to get a better view of the driver.

"Oooh gross! He's not cute at all." She wiped up the tea with the corner of her shirtsleeve.

It was him. He kept his face straight on as he passed, trying not to draw our attention, but I knew it was him.

"He's a patient at the clinic. And I'm not supposed to tell you that with the privacy laws and all, but he kind of creeps me out."

"Like who am I gonna tell?" Gertie said more than asked. "He looks creepy." She made an *ugh* face, and I laughed, nodding in agreement, but that gnawing feeling I get when something's not quite right had me wondering about creepy Mr. Crane.

＊

I arrived at Gitmo at precisely fifteen after six. I didn't want Jake to think I would come when called, so I took my time getting ready. Since I can't travel with any extra clothes or personal items, I had to ship a few things via FedEx and send a list to Jake's assistant, whom I referred to as Ms. Beotch. Not because I was jealous, but because I knew they had a fling going before he knew I had a fling going with Caiyan. Jake and his double standards, jeez.

One of the black suits was standing at the base of the landing pad, awaiting my arrival. I stepped from my outhouse down off the landing pad. "Hello," I said, smoothing the wrinkles from my lime-green Jessica Simpson sweater.

"Miss Cloud." The man nodded and put a hand to his earpiece. "She has landed," he said and cut his eyes at me. "Right away, boss." He was very tall and muscular, much like the other black suits I had encountered at Gitmo. He looked at me, pressed his lips together, and signaled me. "Follow me, Miss Cloud." He led me down a long corridor and stopped in front of a door with a sign that read, "Women." He held the door open for me. "Miss Cloud, you'll find a locker with your name on it and clothing to wear for training. When you're ready, I'll escort you to Agent McCoy."

"Thanks, and please call me Jennifer." He didn't indicate if this was an option, so I went in the locker room. The room was a small restroom with a sink, two stalls, and a changing area. A row of six double-stacked lockers stood against the far wall. I assumed there weren't many women who worked here, because the gunmetal gray lockers and the white painted walls held no indication of a female touch. I supposed Ms. Beotch had her own private dressing room for all her pencil skirts. I quickly bashed my subconscious thoughts. Jake and I were just friends—business relations, I should call it now. I guess the old feelings of attachment were clinging to me. I shouldn't have mean thoughts if he wants to see his assistant. In fact, it takes the pressure off me if Jake is occupied with other things besides keeping me away from Caiyan. This was a great idea, except my subconscious was dabbing at a small tear. I needed to get some closure on that chapter of my life. We were always better friends than lovers anyway.

I opened the locker marked "Miss Cloud." A pair of folded green cargo pants and a black T-shirt lay neatly stacked under a pair of black Nike running shoes. At least the shoes were awesome. Hanging on a hook was the cosmetic bag I had mailed earlier in the week. I breathed a sigh of relief. My stuff made me feel better. I dressed and pulled my hair back into a sleek ponytail. Checking my work in the mirror, I slapped on some nude lip gloss and felt like I could kick some serious boo-tay. I sauntered out of the locker room and bumped chest-first into the black suit. I jerked back and hit my elbow on the door behind me. "Ouch, don't pop out like that—you scared me!" I scolded, rubbing my elbow.

"Sorry, Miss Cloud." He looked sorry that I had bumped my elbow, but I saw the glimpse of a small smile curl at the corners of his mouth. He was laughing at me. Well, on the inside at least. As if he could possibly pop out of anywhere—the man was huge. We walked down the long corridor and took the elevator back to the main entrance. He showed a badge, and we proceeded through the chain of gates to get outside. The security was very tight. Only one person could pass through a gate at a time. Then it would close, lock, and then a beep would sound before the next gate would open, allowing you to proceed. Both gates were never opened at the same time. Once we were outside, we took a right, and a regulation army jeep was waiting for me. I saluted Mr. Black Suit and hopped in the jeep next to the private escorting me to my next destination.

Gitmo is made up of several camps used to house criminals, from *extremely dangerous*, to *probably know a wealth of information and we are going to keep you locked up until you spill the beans*, to *captured because they were just in the wrong place at the wrong time.* The WTF headquarters is located under Camp 5, hence all the maximum security.

I discovered the private's name was Ryan, and he was from Georgia. We took a right out of the base and drove down to Camp 4, where the *I'm not sure what I did wrong* prisoners are located. We passed through the gate inspection and drove around the hospital. The jeep stopped in front of a small building with aluminum siding. A running track circled the building. A small soccer field was to the right, and a group of prisoners played basketball on a court across from the soccer field. A tall double chain-link fence with the standard razor wire on top separated the prisoners from us, and guards were posted throughout the area.

My escort saw me scoping out the prisoners. "Don't worry, miss," he said with a slow southern drawl. "They can't get out. When it's time for them to play soccer, we open the gate to the soccer field. It's closed because today is hoops day."

I smiled at him, and another jeep pulled up behind ours. Jake was at the helm and was dressed in black army-issue sweats and a gray T-shirt. "I'll take it from here, Private," Jake said as he approached.

"Yes, sir." And he was back in the jeep, pulling a doughnut to exit. I started to give Jake a hug as I always do, and he held up a hand. "The prisoners are watching, and female contact is off-limits." I nodded in understanding and followed him into the small building. The building was a one-room workout space that held cardio equipment, weights, and workout mats on the floor. Two large floor-to-ceiling mirrors were mounted on the right wall, and a small restroom was at the back.

"I wanted to go over a workout protocol with you," Jake said. "You will never move around Gitmo without an escort—got that?"

"Why? Don't you?"

"Some of the prisoners speak very good English, and you shouldn't be any closer to them than you are today, but I don't want to take any chances. We'll be doing some training outside. It's hot, humid, and the prisoners aren't used to seeing many females."

We went outside to the running track. The angle of the building blocked the prisoners' view of half the track. Jake started with some stretching and a two-mile run around the track. I was sucking air by the time we finished and was glad to see Jake heading back inside the building. After a short break for water, we did more stretching, followed by a lesson on muscle building, and then moved on to some self-defense moves. I had taken a self-defense class in college, so I knew a few of them. A large mat ran the length of half the room. We began on the mat, with Jake behind me in the aggressor position.

Jake had me in a head hold, my body was pressed next to his, and that old familiar tingle started to pulse in my head and slide down to my loins. *How does he have that effect on me?* I asked myself. *We're just friends.* I told my hormones to calm down so I could finish my lesson.

I felt his breath on my neck and realized he was speaking to me. "Jen, what do you do next?"

Focus, I told myself. I jammed my elbow into his gut and pulled him over the top of me, pinning him to the ground with my body. My left arm was at his throat, and my legs strained to keep his legs pinned to the ground. My right arm held his left arm secure. He looked into my eyes and broke into a wide smile. "Nice," he said. I smiled back and relaxed, thinking our drill was over. He grabbed my ponytail hard and jerked, pushing me off him with his knee. As I flew through the air and hit the ground hard, I was shrieking.

"Damn you, Jake!" I yelled as I lay sprawled across the mat, rubbing my bruised ego.

He stood next to me and tapped me with his shoe. "Never let your guard down."

"You pulled half my hair out!" I stood and secured my ponytail, which had come loose from its elastic.

"Again," he commanded. I stood with my back to him, waiting for the approach. I felt him come up behind me. He smelled of sweat mixed with cologne and freshly laundered cotton. He wrapped his arms around me, and I felt my insides heat up again. *Stop that!* I gave my body a mental warning. I got ready to elbow the gut, when he spun me around and kissed me hard on the mouth. My body took over and coiled into the snake. His lips were soft and inviting. I felt my tongue slide in and mingle with his tongue. His hand grasped the back of my neck, and I relaxed into his arms. As we parted, I realized this was not what I needed from him.

"Dammit, Jake!"

"You were supposed to fight me off. What if I were a rapist?" His mouth drew up in an egotistical grin. He knew he had awakened that part of me that would do just about anything for him.

"That wasn't fair. If we're going to work together, you've got to stop doing that."

"It didn't feel like you minded so much a few seconds ago."

"I can't help it you're, well…you."

"You still want me." A smile stretched across his mouth.

"No, I want you to teach me how to stay alive." I grabbed the towel off the weight rack I had draped it over earlier and dabbed the sweat from my face. He stared at me for a long moment, and the anguish of girlfriends past washed across his face.

"I'm sorry. That wasn't professional of me," he said, packing up the gear we'd used. "I'll always want to keep you safe."

"I know," I replied. "And I appreciate you wanting to protect me from all this. But for some reason I'm here, and I'm going to need your help to stay safe."

He nodded. I put away the free weights and took a swig of the water bottle Jake had brought. As we returned to the jeep, I noticed the basketball players were lined up to go inside the compound. Most likely going in for their dinner. Most of the men looked like they were of Persian descent. I saw a few who could be Cuban or Israeli. No Americans, for sure. I knew this by the lack of catcalls as I battled with Jake. Was it my imagination or did American men go overboard with their freedom of speech?

The drive back was relatively silent. We took the jeep back to Camp 5, and I returned to the locker room to retrieve my clothes. There was a small shower, and someone had set out towels. Body wash and shampoo were in plastic dispensers that hung on the wall under the shower head. I took a quick shower and used the blow-dryer attached to a wall unit. I didn't find a flat iron or any styling tools, so I made do with my cosmetic bag and finger combed my hair. Jake promised that the apartment I would stay in during the weekends would be available after eight. I was borrowing an apartment used by another woman stationed at Gitmo, who was going home on maternity leave.

I didn't have a purse to put my cosmetic bag in, so I tucked my favorite lip gloss in the pocket of my black slacks and stored the bag back in the locker. Jake was waiting for me in the hallway, freshly dressed in his dress shirt and slacks.

"Nice hair," he said. "I like the tree hugger look on you." He smiled big, and his dimples made me smile in return.

"I'm going for the *I don't have my flat iron* look."

"Are you hungry?" he asked.

"Yes." My "best friend" Jake was back, and I was glad to see him. We left Camp 5 through all the security gates, and Jake drove us to his apartment building. Jake led the way up to the deli, located on the roof of the building. We grabbed a couple of subs and beers. We made small talk about friends back home and enjoyed sitting outside. Jake's phone pinged, and he read the text and then pocketed the phone.

"Your apartment is ready," he said.

I followed him back downstairs, and we stopped in front of Jake's apartment door. The first time I was at Gitmo, I had a tour of Jake's apartment, and I found it to be sterile, a complete opposite to the warm and cozy flat he owned in Dallas.

"Do you need something from your apartment?" I asked.

"No, I'm taking you to the apartment you'll be staying in for the training time." He stepped across the hall from his door and unlocked the door opposite his. How convenient, right across the hall from Jake. I didn't know if I liked the location. Jake would know my every move and every visitor. Well, we never really kept secrets from each other before. If you don't count all the coeds he forgot to tell me he was dating in college. I huffed and entered the small apartment. It was clean and had the same standard brown couch and coffee table as Jake's. A kitchenette was against the far wall with a small dining area, and a bedroom flanked off to the left. There was a female touch to the small space. A jug of flowers sat on the coffee table, and there were pictures of the ocean hanging on the walls. A cherry bookshelf held a dozen paperback romance novels, a copy of the Bible, and a basket of seashells. I paused to look at a picture of a pretty brunette girl, laughing on the beach, holding hands with a dark-haired man. They were both wearing military fatigues rolled up to the ankles as they stood posing in the waves.

"My roommate?" I asked.

Jake came over and looked at the picture. "Yes, she's about six months pregnant. She took a desk job, but then her doctor put her on bed rest, and she went home on sick leave."

"What will happen after the baby comes?"

"After six weeks, she'll have her mother care for the baby until she completes her tour."

"Wow, that must be difficult."

"That's military life for these people."

"And for you?"

"No. The CIA doesn't operate that way, but we do have our own rules."

I thought that maybe they made up some rules, like placing me across the hall from Jake. Temptation to fall back into my old ways versus the annoyance of him watching my every move on my only days off from the clinic were opposing thoughts, duking it out inside my head. I wonder what the WTF has to say about an agent mixing it up with one of the travelers. My inner voice was reminding me of that thing that Jake did in bed that I really, really liked. I reminded her there was no comparison between Jake and Caiyan. They were both very qualified in that area. She cut her eyes toward the bedroom, and I made a beeline for the kitchenette. A microwave and fridge were all I really needed, and the space had both. Someone had stocked the refrigerator with the basics: milk, eggs, cold cuts, and bread. The boxes I'd shipped with my essential clothing, makeup, and hair products were on the floor by the couch.

"Good," I said. "My stuff arrived."

"Do you want me to move any of the boxes for you?"

"I thought I was in training." I pointed to what Jake referred to as my spaghetti arms. "Shouldn't I try to move them myself?"

"True, but I don't want you straining your back and then whining through the rest of our weekend sessions." He bent at the knees to pick up the biggest box and huffed as he stood up, box in tow. "What's in this one? It weighs a ton."

"Shoes." I smiled as I picked up the other box and headed for the kitchenette.

Chapter 8

The training session was tough, and after the first lip-lock, Jake acted strangely distant. When we were training together, he was all business. Every inch of my body was sore from trying to keep up with the rigorous schedule Jake demanded. He assigned one of the black suits to teach me combat training in the morning. The guy was huge, and taking him down in self-defense moves required all my strength. After combat training, I had linguistics and history lessons. I enjoyed learning the different dialects, and I was picking up the basics of Spanish and French pretty well. We trained all day with a short break for lunch. Jake would appear after lunch for weapons training. I was amazed at how much he knew about weapons and how accurately he fired a semiautomatic. It would be very sexy if I still felt that way about him. Following weapons training, Jake taught me the can dos, cannot dos, and definitely must never dos of the WTF. Afterward he would dump me off at my apartment, and then I wouldn't see him until the next morning because he had "work to do."

I still had not heard from Caiyan. I finally broke down and sent a text to him. No response. I called and left a voice message on his generic voice mail. I didn't want to tell Jake I thought I was being dumped. I knew we were not exclusive. Well, we didn't talk about it, but I was heading down girlfriend lane. Considering his past, he might have been cruising Jen for a short drive and had moved on, but I didn't get that vibe. When we were together, he was all about me. I texted Ace a few times, but he was no help. He told me that was Caiyan's MO, or method of operation. It was how he snagged all the ladies, making each one feel special—like she was the only one. It was one of the many reasons the WTF kept him at arm's length, although he was one of their best defenders. "They couldn't trust him to go back and not get his knickers in some kind of jam with the women from the past," Ace replied in a return text message. I thought about his last response. Was the WTF happy I was screwing Caiyan because it kept him out of trouble during his travels? Maybe I was an asset. My inner voice went all preacher on me and reminded me prostitutes provided the same type of service. I debated asking for some medication to quiet the voice in my head, and she shut up.

Thanksgiving was on Thursday, and my parents were making noises about the family getting together. I enjoyed our family Thanksgiving. My mom usually tried out a few new recipes on us. Dad and Eli watched football, and fall truly was here for Texas. Occasionally it was still eighty degrees outside, but sometimes the cool air moved in, and the crisp scent of fall would fill the air.

Last year my mom made us go to Black Friday. My oldest sister, Melody, was in town, and we ended up sitting on the floor of Walmart for four hours, waiting for a toaster to go on sale. Go figure. There is not a toaster in this world that would make me do that again. I did get some sisterly bonding time. She told me about her crazy boyfriends and all the fun she was having in New York City. After high school, Melody got a scholarship at an elite dance school in NYC. At that time, I didn't know I would be able to travel anywhere I desired in the blink of an eye, and I was always bugging my parents to go visit her. The shoe shopping alone was inspiration for a trip. Melody graduated from the dance school, and she has been pirouetting her way around New York in off-Broadway productions for the last three years.

This year my sister bowed out of Thanksgiving because it was taking place in Mount Vernon, my father's birthplace. Melody was starring in an off off-Broadway play and couldn't get away. I was spared from Black Friday and Walmart. It would also allow me to get back to Gitmo for training.

When my great-aint Elma passed, leaving me the key and my new life, she left her home in Mount Vernon to my cousin Trish. Trish packed up her double wide and moved Gertie and her twin half brothers into the small white frame house in the woods. Not too long after, she met Vinnie and moved the kids to a mansion in New York, but she kept her small frame house for family get-togethers. This year she wanted to have a big family reunion, "Thanksgiving at the farm," as she now referred to her small house. She invited all the relatives, even the ones "we don't like very much," Trish confirmed.

My parents picked Eli and me up at my house. Eli was living in a rented space above the chiropractic office in Coffee Creek, and my house was "on the way." It made sense for him to come ride with us. It felt like serious déjà vu when Eli and I climbed in the backseat of my mom's Lexus. This ride would be smoother than the Ford Explorer from my youth, and since Melody wasn't with us, I was entitled to a window seat instead of being squashed in the middle. My dad's dark-black hair had turned gray over the years, but he still held every hair in perfect position with a can of Consort hairspray. He might be a health nut, but he was never giving up his aerosol hairspray. George Jones played on the radio, and my mom scanned her latest cooking conquest for errors. Eli and I looked at each other and smiled. This was family time. There would be nagging at Eli to find a nice girl and settle down. There would be subtle hints dropped about me taking some online classes toward a master's degree, and there would be a degree of not understanding why Melody couldn't make the Thanksgiving reunion. But we were family, and the two-hour drive to Mount Vernon let us catch up on one another's lives, except the part of mine that was a secret.

The car smelled of sweet potatoes and cookies because everyone brought a dish to the reunion. That was family tradition. This year my mom made sweet potato casserole (a recipe of Paula Dean's). I made a tray of chocolate chip cookies (slice and bake), and Eli opted out because his cooking skills were not so great. I checked my cell to see if there was any word from Caiyan. No text. I hit the app that opened my e-mail and scrolled through the shopping ads. An e-mail from Jake read, *I hope you and your family have a happy Thanksgiving.* Nothing from Caiyan.

We exited off the highway at the Dairy Queen, the only landmark available, and took the asphalt road through the tree tunnel, bumped along for a few miles, then pulled up in Trish's yard. The white house sat back from the road, and a few kids were playing on an old tire swing that hung from one of the giant oak trees that populated the yard.

"I thought Trish had that swing taken down?" Mom asked.

"Aint Mable's daughter is bringing all her kids. She has eight of them, and Mamma Bea suggested to Trish that if she didn't want her buffet torn to shreds before suppertime, she should put the swing back up," Dad replied.

Mamma Bea was my dad's mother. She looked like Dolly Parton, smelled like White Shoulders, and could yodel like a Swiss milkmaid. She told me this was good for calling the sows in for feeding. A porch wrapped around the house, and I dreaded the stuffy smell that always hung in the air inside the small home. Dried flowers and bleach would stop you in your tracks as soon as you crossed the threshold. I took a deep breath of fresh air before entering. I was shocked. Gone were the smells of the past along with the furniture. The old brown flowered sofa that sat on the wall underneath the window AC unit was gone. The window unit had been removed, and a big picture window took its place with a perfect view of the tire swing tree. Cousin Trish was burning a vanilla-scented Scentsy on the mahogany entry table, and the whole room felt cozy. As usual, relatives came forward to greet my family. Aint Mable had had gastric bypass surgery and was no longer pushing three hundred pounds. Dad was making a comment about how he hardly recognized her, being so slim and all. There was still about a hundred pounds extra, but who am I to judge?

Mamma Bea entered the room, and her scent of gardenia mixed with the vanilla smelled like heaven. I wrapped my arms around her and felt that warm tingle that always made me feel special when I was little. She looked at me and smiled. Her hair was dyed a honey color and piled up on top of her head. Turkeys dangled from her earlobes, and she wore an apron that claimed her spot in the kitchen.

"I like your earrings, Mamma Bea."

"Thanks, dawrlin'. I got them at Target. They were on sale two for one, so I bought these and a pair of reindeer earrings that have blinking noses."

"I can't wait to see them."

She laughed, took my mother's casserole, and returned to the kitchen. Gertie had driven down the day before, and I could hear her laughter from the backyard. The weather was crisp but not too cold today, and I had worn my black-and-white tribal sweater with my black Uggs just in case it was nippy. I followed Gertie's laughter outside.

When I stepped off the back porch, I walked into backyard glory. Trish had gone all-out. A large white canopy tent was set up, and I could see tent heaters inside, making the area toasty. A long buffet table loaded with casseroles ran the length of one side of the tent. Round tables with rust-colored tablecloths were scattered about. On each table, a centerpiece of the horn of plenty spilled gourds and fall leaves onto the tables. A small squatty pumpkin carved with tiny holes sat in the center, illuminated by a flickering candle.

Gertie sat at a table and had her head thrown back in a roar of laughter. Her twin brothers bookended her and were also laughing out loud. Bobby Ray and Billy Ray were about six five and played tackle for the University of Texas. They never did very well in school, but once a college coach caught sight of them, their grades magically improved. Bobby Ray or Billy Ray was telling a joke. They were both huge with curly black hair, and their skin was the color of Milk Duds. Gertie had her ways of telling them apart, but to me they were just Gertie's brothers. One of them had a gold cap on his front tooth, sporting the Mike Tyson look, but I couldn't remember which one, so I just addressed them as *hey, guys.*

Gertie waved at me, and the man sitting across from her turned and stood as I approached. Marco.

I hadn't seen Marco since the shooting last month. He was Vinnie's nephew and a traveler from his father's bloodline. It must have been karma that Vinnie met Trish at Marco's grandfather's funeral because their marriage brought Marco into my life.

Marco refused to travel but helped me save Gertie last month when a brigand was holding her hostage. He was six three and had washboard abs. He raced Formula One cars as a hobby and did nothing for a living. He came from the Ferrari family, a long line of Italian race car drivers and travelers. Working for anything but fun will never be an option for Marco. He took a bullet in the chest saving my life. He was my first kiss when I was sixteen, and the sexual tension that sparked between us was like lightning.

"Marco." I approached, knowing he would greet me with the Italian gesture of kissing both cheeks. That's just the way they roll in that family. I held out both hands and he grasped mine in his, leaning down to greet me. The electric shock raced up my arms and made my face blush.

"You look much better," I managed to get out. His blond hair, compliments of his Swedish-born mother, had grown longer and curled around the collar of his white button-down.

He cocked a wolfish grin, knowing what his touch did to me. Continuing to hold both my hands, he said, "The doctor says I'm one hundred percent, and I'm going to start racing again soon."

"That's good to hear," I said, pulling loose of his grip. "I didn't know you would be here."

"My parents are traveling abroad, and Uncle Vinnie didn't want me to stay in New York all alone."

I doubted anyone who looked the way he did would be alone, but I'm sure he had his reasons for being here. Hopefully they didn't include me. I'd met Marco here, in my aint Elma's garden when Trish married Vinnie. Trish was living here, and she wanted to marry her rich Italian boyfriend at home. Gertie told me it was so all her friends could attend the wedding and be green with envy.

I grabbed a seat next to Marco, greeted everyone, and the conversation continued. One of the brothers was telling a joke, and that started a round of crude jokes at the table. Marco just sat back and took it all in. He had his reasons for not traveling. The WTF and the Mafuso family of brigands were constantly trying to entice him to travel. The Mafusos went so far as to sponsor his racing team, but to no avail. Marco was firm. He refused to go back in time. His vessel was a shiny red Formula One race car he housed on the rooftop of his apartment building in SoHo. When I first figured out he was a time traveler, I looked him up on the Internet. He was featured in the top one hundred sexiest men alive article in *People* magazine. Here he was sitting at Thanksgiving dinner in Mount Vernon with my country relatives, oozing his machismo and making my knees tremble.

I blamed Caiyan. If he hadn't left me high and dry, my libido would be swaddled in the aftermath of glorious sex rather than teetering on the edge of horny.

I loved being surrounded by my family. Many of my dad's relatives were elderly, and a journey outside of Mount Vernon was too much for them. I think this was the reason Trish kept the "farm." Unfortunately, my aint Elma was the only sibling who inherited the time travel gene. At least that we know of. There was no mention of anyone else in the family by the WTF, which monitors all the relatives of the families with known time travelers. Aint Elma was the last remaining relative to travel, until I came along. She never had any children, so the gene was passed down to me. The WTF is perplexed by this because the gene normally passes from a direct line. From a grandparent to a grandson or granddaughter, and normally skipping a generation in between. As far as we know, my grandpa didn't travel, but no one really knows the truth. He died when my dad was young, and Mamma Bea won't talk about him. She says it brings back too many painful memories. He passed away before the WTF was formed, so the records are a little sketchy, but when I traveled back in time and came face-to-face with the notorious Poncho Villa, there was an indication my line ran from both great-grandparents, so who knows.

It's always a little touchy for Marco to come to Mount Vernon. Marco's grandfather and Aint Elma were having a secret love affair. Marco was with her the night she was killed, defending her lover, his grandfather. Ever since, he rolls in and out of my life, creating this sexual heat that boils up from deep inside me and explodes out the top of my head. Sometimes I wonder what it would be like to have sex with Marco. I know he is curious and he wants the same, but he is also one of the wandering playboys who my life seems to be full of at the moment.

I was admiring the work cousin Trish had done to make this Thanksgiving nice for the family. My mom and cousin Trish were up on the back porch swing sipping cosmos and gossiping about New York fashion. All the older relatives were in the house because until the food was served, it was too "cold" for them to be outside. If it gets below sixty degrees in Texas, we call it winter. Today was a mild sixty-five degrees, so we were still at fall for my family thermometer. I found it ironic the older generation of my family who told stories of working on the cotton farms and in the oil fields from dawn until dusk, rain or shine, walking miles in ice and snow, couldn't leave the warmth of the small house to mingle outside.

My dad and his brother were having some fun at a horseshoe pit. Mamma Bea named all her children after movie stars, I have Aint Loretta Lynn, Uncle Buster Keaton, and then of course my father, John Wayne Cloud. My dad was throwing a horseshoe and laughing at something Uncle Buster said. Aint Loretta's husband, Wayne, stood nursing a beer, smiling at the crude remark. The only time Uncle Wayne smiled was if there was a dirty joke or a crude remark said.

"Marco, are you staying here tonight or are you going to 'poof' back home?" Gertie asked.

I gave her my best *you better shut your yap* look. The WTF made her take an oath after our last time travel. If she revealed the travelers, she could be imprisoned for treason.

"Guys don't poof," said one of the twins. The other one nodded his head in agreement.

Gertie waved her hand in the air. "Whatever. Are you staying the night?"

Marco looked at me, and I felt a tingling start in my toes and work its way upward, pausing long enough by my boy howdy to make me clamp my legs shut. He licked his bottom lip, stared straight at me, and said, "Some other time."

Trish came out to the tent and held up a metal triangle, giving it a couple of clangs with a metal rod. "Dinner's ready—y'all come and get it."

You can take the girl out of the country, but you can't ever take the county out of the girl.

The twins looked at each other and made a dash toward the buffet table. It was like two rhinos charging the last blade of grass. Various relatives followed, and a line began to form down the side of the tent.

Gertie stretched and said, "I'm going inside to heat up the special dinner I brought."

"You brought your own food?" I asked, because I knew how much Gertie loved turkey and all the trimmings.

"Yep, and it's good and it's low fat." She sauntered off in the direction of the house, leaving me alone with Marco.

"How are things at the compound?" Marco asked.

"You know I can't talk about that," I said.

"Still with Caiyan?"

"Yes," I answered, but my shoulders slumped, and I looked away.

"Uh-oh, trouble in paradise?" He reached out and tugged a strand of my hair.

"No, it's just that I haven't heard from him in a while, and I'm worried something might have gone down."

"Aren't the wardens tracking him?" Marco asked, with a sarcastic air to his question.

"I don't know." I shrugged, trying not to look directly into his blue eyes for fear of throwing myself into his arms for a comfort hug. "Every time I ask, they avoid my questions. I've been training there every weekend for a few weeks now, and I haven't seen or heard from Caiyan the entire time."

"You know that's pretty common for him, right?"

I pursed my lips together. A few relatives started to sit down at the table next to us, making conversation about the WTF difficult. Their paper plates were stacked to the brim with food.

"Let's go for a walk," Marco said, standing up and holding his hand out for me. "Unless you would rather eat?"

"No, I'm good for a walk."

I grasped his hand, and hot flames licked at my fingertips. We headed down past the hedge of photinias to the white picket fence my aint Elma used to divide her garden from the yard. My aint Elma had the most splendid garden. My outhouse lived in the center of the garden under a huge weeping willow tree. I am pretty sure it was the reason all the vegetables were huge and the flowers grew like they were wild. It's where I first met Gertie when I was nine, and later Marco at sixteen. We found the gate, and Marco flipped the small latch, pushing the gate open for me. I paused a minute.

"Something wrong?" he asked.

"No, this is where I first met you, remember? You had a flashlight, and it was so dark."

"July fourth, right?"

"Yeah, Trish's wedding. The fireworks were amazing that night."

I walked through the gate, and he followed. The vegetables had long since died. No one to maintain them, and without the magic infused from the outhouse, the back garden looked like any Texas backyard. We walked the part of the path that wasn't overgrown with wild rose bushes and crabgrass.

The huge trees that shadowed the path kept the crabgrass down, and we walked without too much trouble, catching the occasional root or weed on the tip of my shoe. We walked hand in hand, not speaking. The warmth had settled down to a feeling of melting heat. The area where the old vegetable garden used to be came into view, and I sighed. "I wish I had known Aint Elma better."

Marco didn't make a comment on this because it was Aint Elma who was the other woman in his grandfather's marriage. His grandmother was the one who raised him while his parents were off crisscrossing the globe. The mention of Aint Elma was a sore spot for him.

We passed through the garden area and turned left. The willow tree stood tall in all her glory. Her long branches swooped down to the ground and sagged, almost as if she missed the outhouse. "This is where my outhouse used to sit," I said, pointing to the willow.

"I remember," he said, and pulled me toward the tall tree. Someone had placed a wooden bench at the base of the tree. He divided the hairlike leaves of the tree, and we ducked underneath. Alarm bells went off in my head. This kind of closeness with him could only lead to trouble. I hesitated, and he gave a hard tug. My shoe hit a clump of crabgrass, and I fell forward into his arms. He caught me against his chest, and his mouth came down on mine. The kiss started out gentle, and then the temperature rose slowly. My entire body began to tremble, and he parted my lips for a deeper kiss. At first, I held back. Mixed emotions of Caiyan and Jake swarming through my mind. I didn't want to be a player. I always considered myself to be faithful in my relationships. But was I in a relationship? As this realization crossed my mind, I gave in to the heat and responded to the kiss. My inner voice screamed, *What the hell are you waiting for? Go for it!* The heat soared, and I felt the climax start from somewhere down deep inside. It grew like a ball of fire, licking and burning my insides until it spilled out and made me spasm with ecstasy. Marco pulled me back and held me at arm's length.

"Holy shit, Jennifer." Time stood still for a few beats while we stared at each other. I knew Marco was slowing things down, so the fire would die a lonely death.

"We have to get out of here," I said, pulling the curtain of branches back and making a quick exit.

"Jen, wait." Because of his height, it took him longer to maneuver from under the tree. When he caught up with me, he said, "Do you think we would combust if we ever had sex?"

I smiled, still trying to come down from the sexual high. "I don't know, but I'm not sure I'm ready to find out."

He frowned and said, "Whenever you're ready, let me know."

I laughed, and we walked back toward the gate.

"It's not like that with Caiyan?" he asked.

I thought about this for a moment. Yes and no. The fire burned and it certainly had a fantastic ending, but the speed of the heat that engulfed me when I was with Marco was different. Finally, I said, "It's different."

As we walked back through the garden, his cell phone buzzed. He read the screen and then pocketed the phone back in his jeans. "Looks like I got to go." He didn't make any comments about who had texted him, and we returned to the table where Gertie sat staring at two large brown balls placed side by side on her paper plate.

"I gotta bounce, Gert," Marco said.

"Already?" she asked. "You haven't had anything to eat."

He glanced at her plate. "If that's what they're serving, I'll grab something on the road." He laughed, and his glorious smile appeared, making me wish I hadn't run from the tree cave. He caught my look, and his eyes went from laughter to smolder. I shook my head no. He leaned in, kissed my cheek, then bent down and did the same to Gertie, and he turned and walked away.

"I swear," Gertie said. "If you two would just get the nasty over with, all that pent-up tension wouldn't float around like a humid Texas summer."

"What are you talking about?" I asked, sitting down at the table.

"You know what I'm talking about." She took a sip of a green shake she had in a plastic cup. "Every time you two are together, the static electricity goes up so high my hair starts to frizz."

"I'm with Caiyan," I said.

"And when was the last time you heard from Caiyan?" she asked. I shrugged. "That's what I thought. Jen, I don't think Caiyan knows you're with him. So I don't see what the hurt is if you have some fun with Marco." She picked up a knife and sliced through one of the giant brown balls on her plate. "He obviously wants to hook up with you. He's rich, gorgeous, and he has that travel thing you two have in common."

I decided it was best to change the subject. "What are you eating?"

Gertie looked at her plate and nudged a brown ball around with her fork. "This here's fried Thanksgiving dinner. It's everything—turkey, dressing, gravy, and cranberry sauce, all rolled up into a ball and fried to perfection."

"And that is low calorie?"

"It's gluten free." She took a bite and made a face.

"Are you sure it's going to help you with your diet?"

"Yep, I am going gluten free, and with my healthy fruit and veggie shakes, I should be able to get in that little red dress of yours by Christmas."

Gertie wanted to borrow my red Valentino gown Ace and I had picked up super clearance at one of his shopping spots in Paris. Gertie had been eying it since the day I brought it home, and there was a big New Year's Eve party at her stepdad's house in the Hamptons every year. I wondered if Marco would be there, and the thought was quickly pushed aside when the twins returned with their plates loaded with food that made my stomach growl with desire.

Chapter 9

I had been training at Gitmo every weekend for three weeks. Jake bought me a gym membership at a local gym and had me scheduled with a personal trainer three nights a week doing a cross-fit workout. Every morning I had to drag myself out of bed because of all the aches and pains. My muscles felt like they were getting stronger, but boy, they hurt in the process. Caiyan was MIA. My heart ached as much as my legs. I didn't understand how a man could act like he was all about the girl and then not call her for three friggin' weeks. I stumbled down the stairs and stood at the open refrigerator, drinking milk out of the jug. One more week, and then it would be time for the full moon. All the travelers meet at the WTF for their itinerary. If Caiyan didn't show, I would know there was a problem. I guess if he did show up, there was still a problem. Gertie came in dressed in her librarian outfit—a brown sweater and skirt—and reached around me to get a carton of yogurt.

"That's a good look for you," she said as she grabbed a spoon from the drawer.

I was so tired last night I crawled into bed wearing my camouflage socks from Gitmo. I vaguely remembered pulling my pink Victoria's Secret nightshirt on over my head. My hair was piled in a bun on the top of my head, and I'm sure I had raccoon eyes from the forgotten mascara.

"I'm just really tired."

Gertie left for work and school, and I crawled back upstairs to get ready for work. After I showered and made myself presentable, I headed to the clinic.

The week progressed as normal. No creepy Mr. Crane lurking about. Su Le still hadn't returned from China, so I basically followed Eli around and helped the other employees when needed. Paulina and I went shopping Wednesday after work, and I skipped my workout. Screw Jake, screw Caiyan, screw them all! My inner voice shook her head in dismay and pulled up the contact in my cell phone for Marco. Paulina and I drowned my pity party with margaritas at the local Mexican restaurant, and I might have drunk dialed him. I couldn't remember. Thursday morning I woke up and my inner voice had an ice pack across her forehead and reminded me I needed to clean the bathtub because I threw up in it last night. I struggled to overcome my hangover and get to work on time, almost.

After work, I was sitting at the table trying to stab the remnants of my lingering hangover by eating a peanut butter and Craisin sandwich, waiting on Gertie to get home from school. My dad encouraged the Craisins instead of jelly.

"More nutritious, less sugar than jelly," he told us as kids, and it stuck with me. I was licking the peanut butter off my fingers when Gertie entered through the sliding glass door.

"Hey," she said, hanging up her jacket and tossing her book bag on the floor by the door.

"Hey, how was school?"

"Good, but the best part is I'm on break for two weeks." She walked over and put water in her teakettle, then set it on the stove to heat. "What's wrong?"

"Why do you ask that?"

"Because the peanut butter jar is out and you have that look like you might stick your finger in it any second."

"Nothing, I'm fine." I shrugged. "I just made a PB and C sandwich."

"Still haven't heard from Caiyan?"

"No, and Ace is in England having family time. I'm spending all my free time with Jake on the weekends, and his 'treating me like a victim' attitude is starting to grate on my nerves."

"I wouldn't mind being stuck with Jake all weekend."

"No, you don't understand." I tossed my hair behind my shoulder, avoiding my sticky fingers. "He trains me like I'm some kind of animal. I'm so sore afterward I can't even get off the toilet. We usually grab something to eat afterward, where he avoids all my questions about the upcoming moon cycle and where he thinks the defenders will be traveling, and then he drops me off at the apartment with not so much as a pat on the ass, and I don't see him again until the next afternoon. Then the whole thing starts over."

"So are you mad he's not making a play for you?"

"No, I'm sort of relieved, but I would like to know where he disappears to in the evening. I bet he's with that secretary."

"So you're mad he might be dating someone?" Gertie stirred some honey in her tea and eyed me like an old wise woman.

"I don't know what I feel. Maybe I am a little jealous that Jake might be having a life and mine is in limbo."

"Last month you had three hot guys fighting over you, and this month nothing." She quirked her mouth. "I can see where this has left a hole in your ego and you're feeling depressed."

"Thanks for your insight, Gertie, but I thought you were a history major, not a psychology major." I stood to put the peanut butter away, then reconsidered and grabbed a long-handled teaspoon instead.

"I watch a lot of *Dr. Phil*." She laughed. "Why don't you call Brodie? I bet he knows how to locate Caiyan."

"I would feel dumb. Anyway, the moon cycle is next week, and Caiyan will probably just show up for duty. And if not, I'll most likely see Brodie."

"Really?" Gertie perked up.

"Maybe." I opened the peanut butter and stuck my spoon inside, scooping up a glob of anxiety relief.

"Are you going to travel this time?"

"Jake tells me he is not releasing me yet. The full moon is on Monday. I figured if I call in with strep throat, that will give me three days off work, and I can be at Gitmo when the travelers arrive." I hated lying to my brother, but if I told him I couldn't come to work because I might be needed to travel through time and capture a bad guy, he would have me committed. "If my brother calls, just say I'm asleep."

"No problem," Gertie replied, flipping through a *Vogue* magazine I had left on the table. She looked up and smiled. "Telling tall tales is my specialty."

⟡

The next morning was Friday. I was due at Gitmo that evening for training, and I was going to be at Gitmo when the travelers arrived, come hell or high water. I went into work complaining of a scratchy throat. Eli felt my forehead and neck, looked down my throat with a lighted scope, and claimed all to be well. I had to be very careful because if my dad, the health food nut, and my mom, the recipe fanatic, got wind of my illness, they would be at my house immediately with homemade chicken soup and vitamin concoctions to restore me back to health. My plan was to make a few noises around the staff and look tired, which wouldn't be that big of a jump because between the training at Gitmo and my personal trainer, I was sore and tired all the time. On Monday, I would call in early before Eli arrived at the office and tell Mary I went to a doc in the box and had a positive strep test. I should probably send Eli a text as well and let him know I was fine and not to worry Mom and Dad.

My plan was going as premeditated. I coughed a little in front of Mary and complained to Paulina about my throat. She took two steps away, grabbed a bottle of hand sanitizer, and said I should go have it checked. I was about to tell Elvira of my woes when the bell on the front door sounded and in walked my stalker. Mr. Crane dragged his bulk up to the window and eyed me like a rib roast. I stood frozen in the center of the office. Mary scowled at me and took the window. "May I help you?"

"I received a call I need to reschedule my acupuncture appointment because Su Le is out of town." He was looking at Mary, but I still felt his beady eyes on me. His body odor crept around the room, and Elvira stopped what she was doing to locate the foul smell.

Mary explained Su Le was on extended leave for family reasons and gave Mr. Crane a referral to another acupuncturist.

"Why can't she do it?" He pointed a stubby finger at me. Mary and Elvira looked at each other and broke into a fit of laughter.

"Jennifer is only allowed to remove the needles. You have to be licensed to put them in," Mary explained.

Mr. Crane slammed his fist on the counter and left the office.

"That man really needs a bath," Elvira said.

"I think he has serious gout," Mary explained. "My uncle had it, smelled real bad."

"I saw him coming out of the new plastic surgery place that's going in next door."

Both Mary and Elvira looked alarmed at this information. "Do you think he's doing the gastric bypass?" Elvira asked.

"The place isn't even open yet, but Dr. Cloud never recommends bypass." Mary removed the pencil from behind her ear and used it like a conductor's wand to emphasize her point. "He says without the proper psychological counseling, most gastric operations fail within a year." She swung her chair back around to her computer to grab the phone that had begun ringing.

Elvira looked at me and made a face. "That man creeps me out."

My brother is six feet tall and Elvira towers over him. She has shoulder-length brown hair that gets washed about once a week, and she ties it back in a ponytail to avoid the greasy look. In her days of driving a semitruck, she whooped ass on more studded-leather-jacket-wearing bikers than I have digits. If Mr. Crane gave her the creeps, I was sure staying away from him was a good idea.

"Are your legs broken?" I heard Mary's voice behind me, and I realized I was still standing like a statue in the middle of the office.

"Nope, just feeling a little under the weather today." My lie was back in action.

Eli entered the office. His dark hair was perfectly groomed, and his wire-rimmed glasses reflected the light from the incandescent fixture in the ceiling. "Jen, I need a favor. Su Le is having problems getting back into the United States. Her work visa expired, and it may take a couple of months before she can return." Everyone in the office looked privy to this information except me. Eli pushed a piece of paper he had in his hand in my direction. I took it and saw a list of names and addresses printed neatly in Eli's handwriting.

"These are massage therapists," he explained. "I want you to book yourself a massage at each of these offices and give me some feedback on their ability. If they're good, I want to offer them a few days to come work here using Su Le's room."

"Let me get this straight. You want to pay me to get a massage?"

"That's right. It would be easier to rent her room for massage therapy while she gets her visa than to find a temporary acupuncturist."

"If she won't do it, I will," Elvira said.

"Me too," said Mary.

"Count me in." Paulina poked her head in through the front desk window.

"Thanks, girls, but Jen is the only one I can give the time off to right now."

This will work out great, I thought. There were about six names on the list, which would take about three days to complete. Maybe I wouldn't have to lie about being sick, and I could get free massages.

"You can count on me," I said. "Can I get started after lunch today?"

"Sure, thanks. I really appreciate you doing this for me," he said, giving me a brotherly hug.

This would work out great. I would do my calling this afternoon and book some massages on Saturday morning. I would tell Jake I needed to come in late Saturday and be there when the travelers came in for their assignments Saturday and Sunday. Then I would have the first part of the week free in case they needed me to travel. My inner voice gave me a high five for the perfect plan.

91

texted Jake and told him something came up, and I needed to report in Saturday afternoon at one. I scheduled the first massage on Saturday morning at nine, the second one at ten thirty, and the third at noon. I would get the first few out of the way and then report to Gitmo. If I persuaded Jake to let me stay until the travelers got there sometime on Sunday, I could either see Caiyan, if the ratbastard showed up, or find Brodie and get the down low on Caiyan's whereabouts. Jake responded with a firm, "FINE."

Gertie was having a book club meeting at school, so I took a long bath and mentally planned my outfit for Gitmo. I decided to wear my Rock Revival skinny stretch jeans with the blingy rhinestones embroidered on the pockets. All the jostling around during travel made pants my smartest choice. When I first started to travel, my outhouse would repel me three feet upon landing. I usually ended up facedown on the ground with scraped knees and elbows. Ace told me, *"The vessel feels what you feel, love—just chillax."* I tried some deep breathing, and sure enough, the travel was still bumpy but not damaging. I finally figured out if I relaxed, the travel was much smoother. It was almost as if the outhouse was part of me. Like somehow my thoughts connected to the container of potties past. I had a funky new Risto miniskirt I was dying to wear, but I didn't want to land with a skirt over my head if my outhouse decided to get cranky. I added my Tory Burch V-neck bright-orange belted tunic top, and my high-heeled Naughty Monkey gray leather boots trimmed up the outfit nicely. Too bad I couldn't take my new Brahmin cross-body bag I had bought as a pick-me-up gift to myself. It would complete the outfit. Everyone at Gitmo was dressed in either three-piece suits, military uniforms, or orange jumpsuits. Only the travelers and the occasional visitor stood out when on the base.

The next morning I showered, dressed in a pair of sweats, and flat ironed my wavy hair stick straight. I was rockin' Keisha on my iPhone as I skipped the makeup and glossed my lips. I could hear Gertie snoring behind her door, so I left her a note on the kitchen table, saying that I had dropped my plan for strep throat. I explained about my research for a massage therapist and asked her to inform any callers that

I was out getting a massage. Sometimes having Gertie as a roommate held certain advantages. She could lie without looking down and to the left. She was a walking history book and my main go-to for information before I traveled. She wasn't extremely messy, and she paid her rent on time.

After I put on my gray Michael Kors trench coat my mom had given me for Christmas last year, I pulled open the sliding door and locked it behind me. I didn't want any intruders to grab Gertie. After last month when Gertie was kidnapped, I learned that locking a few doors was mandatory in my new profession. Snatching attack cat was another matter, but I figured the chances of that were slim.

The wind whipped my straightened hair. I pulled my coat around me and walked head down to my car.

I hopped in the car and entered the address to my first massage appointment into the mapping app of my iPhone. The massage therapist was in the next town over from Coffee Creek. Growing up, we referred to the town as Trashy Terrell because of the town's locals, not the roadside waste. Apparently, the therapist rented a room in the back of a boutique named the Salon. I sang along with Rihanna as I drove the short distance to Terrell, looking forward to a relaxing massage. I found the place and grabbed a parking spot near the door. A flashing neon sign hanging in the window indicated they were open, so I went in and was greeted by a receptionist with purple-and-green-streaked hair.

"I'm here to have a massage with"—I glanced down at the paper Eli had given me—"Cherry."

She told me I could wait down the hall while Cherry finished with her client. I walked down a narrow hall that had multiple rooms branching from it. Many were hair salons, and the smell of hair tint and styling products wafted down the hall, making my nose run. Laughter pealed from one of the rooms, and I found a seat outside the room with "Cherry—Massage" plated on the door. While I waited, people came and went. Finally, a heavyset woman in neon-green tights and a purple spandex minidress emerged from the room marked "Cherry—Massage." She looked me up and down and asked, "Are you my nine o'clock?"

"Yes, hi, I'm Jennifer."

"Cherry." She quirked her lips. "You got anything wrong with ya?"

"Uhm, no."

"Good, 'cuz I'm outta the paperwork you're supposed to sign."

The door to her room opened, and an older man walked out and gave her a long kiss with a lot of tongue. "Later, Cherry pie," he said as he put on his coat and left out the back door. Ick.

"OK, sweetie, you're up."

I stood and entered the massage room. It was an eight-by-ten space stuffed to the gills with garden art. There were little garden signs that hung on the walls. Ceramic snails and frogs stared up from the small table that sat next to a wooden bench. A tall bookcase filled with magazines leaned against the wall, and garden gnomes lined the top, staring down at me with their slanty little eyes. A massage table stood in the center of the room.

"Go ahead, honey, take off your clothes and lie facedown on the table, then holler at me when you're ready. She stepped out of the room, and I took off my clothes and draped them over the bench. The table looked clean, but when I slipped under the satin sheets, they smelled like cigarette smoke. Apparently, changing the sheets wasn't a high priority for Cherry. I took part of the sheet and wiped the headrest clean, just in case. This was better than nothing, and I made a mental note to bring hand sanitizer for my next massage. I told Cherry I was ready, and she entered the room.

"Is coconut oil OK?" she asked. "I'm all out of cocoa butter."

"Fine." I guess. *This woman seems to be out of everything,* my inner voice chided and started making strike marks against Cherry.

"I'll infuse it with a little peppermint. That will get your circulation moving," she said as she began rubbing my back. She had firm hands; maybe she could be a candidate to fill in at Eli's office.

I felt myself being drawn into the first stages of REM sleep. Cherry moved to the top of the table and began rubbing her hands from my shoulders down to my buttocks. As she neared my butt, her large breasts lay like two huge water balloons across the back of my head, pushing my face into the headrest and making it difficult to breathe. I sucked in air through the small hole in the face cradle.

"How's the pressure, honey?" she asked as she held me hostage with her massive boobs.

I gave her a muffled "A little less please," and my inner voice marked a definite NO next to Cherry's name. I left Cherry agreeing with my inner voice and smelling like a piña colada.

I had another scheduled at a place back in Coffee Creek. When I arrived, the building was boarded up. No piece of paper for a forwarding location was hanging on the door. I crossed that name off my list.

My next massage was back in Sunnyside. Last time my sister, Melody, was in town, we went to Massage Appeal for a hot stone massage. An inexpensive chain massage center, it offered various types of massages. My potential massage candidate was a guy named Ahwad. He didn't do the hot stone, so I downgraded to a scalp and upper body massage. Because Cherry had rubbed my buttocks until they hurt, I felt like thirty minutes would allow me enough time to check this guy out and get to Gitmo in time for my lesson with Jake. Massage Appeal was located in a strip shopping center across from my dad's health food store. I parked in front of a big plate glass window that read, "Couples' One-Hour Massage Special—$40." As I entered, a chime sounded from the doorway, letting the staff know I had arrived. An older lady in head-to-toe black greeted me and handed me a clipboard with three pages of information to complete. This must be Cherry's missing paperwork. The reception area had floor-to-ceiling shelves across the back wall that displayed the Massage Appeal products. Three brown leather sofas formed a triangle with a large round rattan table as their centerpiece. I sat at the end of one of the sofas and completed my forms.

After I turned in my paperwork, a thin Asian gentleman took me to the dressing area and gave me a complimentary white bathrobe to change into for my massage session. My inner voice cooed at the soft robe and put a check mark next to Massage Appeal. I rolled my eyes and changed into the robe. The Asian gentleman was waiting for me outside the dressing area and took me to a small waiting room that was playing relaxing music. He offered me a glass of water infused with cucumber. It was delicious, and another checkmark was given. I reminded my inner voice we were looking for a therapist. I sat waiting on a brown chenille chair and sipped my cucumber water.

About five minutes later a dark-skinned man with thick black-rimmed glasses called my name. He introduced himself and escorted me down a hall and into his therapy room. Like Cherry minus the garden gnomes, he asked me to get on the massage table that was centered in the dimly lit room. I crawled under the plush sheets, and he returned with hot towels that he wrapped around my feet. Cozy. He began massaging my back in the same manner as Cherry had previously. I started to drift off when I felt Ahwad place his entire forearm across my bottom. Wait, I was supposed to have scalp and upper body only. Ahwad did not read his paperwork. He began dragging his arm over my butt and up toward my back. His very long arm hair dragged across my back like seaweed floating in the high tide. Goose pimples rose all over my body as he repeated the process over and over. About the third pass, my inner voice screamed, *MAKE HIM STOP*, so I asked Ahwad if he could just move on to the neck and scalp massage. He asked me to flip over, and he worked the knots in my neck and shoulders. He told me I had "much tension" in my neck muscles, and he proceeded to push on each and every one of them until I begged him to stop. He began working on my scalp, gently rubbing in the beginning, which felt nice. I gave a sigh of relief and tried to relax once again. Ahwad said, "And now for the finale."

My eyes popped open. *Finale? What the heck is that?*

Ahwad grabbed me in a headlock and began ferociously rubbing on my scalp with his fingers. The same way that Eli used to give me a noogie when we were kids.

"This increases the blood flow to the scalp and makes beautiful hair," he explained.

Ahwad ended my session with three final taps to the head. He announced the massage was over and told me that he would meet me in the hall after I was dressed. He turned on his heel and left the room.

As I stood up, I glanced in the mirror to see my perfectly straightened hair standing up on its own as if I had recently stuck my finger in an electric socket. I stifled a scream and quickly put my robe back on while trying to smooth my static-ridden hair. Ahwad was waiting for me in the hall as promised.

"Here you go," he said as he handed me a small cup of water and held out his hand, palm up.

I downed the water and set the cup balancing on his open palm. He raised an eyebrow and gave a sigh of indignation. I gave him a thumbs-up and returned to the dressing room to fetch my belongings. My inner voice drew a line through Ahwad's name and shook her head back and forth.

Chapter 10

$\mathcal{A}$rriving back home, I ditched my coat because it would be warmer in Gitmo. Gertie was already gone. I ate a carton of strawberry yogurt and went upstairs to shower off all the massage therapy oil. After my second shower of the day, I applied my makeup with the precision of Michelangelo and ran the flat iron over my hair again. I put on my subtle but sexy outfit I had planned the day before. I was ready to head to Gitmo for combat training. Many of the travelers would be arriving to get their assignments, if Pickles had any idea of where they might go. Hopefully, Caiyan would be one of them.

Attack cat was sleeping lazily on the back of the couch. I gave him a gentle rub on the head, and he gave me a swat, snagging my tunic.

"Thanks, cat," I said, finding a pair of scissors to cut the thread he'd pulled loose. I stepped outside and locked the door. Wrapping my arms around myself, I made a run for the outhouse. I jumped in, took a deep relaxing breath, and braced myself. Focusing on Gitmo, I said the magic word *hanhepi*, and my world went spinning.

The landing at Gitmo was a few bumps, similar to a plane's wheels touching down on the runway. I stepped from my vessel to find Jake waiting for me. We greeted each other with a quick, awkward hug. I hated that our relationship was strained. In the past, that would have been a big brotherly hug. In the not-so-recent past, it would have been followed with a lot of tongue.

"Are you trying to kill me?" he asked, pointing at my heels.

"What? I love these boots."

"The last time you wore those, we were dancing at the Longhorn Ball, and I had to rub your feet afterward because they gave you blisters."

I had forgotten the ritzy ball we'd attended last year. I had also forgotten the passion-filled night that we'd spent together after the ball at the W hotel. The way Jake looked at me, I could tell he had not.

"He's not here," Jake said.

"Who isn't here?"

"Jen, I've known you since grade school. I know why you're wearing those shoes, and I'm taking you to change and dropping you off at combat training."

I sulked as we headed down the long corridor toward the elevator to the exit.

Jake's cell beeped as we turned the last corner. "I'll be there right away, sir." Jake tucked his phone back in his jacket and turned to me. "Sorry, Jen, I need to go see General Potts. Please wait for me in the lounge."

"Yes, sir," I responded with a salute. "And tell General Poopy Potts hi for me."

Jake grimaced at this remark but didn't disagree. The general was a grouchy, overweight man who reminded me of Buford T. Justice. In fact, I sort of felt like Sally Field in *Smokey and the Bandit*, an upstanding young girl accidentally thrown in with a bunch of outlaws. My inner voice reminded me Sally Field was wearing a wedding gown when she hopped in the bandit's car. OK, maybe *upstanding* is too strong a word. Jake deposited me on a couch in the lounge and left for his meeting. The lounge was a break room of sorts for the guards and personnel of floor B. There was a refrigerator stocked with sodas and water, a wall of cabinets, a sink, and a microwave. Several round tables were scattered around the room with black plastic resin chairs set up around them. The room was quiet except for a television mounted on the wall opposite the black pleather couch I was currently occupying. CNN piped through the room, and I skimmed a *People* magazine that I had picked up off the rectangular coffee table.

After ten minutes of finding out the latest celebrity gossip, I decided to pay the lab a visit. The little voice inside my head reminded me that Jake told me to wait in the lounge, but I dismissed it by telling it Jake probably didn't think to tell me to wait in the lab. Besides, the last time I was here, he took me there himself to say hello.

I walked down the hall and found the wall with the keypad. I didn't have a code. Maybe I could just knock. I reached my fist up and gave the door a three-tap knock. The door slid open, and Al was standing on the other side. "Jennifer, my dear, this is a secured area. You can't just walk up and knock on the door."

"But you answered," I pointed out.

"I did indeed, but I saw you on the security camera." He pointed at a wall of small screens. "Come in." He stepped aside, and I entered, waving to Pickles, who sat behind his semicircular desk that allowed access for his wheelchair.

Pickles had on a Bob Marley T-shirt and jeans. Several rope bracelets stacked up his left forearm. He had a diamond stud earring in his left ear and his dreadlocks pulled back in a yellow bandanna. His key hung from a black leather cord around his neck, and the tornado on his medallion shone brilliantly against his dark skin.

"Hey dare, you are lookin' veery nice today."

"Hey yourself." I walked over to his workspace, and he leaned back in his chair.

"I heard you was going to come fer training again tis weekend."

I smiled at the tone of his voice. It was that *I can't believe she really showed up* tone.

"Yep, here I am. I am combat training for about two hours today, and then we're hitting it heavy tomorrow—weapons training." I made a gun with my hands and did a *Charlie's Angels* pose.

"Jeez, next dey be askin' Al to suit up for combat."

"Don't think I can't take out a few brigands." Al threw his shoulders back and puffed his chest out. "I was mighty in my day."

Pickles leaned his head back and gave a deep, throaty laugh. "Sure thing, man." Then something on his screen caught his eye.

"Dey are at it again, Al."

Al came over and peered through his spectacles at one of Pickles's monitors. I moved closer to get a better look. There was a blue dot flickering around the screen and a black dot and a red dot not too far away.

"Who is doing what?" I asked.

"This dot here," Al said, pointing to the black dot, "is a brigand. We don't know who yet, but we're working on it. The red dot keeps popping up, but we still haven't identified it yet, either."

"But the moon cycle is over," I said. Both men looked at each other and shrugged. "You mean the mystery traveler really stayed in the past?"

"Not only dat, but de brigand stayed, too. Dey both stayed after de last cycle ended," Pickles explained. "De moon is beginning her waxing phase, so we can see dem again."

I knew this was a very difficult thing to do. Caiyan had explained it to me. There would be a lot of pain as the full moon cycle ended, but if the traveler could endure, he or she could stay until the next full moon cycle. The longer the traveler stayed in the past, the less chance he or she would be able to travel back to the present safely. Caiyan told me he and Ace had stayed in 1969 because they wanted to see Woodstock live. He told me it was extremely painful, but the LSD everyone was handing out helped diminish the pain.

I remembered from my last trip to the time lab that the red dot was an unidentified traveler. We didn't know if it was a brigand or a new traveler who could become part of the WTF, like myself. I had shown up as a red dot until they figured out who I was, thanks to Caiyan and his womanizing ways. "Do you think the red dot might be someone the brigand is after?"

"I don't tink so," said Pickles. "In fact, we are almost positive de brigand is with de red dot—dat we are fer sure."

"How are you going to find out who it is?" I asked, watching the red and black dots dance across the screen.

"Caiyan is doing dat fer us," Pickles responded, watching the screen intently.

"Caiyan?" I questioned, and then my eyes saw the blue dot jumping a few inches away from the other dots. "Is Caiyan back there?" My voice started to raise a few octaves, and Al's and Pickles's heads snapped up in alarm.

They turned and looked at me, oblivious to the fact I might have feelings for Caiyan. They knew something was amiss. "How did he get back to—where is he?" I stuttered.

"He's in 1985," Jake said as he entered the room. "I told you to stay in the lounge."

"How did Caiyan get back to 1985?" I asked, hands on hips. "We just returned from a travel."

"He volunteered to go back as the moon cycle closed," Jake answered.

"Isn't it very painful to stay between moon cycles?" I asked. Pickles and Al looked like they were watching a tennis match as Jake and I squared off.

"Hurts like hell if you're caught between cycles, but he volunteered."

We stood staring at each other for a minute. The room was silent except for the whirring of the computers and the blipping of the dots on the screens.

"You knew and you didn't tell me?" I asked, and Jake stared me down.

"This was a classified mission." He was eye to eye with no regrets leaking out. At this moment I wasn't the best friend who was privy to all Jake's secrets, but a member of the WTF. Focusing on Caiyan rather than being mad at Jake might be the smarter hand to play.

"How do we get him back?" I asked.

"He's on a mission. When he finds out who the red dot is, he can come back," Jake said, pointing to the screens. "I expect him to return this moon cycle."

"What if something is wrong and he can't come back?" I stomped my foot in protest. "What if the red dot has him held prisoner like Pancho Villa did with Gertie and me?"

Al chimed in, and I jumped slightly. I was so caught up I had forgotten he was there. "We can see Caiyan moving around." He placed a fatherly hand on my shoulder and directed me toward the large screen centered in the room. Pickles tapped a few buttons, and the map projected on the screen. I saw the tiny dots blinking on the map.

"See." Al took a metal object from his shirt pocket and expanded it into a long metal pointer. "Here is Caiyan." He pointed at the blue dot. "He seems to be moving around freely and follows the red dot to different locations."

"Where are they?" I asked.

"Los Angeles, 1985," Al answered.

"LA?" I looked at Jake, and the corners of his mouth turned up in a smirk as if Caiyan was out partying in Hollywood with Tom Cruise.

"Yeah, mon," Pickles piped up from his chair. "We know dat is de location, but we don't know why or who is dere."

"Traveler X, as we now call the red dot, has been jumping back to 1985 for the last few months, but this last time he didn't return." Al shrugged, telescoped his pointer back to pen size, and returned it to his pocket.

Jake came over and stood next to me, staring at the screen. "We had just enough time to send someone back to try to get this guy before he does something we can't fix. If he's a new traveler, he doesn't understand what can happen if he screws up the past."

"The problem is we think the brigand is Mitchell Mafuso. If it is Mafuso, he has a new key and a new vessel. We have proof he was in the same location as Traveler X in November, but we're not sure if they're working together."

Caiyan had captured Mitchell, the sixteen-year-old bundle of trouble, on our trip to the past in October. We took his key but had to trade him back to the Mafusos in exchange for Mortas, his older brother. Mortas was sent to prison. The WTF thought the older Mafuso would be more dangerous, so the exchange was made.

"I thought Mitchell couldn't travel?" I asked.

"Der is always a way fer the sneaky," Pickles replied. "He is probably jest using Mortas's key. When Mortas gets out of jail, der will be a fight between those two over dat key unless dey find a new one."

Everyone nodded in agreement.

"Are we going to send someone back to help Caiyan in the next moon cycle?"

"There isn't anyone else," Jake said. "All the other defenders are either too old to go back to this time or too inexperienced to travel alone."

"What about Ace?" I asked.

"Already a babe in arms." Pickles giggled at the thought of Ace as a baby. The mood in the room seemed to relax.

"What about me?" I knew Jake would object, but I had to ask. "I can go. I'm younger than Caiyan."

Jake shook his head no. "You don't have enough experience to travel alone."

"We can't just leave him there," I stammered.

Al looked at a printout he held in his hand. "If we could figure out who the traveler is, it might give us a clue if he could be swayed to our side. The last emissions from Traveler X's vessel were from Florida." He crossed the room to the giant world map that stretched across the wall. "I think here." He pointed to an area on the map. We walked over and stood staring at Al's finger. He reached into his lab coat pocket and pulled out a box of pushpins. He selected a red one and put it up on the map next to a green one. "I think Traveler X originated from this area. I don't know if he stole a vessel or if he's a new traveler."

Jake motioned toward the map. "We've been over this before; the only traveler in that vicinity is Italina." He moved around so he stood facing us, as if to make his point clear. "She's retired and doesn't have any living children. In fact, we've searched the entire state of Florida and haven't found anyone."

"Have you talked with Italina to see if she knows anyone or has seen anything strange?" asked Pickles, tapping his index finger to his lips.

"Yes," Jake replied. "Caiyan went to see her right before he left for the November travel."

Everyone was staring at Jake, waiting. "Damn, do you think he knows who Traveler X is?" Jake finally asked.

Pickles nodded. "Maybe. I tink we need to have a chat wit Caiyan's aunt."

"Caiyan's aunt?" I asked.

"His great-aunt, to be more precise. Italina is Caiyan's grandfather's sister. She's about eighty years old and was quite the dynamo in her day," Al said with a slight smile.

"She was forced to retire because she's a little forgetful," Jake told me. "The green pin indicates retired travelers."

I must have been blind before because I suddenly noticed a number of green pins spread across the continents on the map. In fact, there were also blue pins for the travelers' home locations, black pins for the brigands' base locations, and many yellow pins.

"What are the yellow pins for?" I asked.

"Dey are de travelers who have died," Pickles responded from his wheelchair. He had wheeled closer to his computers. "But we still mark their home locations in case a new traveler appears in a past lineage who went undetected, like yourself."

"I see," I said, and I did see. There were many more yellow pins than any other color. The reality of it caused goose bumps to stand at attention on the back of my neck. I found Texas, and sure enough, there was a yellow pin in the small town of Mount Vernon. Each pin had a tiny number on it that Al told me cross-referenced with the computer files of all the travelers. There were also two pins in Mount Pleasant, a neighboring town, for my great-grandparents, Mahalo Jane and John Cloud. We discovered they were both travelers on my trip in October.

"Let's go, Jen. I need to get in touch with General Potts and plan our next move," Jake said as he walked toward the door.

I followed him, looking back at Al, standing in front of the map for one last glance at the sea of yellow pins on the map.

*G*eneral Potts called for an emergency meeting. There were only a few days before the next moon cycle, and we had to figure out the semantics of the travel. I wanted to figure out how to get Caiyan back in one piece.

Jake and I were waiting in the conference room for the other travelers to arrive. General Potts was in his office on the phone, and I could hear his booming voice all the way down the hall.

Jake was explaining that not all the travelers would be here for this meeting, only the ones who collaborate with Caiyan on a regular basis. The next moon cycle was approaching, and there would be other problems to chase in addition to the one in 1985.

There were many travelers I had not met from all over the globe. When we were in the travel lab, I took note of all the blue pins spread out over the map. There were more blue pins than black pins, so that meant the good guys were ahead. Right?

I was helping myself to a second cup of coffee when Brodie arrived, wearing his Crocodile Dundee hat and a worn pair of Levi's. He swaggered when he walked, and I could see why Gertie found him attractive. He had a gorgeous smile, and if I squinted, I saw the resemblance to Keith Urban that Gertie had pointed out on our first meeting with him.

"Hey. Ow-yar-doin?" Brodie asked, leaning in and giving me a peck on the cheek.

"I'm all right," I said, returning the affection by giving him a side hug. I wasn't too sure he was the "hugging" type, but he wrapped an arm around my shoulders and responded with a tight squeeze.

"Good, mate. Why are we meeting t'day instead of Sunday?" he asked Jake as he grabbed a few of the chocolate chip cookies off the plate next to the coffee maker. "I thought you had me pegged to follow one of the Cracky clan fer the next cycle."

"Yes, you are still going wherever they decide to go next week. This meeting is about Caiyan," Jake said.

"Oh, crimany, did he stay?" Brodie asked with a mouth full and cookie crumbs cascading down the front of his flannel button-down.

"Yes," I said, hands on hips. "Did you know about this?"

"Uhm..." Brodie looked at Jake, who was taking the fifth. Before he could respond, Ace sauntered in, wearing clogs that clicked on the tile floor as he walked.

"What the 'ell is so important?" he demanded. "I was taking an Irish clogging class." He was dressed in black tights covered, thankfully, with a pair of neon-green running shorts and a skintight T-shirt. His long brown hair was on top of his head in a sock bun, and his lightning bolt key gleamed in the reflection of the fluorescent lights overhead.

"How am I supposed to go to Ireland next week if I can't clog?"

I fixed Ace a cup of coffee, cream no sugar, and handed it to him. "This meeting is about Caiyan," I said.

"Oh, thanks, love," he said, taking the coffee from me and flopping down in the closest chair. "What's wrong with that gorgeous playboy now?"

"He stayed in 1985," I said.

"Oh, he's probably just shagging Madonna, or even better, Rocksanna," Ace said as he blew the steam on his coffee.

"Uhm, Ace," Brodie said and gave a head nod my way.

Ace looked up at me. My face was stone-cold mad.

"Oh, what I meant to say was he must have a lead on our little unidentified dot and had to stay to protect the greater good of mankind." Ace shifted uncomfortably in his seat.

"So you knew about the dot?" I pointed my finger at Ace.

"Well, yes, love, I thought everyone knew there was a UBD."

I crinkled my face with confusion. "UBD?"

"Unidentified blinking dot." Ace rolled his hand as he said the words and continued to sip his coffee. Grrr. He knew Caiyan hadn't contacted me and that I was worried about being dumped. Why didn't he tell me about the UBD? My inner voice clicked her tongue, and we did a pinky swear never to trust a man in clogs again.

Jake left the room to inform General Potts we were assembled and ready for the meeting.

A small man poked his head in the room. He was only about five feet tall. His arms and legs were much shorter in comparison to his head and body. He was in a navy suit and tie. "Hello, all," he said as he entered the room and stopped in front of me. He let out a long wolf whistle as he looked me up and down. "The staff here is getting better all the time. That Potts really knows how to get the good ones." He smacked me on the ass and ordered me to pour him a coffee, no cream, lots of sugar.

"I beg your pardon," I said, looking down at him, hands on my hips.

He reached up and pushed back a strand of his copper-colored hair that had fallen across his face, obstructing his line of vision. His square jaw and long nose had the makings of a very attractive man. He poured his cup of coffee, grabbed three sugar packets, and moved a few steps away from me. He turned to Brodie and asked, "What's with the new cookie?"

Brodie opened his mouth to reply, but I cut him off midsentence. "For your information, I am Jennifer Cloud. I am the new transporter. I am NOT a cookie."

"The new transporter?" He looked around the room. "When did we get one of those?" He struggled up into one of the chairs next to Brodie. "Who do you transport for? Because I'd like to switch. My transporter is always late. See," he said, taking a survey of the room. "She's not even here yet, and we're about to start the meeting. I call dibs on the new girl." He nonchalantly took a sip of his coffee.

"No can do, Gerry." Brodie slapped him on the back, splashing his coffee on the table. "Jen is Caiyan's transporter."

"Damn, why does he get her?" He motioned up to the heavens as if God had personally deprived him of something. "I need a tall blonde to help me reach all the high things."

Al and Pickles joined us, so I ignored the little man and sat down next to Ace. Pickles and Brodie were doing some kind of complicated handshake as General Potts walked in the room followed by Jake and his personal assistant, Ms. Beotch. Since General Potts wasn't always on the base, Jake's assistant was pulling double duty.

The general took his seat at the head of the table. "OK, people, let's get down to business," he said, placing his notepad on the table in front of him.

Ms. Beotch squeezed a chair in between the general and Jake.

General Potts looked around the table and tapped his pen on the notepad he had in front of him, which never received even a smidge of ink. Ms. Beotch set her laptop on the table and began to type the minutes of our meeting. Just as General Potts took in a deep breath to begin, the door burst open and a tiny Asian lady rushed into the room.

"So sorry, me so late. I stopped to get everyone a fortune cookie from my family restaurant." She held up a white pastry bag and began passing out fortune cookies.

"Ooh, I love those!" Ace ripped the plastic bag off his cookie and broke it in half, freeing the small white piece of paper from the cookie.

"You will travel to the land of fun," he read aloud. "Oh goody, I love fun."

General Potts cleared his throat and asked, "Can we begin now?" Everyone nodded, even though I thought it was a rhetorical question. The Asian lady took her seat next to the dwarf, who frowned at her. She stuck her tongue out at him, and the meeting proceeded.

Jake explained about the mystery dot and the starting location of the last travel made by Traveler X. He went over how Caiyan had stayed in 1985, and I watched faces grimace at the thought of staying after the moon cycle closed. Al and Pickles explained the theory that they didn't think the brigand was working with Traveler X, but may be following him to try to steal his key.

"Gerald." General Potts pointed at the dwarf. "I want you to go to New York and find Mitchell Mafuso. I want to know where he is and what he's up to. If you can't find him, find out where he is. I also want recon on that family of his. Find out if anyone is planning to travel and where."

The general pointed to the pad of paper like it was a carefully mapped out strategy of war.

"Brodie, I need you to go to Caiyan's homes in the States and Europe and look for any clues to this new traveler. If Caiyan knows who this guy is, I want to know about it."

I wanted to go with Brodie. In the four weeks that Caiyan and I had been seeing each other, I had never seen his home. He had his "normal" job of managing his *accoonts*, as he would say. We would meet up when I wasn't working at the clinic and he wasn't working wherever. We had an amazing night in Rome and another equally amazing night in Abu Dhabi.

"I can go with Brodie," I blurted out.

All eyes turned toward me. Jake frowned. "Jen, I'm sending you with Ace to check on Italina."

"No way!" Ace slumped down in his chair. "Last time I checked on Aunt Itty, she popped my knickers off right out from under me clothes and then forgot where she popped them to. I had to walk around all day commando, and I'll tell you, going without knickers under your jeans causes chaffing."

General Potts gritted his teeth as if to contain a growl, and Ace straightened up a little.

I wasn't thrilled about losing out on going through Caiyan's private homes, but maybe Caiyan's aunt could tell me a few things. "Where does this aunt live?" I asked.

Jake smiled. "Wonderland."

Chapter 11

Wonderland, the theme park that all children in the universe prayed would be their family vacation destination, was now my destination. After the meeting was adjourned, I was ushered back to my apartment to change into clothes appropriate for a theme park. My choices were limited because I'd only FedExed clothes for sleeping and exercising. I finally settled on a pair of khaki capri pants and a navy Gap T-shirt. Ace told me to wear tennis shoes because there might be some walking involved if Caiyan's aunt wasn't at home. I settled on a broken-in pair of Sperrys. Ace received permission to return home to change clothes, and I met him one hour later in the landing hangar. We boarded his vessel and left with "It's a Wonder World" ringing in my ears.

Ace's vessel made a smooth landing, and I pulled back the curtain to the happiest place on earth. My heart was pounding, and I had to control myself from jumping up and down in an excited stupor. I hadn't been to Wonderland since I was five. Ace stepped out around me. He had changed out of his "Lord of the Dance" outfit and looked almost normal in his black Lucky Brand jeans and white V-neck T-shirt. The shirt was studded with rhinestones and had a big skull across the chest with the logo *Love Hates* embroidered on the bandanna worn haphazardly by the skull.

"Maybe we ought to buy you a new shirt, a souvenir," I suggested.

"Are you afraid I'm going to scare the little tykes, love?" Ace grinned, pulling his wavy brown hair into a ponytail.

"Possibly." I shrugged, taking in my surroundings. We had landed in a clearing in a small patch of trees. Off in the distance, I could see the peak of the royal castle. The uppermost tower sparkled like a cupcake sprinkled with tiny diamonds. I smiled—even imaginary royalty gets the best.

Ace stood beside me, shielding his eyes from the sun, and suggested we move through the trees to get a better idea where we were exactly in the park. A purple tent that reminded me of a circus came into view. A long gold cord indicated the current residents were on break and would return at the top of the hour. There was some kind of ruckus going on inside the tent. Ace and I paused outside the entrance, and gold silk bloomers flew out past us, followed by a set of gold shoes that curled at the toes and had tassels on them.

"Why do ya got to bring that up now?" said a shirtless young man in white boxers as he came out after the pants. He looked Ace and me over, and he blew the feather attached to his large gold turban out of his face. "Sorry, I'm not doing autographs right now. Women always want their prince. Well I've had it. She can try kissing toads, for all I care." He scooped up the clothes and huffed off in the opposite direction of the tent.

Ace quickly followed. "Excuse me, sir, uhm, Mr. Sultan."

The man stopped abruptly and stood staring at us. "I'm not a sultan. I'm just a prince by marriage."

"Do you know where we might find the fairy godmother?" Ace asked.

My mouth dropped open. Jake had told me Caiyan's aunt worked at Wonderland. He didn't tell me she was the fairy godmother.

"Godmother, huh?" The man rubbed the small beard on his chin. "She normally works her routine at the castle this time a day." He paused and looked at the sun. "If she's not there, you'll probably find her at the Hibbidi Bobbidi Boutique. She likes to do hair." He pointed toward the castle. "When you find her, tell her I'll be in for my trim tomorrow." He turned and proceeded up the hill to a small outbuilding that was conveniently camouflaged to resemble bushes.

"Poor guy. Maybe I should go after him," Ace said. "He might need a shoulder to cry on."

"Sorry, your shoulder is coming with me to find the freakin' fairy godmother." I did a little spazzy dance. "How cool is that? She is like the best character in the park."

Ace looked down his nose at me. "You have obviously never met her. Oh, she looks so sweet, and then she zaps off your knickers, and you're standing there bare-assed in front of the teacups."

"She didn't really do that, did she?"

"Let's go find the old dearie and see what she zaps off you when she finds out you've been climbing all over her favorite nephew."

Yikes!

ce and I walked through the park, avoiding the cotton candy–filled hands of the small children we passed.

"Why didn't you tell me Caiyan's aunt was THE fairy godmother?" I asked, arms crossed over my chest.

Ace shrugged. "Sorry, I thought Agent McCoy told you. Aunt Itty has the gift to move things small distances. She loves entertaining the children with her 'magic,' as they call it."

"Aunt Itty?" I looked at Ace.

"She goes by Itty, always has as long as I have known her."

"Didn't the people who hired her wonder how she did the tricks?"

"You'll just have to meet her to understand." Ace shrugged.

We crossed over a small footbridge. Wonderland was built on swampland, so there were many little ponds and waterways scattered throughout the amusement park. Futureland peeked out across the water. The colorful spaceships of the Mars Orbiter spun and tilted, while the inhabitants screamed their heads off.

"You don't want to go on a ride, do you?" Ace asked, looking down at the ground and scuffing his feet around. I knew he would rather be anywhere else. Las Vegas, Hollywood, Monte Carlo, maybe. Wonderland was certainly not his scene.

"Nah, I just like watching people having fun." I heard his sigh of relief as we continued across the bridge.

The royal castle was beautiful. A purple glow was cast around it, reflected from the midafternoon sun, turning it into a shimmering wonder. The boutique was to the left of the castle as we approached from the front. A huge mouse was taking pictures with a small boy, while his parents tried to snap a quick shot with their iPhones. Amazing, I thought to myself—from the mouse's lap directly to Facebook in a matter of minutes. A long line of not-so-patiently waiting kids wrapped around the side of the castle. We followed the line around the side and into a little magical town. A crowd of people had gathered, and Ace was standing on tippy-toe, trying to see what everyone was watching. Pretty soon a flash of blue smoke and a screeching "Hibbidi bibbity boo!" sounded from within the crowd. The people next to me cheered and clapped. The crowd parted, and a short stout lady dressed in a blue coat came barreling down the cobblestone street. Her hair was pulled up into a loose bun, and she carried a long white wand. She ran down the street amid the cheers from the crowd.

"Wait," I cried out after she stepped into the street. I was immediately shoved out of the way and fell backward onto my ass.

"I'll show her bibbity boo," said a tall woman in a long green velvet dress covered with orange goo. Two other women trailed after her, both sporting mountain-high hair and long fairytale gowns.

Ace was laughing as he held out a hand to bring me to my feet. "I think we might have missed all the fun."

"You think?" I asked, brushing off the dust from my fall.

"Oh yeah, you guys totally missed it," said a teenage girl dressed in a leather vest and an imitation sleeve tattoo up her right arm. "The ugly stepmother and her two daughters were telling everyone it was time to go, that they wouldn't be giving any autographs to all us people who've been waitn' for over an hour. I'm a big fan, you see. I'm tryin' to get all the villains on this trip." Ace nodded, and she took a bite of her candied apple, smearing red on her cheek. "Anyhow, a boy stood up and hollered at them and told them they couldn't leave these fans after they waited so long. The stepmother just rolled her eyes at him and said, 'Who's going to stop me?'" The girl started talking faster, trying to get in all the details. "The boy took one of them small punkins over there by the fairytale garden and chunked it at her like a bowling ball. It took a bounce and hit her in the butt." The girl slapped her thighs in a fit of laughter. Ace and I stood looking questioningly at her and each other. Tattoo girl continued. "The stepmother got that evil look, just like in the movie, ya know, then went after the boy with her long fingernails. She had her talons hooked around his jacket, ready to give him the what for, when here comes the fairy godmother shouting bibbity whatever and waving her magic wand. The punkin rises off the ground, dances above the stepmother's head, then cracks open like an egg and spills orange goo all over the her," the girl said, using her candy apple as a wand for emphasis. "I dunno how she did that trick, but it was the best. I'm gonna go see what time the next show is. You guys really missed it."

"Well, I guess that's one way to use your gift and no one figures it out," I said to Ace while we made our way toward the puppet maker, who had just taken a break from making wooden boys to see what all the fuss was about.

"Do you know where the fairy godmother went?" I asked.

"I bet she went on home. If I were to make the stepmother that mad, I would definitely head for the hills."

"You mean she left the park?" I asked.

"No, she's one of the few who has housing right here on the grounds."

"I know where it's at, love," Ace said as he thanked the man and locked elbows with me. "Onward, soldier."

I laughed. Jake had given us exactly eight hours to find out what we could about the mysterious blip on the travel screen. There wouldn't be any fun on this trip. Ace's fortune cookie had revealed he was going to the land of fun, but it didn't say he was going to have any. With the full moon on Monday, we needed answers, fast.

ce and I power walked through Wonderland, keeping our eyes peeled for any signs of Aunt Itty. Ace stopped at the edge of the park in front of a group of pine trees. The trees were separated from the park by a fence. A golden cord was drawn across a narrow path that led into the group of pines. A sign read, "Wonderland cast members only."

Ace stepped over the cord. "Well, come on, love. We haven't got all day. Hike up your pedal pushers and get over here."

"These are capri pants, not pedal pushers," I replied, ducking under the cord instead.

"You can call them whatever you like, but they aren't going to take you into the fall season. They scream summer, darling." He had his hands on his hips, staring at me.

"Are we here to get some answers, or are we interviewing for Project Runway?" I eyed him.

Ace laughed, grabbed my hand, and we walked down the path like Hansel and Gretel. As we cleared the trees, a quaint cottage sat square in the middle. It looked exactly like the house I would picture for the fairy godmother. Made of creamy stucco, it stood with a round door and vines trailing up the sides and hanging from the eaves. A white picket fence surrounded the cottage, and a little bell tinkled as we opened the gate.

Ace rolled his eyes, and I giggled at the whimsy of it all. As we approached the porch, we saw that the round door was ajar. Ace walked in and called out, "Yoo-hoo, anyone home?" The inside of the cottage was charming. A plaid sofa sat along the wall across from us, bookended by two end tables. A cozy chenille chair sat to its right, and a small round footstool held a steaming hot cup of tea. The owner obviously was somewhere close by.

"Aunt Itty?" Ace called out again.

The sideboard cupboard opened, and out popped Aunt Itty. She was still wearing her fairy godmother dress. "Ace, oh my goodness! Is that you, dear?" She rustled over to us and pulled up her round spectacles, which had slid to the tip of her nose. "Why, it's been ages. You've grown so tall, but I would know that voice anywhere. Are you still singing, dear?"

Ace blushed from head to toe. I had never seen Ace embarrassed, but his gangly frame seem to fold up in itself as he gave Aunt Itty a hug. "Aunt Itty, why were you in the cupboard?"

"You never know when 'you know who' might be lurking about."

"You mean, a brigand?" Ace asked.

She peeped around Ace, questioning his handiness with the word *brigand*, like Harry Potter using his wand in front of a muggle. Her eyes lit up when she saw me. "Ace, who is this lovely?"

"Aunt Itty, this is Jen." Before Ace could get in another word, Aunt Itty was all up in my business, hugging me and standing back, holding me at arm's length. "Oh, Ace, the door does swing both ways in your life."

Now Ace was truly tail-between-the-legs ready to bolt. "Aunt Itty, no—she belongs to Caiyan." Realizing what he had just said, Ace stammered, "I mean, Jen is Caiyan's transporter." Nice save because both Aunt Itty and I were standing, hands on hips, ready to kick some butt.

"Oh...how nice for you." Aunt Itty seemed a little distraught at the fact that I was a transporter and I worked with Caiyan.

"Can I get you a spot of tea?" Ace and I took a seat on the sofa as she tootled into the kitchen. A few banging pots later, she returned, carrying a tray with two steaming cups of tea and blueberry scones arranged on a delicate china plate. She topped off her tea and placed a teapot wrapped in a little coat on the table between Ace and me. "What brings you to the happiest place on earth?" Aunt Itty asked, sitting down in her cozy chair and sipping her tea.

"Caiyan has gone back to 1985 and hasn't returned," Ace explained.

"Hasn't returned? Oh my, that's bad." She put her cup down and placed her hands in her lap. "Is his key working?"

"Yes, we can see him on the transport screens, but for some reason he isn't returning."

"Did you say 1985?"

"Yes, ma'am," Ace replied. "It's getting near his birthday, and we need him to return this next moon cycle, or you know..."

It dawned on me, if Caiyan didn't return before he was born, he would die. Caiyan had explained it to me on our first travel together, but I couldn't recall the details.

"He'll die?" I asked.

"Yes, love," Ace said. "You can't travel back to a time when you are already living, but if you travel back and then you are born, some kind of cataclysm happens and you die." He shrugged. "Your life becomes an endless cycle. We have sent people back to look for the travelers who have disappeared off the travel screen. It's like you just disintegrate."

A big knot of fear was rolling around inside my gut. I needed to figure out a way to get to Caiyan.

Aunt Itty was wringing her hands. "I haven't seen him since the month before last. He brought Campy here to live in August, right before the fall semester began."

"I didn't know Campbell was living with you." Ace took a sip of his tea.

"Yes, I'm afraid he was in a pinch of trouble back in London. His sister works nights, you know." She smirked as she said this, as if she didn't approve of either the job or the night shift. I became curious about Caiyan's sister's night job. Caiyan never talked much about his family. I knew he had a sister and his parents had died, but I got this information from Jake.

"Who's Campbell?" I asked.

"That's my great-great-nephew, dear." She nibbled on a scone and educated me on Campbell's situation. Caiyan's sister didn't have the gift. She was a single mother who lived in England and worked as a server. Her son, Campbell, was involved in some trouble and came to live here with Aunt Itty. He goes by Campy because he hates the name Campbell. It was his father's name, and he was a big-time loser, according to Aunt Itty.

I leaned toward Ace. "Does he have the gift?"

"No." Ace shook his head.

Aunt Itty said, "Caiyan tested him with the key when he turned thirteen and every year after—nothing." She sighed as if her family tree was hanging on by its last limb.

Ace set his teacup down and picked up a scone. "I haven't seen Campy since he was five. He's probably all grown up."

118

Aunt Itty set her scone down on the pretty china plate and reached into a Vera Bradley tote bag she had hanging on the arm of her chair. It was the new print out this fall, and I had extreme bag envy.

"We toured the park the day he arrived, so I took a few photos." She pulled out an iPad and opened her picture app. Scrolling through the photos, she stopped on one of a teenager, the spitting image of Caiyan. He was standing in the breezeway between the small galley-style kitchen and the back door of Aunt Itty's house. His black leather jacket hung off his narrow frame, and he balanced a skateboard between the top of his canvas shoe and his right leg.

The next photo was a close-up of him and Caiyan surrounded by a group of princesses from the royal castle. Caiyan had his arm slung around the redheaded princess's neck, and she was looking up at him with desire. Campy and Caiyan were centered in the picture, and they both wore the same shit-eating grin. The resemblance was incredible. They both had the same dark hair and square-set jaw. Campy's eyes looked a shade darker, maybe brown. It was hard to tell from the picture because they both had red-eye reflecting back at the camera.

"Maybe he's a late bloomer," I said, considering his thin frame and lack of any outward signs that his hormones were in high gear. He had a smidge of acne across his chin.

"He turned fifteen this August," Aunt Itty said, shaking her head. "Most travelers start showing the signs from early puberty."

"Is he at school right now?" I asked.

"No, his mother sent for him." Aunt Itty sighed. "He only spent a few weeks with me, and she sent him a plane ticket to return home."

"Aunt Itty, did you see the ticket?" Ace asked.

"Well, no," she said hesitantly. "But I took him to the airport."

Alarm bells were going off in my head. *Was it possible Campy had a key and Caiyan knew about it? And if so, why didn't he tell Aunt Itty?*

"Aunt Itty, do you wear your key at all times?" Ace asked.

Aunt Itty looked a little put back at the question. "I wear it every day. I am the fairy godmother, you know." She took a dainty sip from her teacup and placed it gently on the saucer. "After all, I have a show to perform. I just took it off before you arrived."

Ace stood and moved around the room, pausing to look at a photo of a young man hanging on Aunt Itty's wall. "Headquarters had unprecedented activity that came from this area, and they thought you might know what was going on."

"What do you mean by unprecedented?" Aunt Itty asked.

"An unregulated traveler has been blipping about the screen on an almost daily basis." Ace turned and looked at her, eyes questioning.

"Well, I wear my key on my workdays. It's a little heavy, and I'm not getting any younger." She stood, smoothed the wrinkles from her dress, and walked toward the kitchen. We followed single file behind her.

I gave Ace a jab in the ribs. "You didn't tell me that we were coming to interrogate a little old lady." Ace grimaced.

"My memory may be a little fuzzy, but my hearing is top-notch, dear." I swallowed a big piece of humble pie. She pointed to a ceramic cookie jar of the royal castle. "When I'm not wearing my key, I always put it in here."

Ace walked over, lifted the lid off the jar, and reached inside. "Uhm, Aunt Itty, there's nothing in here."

She hurried over to see for herself. "Well, I could have sworn I put it in there. No, wait. It's in the Winnie the Pooh." She made her way over to a bookshelf that held three other ceramic cookie jars. Sure enough, she plucked the key out of the Winnie the Pooh. We all gave a sigh of relief. It was beautiful. A starburst with a large blue diamond in the center and tiny white diamonds lining the rays that emanated from the medallion fit perfectly in the palm of her hand. "I told you it was here," she said with a sly look of satisfaction on her face.

The woman was a cookie jar maniac. They were everywhere. She had two on an entry table in the hallway and four on a shelf in the sitting room, holding books upright.

"Aunt Itty, you know I hate to ask, love, but where is Liam's key?" Aunt Itty's face went all soft, and I could tell this was a painful memory Ace was digging up.

Aunt Itty walked over to the photo Ace had been admiring earlier. The young man looked about twenty, and he was wearing a military uniform. "It's in my bedroom. I'll go see to it." She left the room, and Ace filled me in on the details. Liam was her grandson who was killed in Desert Storm. He'd refused to wear his key to help protect him. He wanted to fight like a real soldier and lost his life in return.

Aunt Itty called from her bedroom. "It's gone! It's gone! Liam's key is gone." She ran out, holding a heart-shaped cookie jar. "I've been robbed."

Ace walked over and returned the lid to the jar, placing it gently on the table. "Let's call Campy. Maybe he knows something." I put an arm around Aunt Itty's shoulders and escorted her over to her cozy chair, and she pulled her cell phone out from somewhere inside her bra.

All three of us huddled around Aunt Itty's cell phone as she made the call. Placing it on speakerphone, she wiped away a tear as the phone connected.

London was about five hours ahead of Florida, and Caiyan's sister picked up immediately. Just as I expected, Caiyan's sister told Aunt Itty she had not seen Campy since the day Caiyan took him to Florida. Aunt Itty explained about the plane ticket, but of course, she said she never sent a ticket. The sister sounded worried. Itty told her she was sure he was with Caiyan and not to worry.

Ace asked to see the room Campy had used. Aunt Itty took us down a short hallway to the back of the cottage. The small room was big enough for a twin bed, a nightstand, and a beanbag chair that pointed toward a flat-screen television mounted on the wall.

It didn't take long for us to go through the nightstand.

"Is this why Caiyan was here last month asking all kinds of questions about my key?" Aunt Itty asked.

"I'm not sure. I think we need to go back to the WTF so we can report in and sort this out," Ace said.

"I'm coming, too," Aunt Itty said as Ace stood behind her, shaking his head and mouthing, "No way."

Aunt Itty began clearing the tea tray. "That key was my responsibility. It's all I have left of Liam, and I swear on Her Majesty's life that no brigand will get that key."

"Aunt Itty," Ace began, but I put my hand on his arm, and he relented. The poor woman was beside herself with worry, and maybe she would be of some help at the WTF.

Itty left the room to change her clothes. Ace left a note for Campy in case he returned, but my radar was revving up in regard to our MIA teenager. If he didn't have the gift, maybe someone who did had him steal the key. Or maybe a brigand broke in and stole it. Or maybe Aunt Itty moved it and forgot which jar it was in. The possibilities were endless. Ace stood smiling with his thumbs hanging out of his front jeans pockets.

"What?" I asked.

"You're doing that thing where you run all the scenarios through your head."

"How do you know?"

"Your blond hair is starting to frizz, and your eyes are glazed over."

"Humph."

Aunt Itty came back into the room. She had changed into a pair of slacks and a flowered tunic top and was hurriedly tying a scarf over her hair in case we might change our minds. Her spectacles had been replaced with a pair of chic sunglasses, and she announced she was ready to go.

We had started to walk toward the front door when she announced, "I'm driving. I hardly ever go anywhere anymore."

Ace paused, started to argue, then sighed, and we turned around and followed her out the back door. Aunt Itty's backyard looked like one you might find out in the country dump. There was a weathered barn with various pieces of mowing equipment lying about. An old refrigerator sat on the back porch next to a soda vending machine. I felt like I had just gone through a time warp. Fantasy world out the front door and John Deere out the back.

Ace started to argue with Aunt Itty again. "Aunt Itty, maybe we should just take our own vessels and meet up at the WTF."

"Horsefeathers! We can all ride along in mine. It holds three, you know." She said it with pride, and I bet in her younger days she was an awesome transporter.

Wonderland was using Aunt Itty's backyard as a retirement farm for their old equipment. We walked past an old single-engine airplane, a minitank, and a weathered carousel. Under a big shade tree sat an old rusted-out Ford pickup. My guess was it used to be red but succumbed to the corrosion of time.

Ace huffed as we walked over to it. Aunt Itty hoisted herself into the driver's seat, while Ace and I stood staring at the broken-down truck.

"Well, come on, kids, this is a 1936 Ford half-ton; they don't make 'em like this anymore." She patted the dash as if it were brand-new.

I figured if I could travel in an outhouse, how bad could it be? I reached up and gave the door handle a pull. The door creaked open, inviting us inside. I looked over at Ace.

"Well, get in, love," he demanded. "I am not riding bitch." I snickered and climbed in, and Ace followed, securing his lap belt. Aunt Itty said the magic word, and with one loud backfire, we were sent spinning into a world of darkness.

Chapter 12

Our arrival at Gitmo went surprisingly smoothly. Aunt Itty was a much better driver than I was. The three of us climbed down from the landing pad and headed single file toward Jake's office. He met us in the hallway. Jake had only been with the CIA a few months. After he completed his CIA training at "The Farm," they sent him directly to Gitmo to maintain order among the travelers. He never had the pleasure of meeting Aunt Itty.

We stopped in front of Jake, and he introduced himself. Aunt Itty smiled at Agent Jake McCoy and looked in my direction as if to say, *Why not him?*

I smiled pleasantly back at her with my *been there, done that* expression. We followed Jake down the corridor to the travel lab, explaining about Campy on the way. Al and Pickles were inside, pecking away on their computers. As Aunt Itty stepped into the travel lab, Al's face lit up like a Christmas tree. He stood and almost skipped over to Aunt Itty.

"Italina, how are you?" he asked, taking one of her hands and placing a kiss on the top of it.

"Alfred, you are looking very well," she responded, stiffly jerking her hand out from under the kiss.

Whoa, where was the mellifluous little lady I met earlier? I wondered what the history was between them because there was obviously something hanging in the air. My inner voice was pushing her poker chips toward relationship troubles. I told her to save her money and ask Ace about this later.

Pickles wheeled over, and Aunt Itty leaned down and gave him a peck on the cheek. The two of them exchanged nice words; no need for anger management with Pickles. The three of us took a seat in the big comfy chairs facing the giant screen as Pickles brought the dots up for us to view. The red dot was still blipping around the screen close to the Hollywood Hills, and the blue dot was in the same city but much farther away from the red dot. Al brought Aunt Itty up to snuff on the details as we knew them. Brodie had not returned, but Jake informed us it may take a few days to research all of Caiyan's properties. We didn't know which one he was at last, so Brodie had to check them all out. I wanted to ask how many and where they were, but I added that to my memo for Ace because asking Jake was not likely to get me any answers.

Jake told us the little dwarf—I think they called him Gerald—was still doing recon on the Mafuso family. He had reported in, letting us know there was no sign of Mitchell Mafuso, and there was a rumor he had stayed during his last travel. Ace caught Al and Pickles up on our theory that the traveler might be Campy.

Al took out his metal pointer and aimed it at the blue dot. "Caiyan, for some reason, cannot seem to get close to the red dot." He looked over at Jake. "It would be a good idea to send someone back on Monday during the moon cycle to see what the problem is."

Jake looked at me and shook his head no.

"Oh come on, Jake, how hard could it be to go check out the situation?" I asked. "If the traveler is Campy, he's probably not dangerous, and Caiyan is there to help me."

"Maybe," Jake said. "We don't know what kind of predicament Caiyan has gotten himself into." He shrugged. "Besides, you don't know anything about 1985, and we've just begun your training."

"What if I took someone who knows something about 1985?" I asked.

Everyone turned to look at me. "You mean take a nontraveler, dear?" Aunt Itty questioned as if this couldn't be done.

"Well, yes," I said. "My cousin Gertie went with me the first time, and she knows a lot about everything. She has a photographic memory, and we still have two days for both of us to study that time period."

"It might work," Pickles chimed in. "If Campy is de traveler, he's no more dan fifteen. He's probably chasing some beauty queen, and Caiyan's having trouble persuading him to come home." He wheeled around in front of us. "I tink it's a good idea to let Jen go have a peek at de situation. Den we would know fer sure if Caiyan is in trouble."

"I'm not comfortable with Jen and Gertie going alone." Jake stood and paced around the room. "I just can't risk it."

"What if I get another traveler to go with me?"

"Jen, we've been over this. There's no one the right age."

"Well, there's Marco," I said and crossed my arms over my chest.

"If we could get him to go, dat might be good," Pickles said. "He has experience traveling, and he knows the Mafusos."

"Also, the Mafusos covet Marco's special abilities, and maybe we could persuade him to work for the WTF. Having him on our side would be very appreciated by the WTF, and you would get all the credit," Al added, putting emphasis on the final words.

Jake sighed. "All right, you three go see Marco." He pointed at Aunt Itty, Ace, and me. "And if you can get him to go with you, and *if* Caiyan doesn't return when the portal opens, and *if* you agree not to screw up the past, I'll let you go."

Ace gave me a high five, and I turned to Jake. "Thanks."

Jake screwed his mouth into a grimace. "I said *if.*"

⌣‿⌐

Jake provided us with black trench coats because we were not dressed for New York weather. Aunt Itty told us she felt like

Dick Tracy, but I thought she looked more like Tracey Ullman. Aunt Itty, Ace, and I rode to New York City together in Aunt Itty's Ford. We landed in a big vacant lot across from a construction site next to the Brooklyn Bridge.

"I think you overshot us a little, Aunt Itty," Ace said, staring at the bridge. Everyone vacated the truck and scoped out our location.

"Oops, my accuracy is a little off," Aunt Itty said, tapping her finger to her lips. "I was aiming for that nice spot in Chinatown, behind that place that sells the delicious eggrolls." She looked out over the water as if the restaurant she was seeking might appear. "Ace, do you know the one?"

Ace rolled his eyes at Itty. "Aunt Itty, it's called China Town."

"Oh, that's right, dear. How could I forget?"

"I could go for some moo goo gai pan; I'm starving," Ace replied, rubbing his stomach.

"Hey, you guys," I interjected. "I thought we were here to talk to Marco."

"True, dear, but we have to eat, too." Aunt Itty made a palms-up gesture with her hands. "We are really close to Grimaldi's." She pointed up the hill. "Let's go have a slice of pizza pie."

"Pizza's good," Ace replied.

We parked outside Grimaldi's, and I was surprised the truck actually worked like a real truck. We were standing in line out on the sidewalk to the pizza place, trying to decide the best way to ask Marco to travel. Ace thought we should just kidnap him and take him back with us. He was sure that was the only way to get him to go. Aunt Itty wanted to go buy some cupcakes at the Magnolia Bakery. She thought bribing him with sugar or sex was the answer. Since I wasn't offering up the latter, she went with the cupcakes.

"How about we just ask him nicely," I suggested.

"It will never work," Ace said. "Marco won't travel. He barely helped us out the last time we needed him."

"What do you mean, barely?" I asked. "He took a bullet saving me and Gertie."

Ace frowned. "Well, I meant initially."

Aunt Itty waved her hands and tsked at us. "Let's get the cupcakes, and then we can ask him nicely." She pulled her coat around her chin when a big wind blew by. "If that doesn't work, we'll do it Ace's way."

I agreed. The cupcakes couldn't hurt. After we finished off what was probably the best pizza I had ever eaten, we piled into the truck for a trip to the bakery. We found the quaint bakery at the corner of Eleventh and Bleecker Streets, but we had to wait in another line.

"Isn't there anyplace in New York that doesn't have a line?" I asked, not used to waiting in lines at pizza places and bakeries.

"No," Ace and Aunt Itty said in unison.

Ace added, "Well, not anyplace you would want to go."

We finally made it inside, and the smell was heavenly. It reminded me of one of the patients at the clinic. She worked in a doughnut shop, and every time she came in, she smelled like a doughnut. It was hard not to lick her.

We bought an assortment of goodies and headed to Marco's apartment in SoHo. He lived on the top floor of a building that he owned. Mainly because the roof was his garage for his vessel, a Formula One race car.

"I haven't seen Marco since he was a baby," Aunt Itty said. She looked lost in thought as Ace directed her toward the apartment building. "I think the last time was at his parents' house in Italy. They were having a wine festival, and he was toddling around in his nappies."

I thought of Marco in diapers. He was so incredible looking, thinking of him as a baby was difficult. He was probably born with muscles. His tall, blond image with the big dimple in his chin clouded my thoughts. He was so cocky, and when we touched, it felt like my world was on fire. Just thinking about him made me squeeze my knees together. I closed my eyes and tried to concentrate on the reason we were here. Damn Caiyan for leaving me alone and horny. Ace caught me out of the corner of his eye.

He patted my knee. "It's OK. He does that to me, too."

I opened my eyes. "I don't know what you're talking about."

Ace laughed. "Sure, hon."

The truck backfired as we parallel parked next to a meter. Ace jumped out and paid the meter as Aunt Itty and I got out of the truck. We walked the short distance to Marco's building. The apartment didn't have a doorman, but there was a secured entrance. Ace pressed all the buttons on the intercom. Thankfully, an unconcerned citizen beeped us in, and the door opened. We took the elevator to the penthouse and rang Marco's doorbell. He opened the door with a sigh. "What did I do to deserve this intrusion?" he asked, stepping aside to let us in.

"Hey, Marco, buddy." Ace shook his hand. "We were in the neighborhood."

"Yeah, right." He looked me up and down as I passed over the threshold.

"Hi." I stopped and gave him a quick, hot peck on the cheek. He raised an eyebrow, and then his gaze dropped down to Aunt Itty. She stood in the doorway, mouth open, gaping at Marco.

"And who is this?" he asked. His blond hair curled around the nape of his neck, and his steel-blue eyes stared at Aunt Itty.

"This is Aunt Itty," I said with a cherubic smile. "She hasn't seen you since you were in diapers."

"My, my," Aunt Itty finally said. "You sure have filled out your nappies."

"Caiyan's Aunt Itty," I explained.

"Well, come in, Aunt Itty," he said, motioning with his hand as if admitting another admirer was fine.

Everyone stood in the foyer afraid to move forward into the living room.

"We brought you some cupcakes," Aunt Itty said, presenting the bakery box to Marco.

He took the box and opened it. "Yum, my favorite, devil's food." He winked at me, picked up one, and took a bite. "Yep, tastes like a bribe to me. C'mon in and sit down so you three stooges can tell me what's going on."

We walked over to the couch, and all three of us sat down side by side on the sofa. Marco set the box down on the coffee table and stood in front of us, arms crossed over his chest. He was wearing faded jeans and an Islanders sweat shirt. His feet were bare, and he wore three rope leather bracelets on his right wrist.

"The reason we're here, Marco, is—" Ace began, but Marco cut him off midsentence.

"Not you, her." He pointed at me.

"Well, it's like this—" And I proceeded to tell him about the mystery traveler, Caiyan being stuck in 1985, and how I was the only one the right age to go back and save him.

Marco reached down and took another cupcake from the box. "Let me get this straight. You want me to go back in time with you and Gertie, who got captured the last time you went back together, to save your boyfriend and some mystery traveler?" He took a bite out of the cupcake and glared at me. A smidge of icing was hugging the corner of his mouth, and I heard Ace gasp in ecstasy beside me. Marco wiped it away with the back of his hand and finished the cupcake.

"That about sums it up," I said. "Except for the boyfriend part. I'm not sure about that."

"Thank you very much for the cupcakes," he said as he walked to the door. "Aunt Itty, it was a pleasure catching up after all these years, and, Ace—well good-bye." He opened the door and stood waiting for us to leave.

"Are you sure you won't help us?" I asked, flashing my baby blues at his.

"Last time I helped you, I got shot. Two weeks in the hospital and three weeks of rehab, and I just started doing test runs at the track."

"Yeah, sorry about that," I said, dropping my head.

The three of us stood up, and I was contemplating begging him to help us. "Couldn't you please do this one last favor?"

"Are you offering more than cupcakes?" He looked me up and down. I cut my eyes at Aunt Itty. *How rude to ask me such a question in front of the sweet little old lady.*

"Nope," I said, but my inner voice was shouting, *Stupid girl!* in four languages at me.

"Are you sure, dear?" Aunt Itty turned and asked me.

My mouth was hanging open, and Marco let out a big bark of laughter.

Ace chimed in. "I'm happy to oblige—"

"Not in this lifetime." Marco's laugh changed to a low growl.

Ace, Aunt Itty, and I trooped out into the hall with slumped shoulders, and Marco waved good-bye from the doorway. He made sure we boarded the elevator before he shut the door.

"Now what do we do?" I asked.

"Plan B." Ace smiled. "This is going to be fun." Aunt Itty and I looked at each other, a little worried, but maybe if we could just get Marco to Gitmo, he would have a change of heart.

"Let's go get your cousin Gertie on board, and then we can put our heads together and have a nice cup of cocoa." Aunt Itty linked elbows with me as we exited Marco's building.

I couldn't help but giggle. "Let's go." I locked elbows with Ace, and we walked off, not down the yellow brick road but the cracked sidewalk of SoHo to our waiting vessel.

⌒

I was pretty sure Gertie wouldn't mind going with me because she was always after me to travel. We took the truck to my house, and once again, Aunt Itty overshot the driveway and ended up in the field behind my house. We drove the rest of the way home and parked under the carport. There was just enough room to squeeze in the truck next to my Mustang and Gertie's BMW. The truck backfired as Aunt Itty pulled it into park.

Gertie came running outside in her pink bathrobe. Her long red hair was pulled back in braids, Hello Kitty pajama pants extended out from under her robe, and she had blue-striped water socks on her feet.

"What the hell, Jen?" she said, holding her hand over her heart. "It sounded like a gunshot out here."

I frowned at her. "So you came running out here?"

She frowned back at me and then saw Ace and Aunt Itty. "Who are y'all supposed to be?" she asked, pointing at our trench coats.

"Don't you recognize us, love? We're the new backup singers for Miley Cyrus. We're all wearing knickers under these." He grabbed his coat and flashed Gertie. She yelped and threw her hands over her eyes, laughing as she saw he was joking.

"Hey, Ace." She gave him a hug, and he introduced her to Aunt Itty.

"Aunt Itty is THE fairy godmother at Wonderland," I said to Gertie.

"I always wanted to know a fairy godmother," Gertie said, genuinely intrigued. "Can you conjure me up a handsome prince?"

"NO!" Ace and I shouted in unison.

Aunt Itty looked a little taken aback at our lack of confidence. "I've been known to make a wicked love potion that can turn a few heads."

I hurried everyone inside before Gertie and Aunt Itty could continue the conversation. I hung up the coats, and Gertie made us some hot chocolate. Aunt Itty took a seat on the sofa, and attack cat jumped on her lap. I rushed over to take action in case he dug his claws in, but he rolled onto his back, and she scratched him under the chin.

"What a good little pussy," she cooed.

That figures, the traitor. If it had been me, he would have snuck up behind me and made me spill my chocolate.

"So what are you up to?" asked Gertie, passing out the mugs of cocoa. "Are y'all on a secret mission?"

"Sort of," Ace responded first. "We need a favor from you."

"From me?" Gertie looked excited and took a seat next to Aunt Itty on the sofa.

"Yes, dear," Aunt Itty jumped in. "You see, Caiyan is my nephew, and he's stuck in 1985. We need you and Jennifer to go get him."

Gertie looked at me and blinked like a deer in headlights. "Me?"

"Yeah, don't you think it would be fun to go back to 1985?" I asked.

Gertie set her hot chocolate down on the coffee table and smoothed the bathrobe out over her knees. She started to bite on her index fingernail, and I knew it was all over.

"I really don't want to go back in time again," Gertie said.

"Why not?" Ace asked. "I thought you wanted to travel with us."

"I do," she answered, finger still in her mouth. She moved her hands to her lap. "I want to go to Paris or London, now, in the present. I don't want to go back in time to 1985. What if we get lost or stuck in the past?"

"We won't get lost," I said. "I've gone back three times now, and I have always come back."

"I don't know—Caiyan is stuck, and he's a good traveler."

I couldn't argue with that statement. Caiyan had a lot of experience, and I couldn't explain why he went back at the end of a travel cycle instead of waiting until the next full moon.

"Gertie, I really need you to come with me. You can learn about 1985 faster than I can, and I need your knowledge."

"Is Ace going?" Gertie asked.

"No, he's too old," Aunt Itty said.

"Marco is going," Ace told Gertie. I gave Ace a dirty look. We didn't know for sure we could change his mind.

Gertie looked a little bit more confident, and then she got a gleam in her eye. "I'll do it on one condition."

"Sure, you name it, love," Ace said.

"I want a date with Brodie." She crossed her arms over her chest, and Ace and I sucked in air.

I wasn't sure Brodie would oblige. The last reference he made to Gertie was, "She's a royal pain in the arse." I looked over at Ace.

"It's a deal," Ace said. "In fact, Brodie was telling me the other day he wished he could see you again."

"He did?" Gertie's eyes glazed over, and I wondered how Ace was going to pull off two miracles.

Ace leaned back and finished off his cup of chocolate with a smile on his face. I wondered what in the devil he was up to, and I thought I needed something stronger in my cocoa.

Ace and Aunt Itty were giving instructions on things we needed to learn about 1985. "Make sure you know who the president is," Aunt Itty said. "I think it was that nice actor fellow."

I huffed. There was a lot of information to learn in such a short time. Ace wrote down a few websites for Gertie and me to look up. He explained they gave a brief synopsis of history based on the year. Since we weren't sure who Caiyan was with, but we knew he was in LA, we should brush up on anything that had happened in that area. He suggested reading old newspapers and magazines.

Gertie became excited. "I have an entire room of periodicals. I can check out magazines and books. The newspapers have been converted to the web."

Ace told us he would clear everything with Jake, and we would meet in the parking lot in Brooklyn where Aunt Itty had accidentally landed when we went to meet Marco the first time.

"Why there?" I asked. "If you're going to convince Marco to come with us, why not bring him to Gitmo?"

"Marco may not be very cooperative for what I've got in mind," he said, and a wicked little Grinch grin spread across his face.

"Ace, you're not going to do anything illegal, right?" I asked. Gertie and Aunt Itty stopped discussing important political leaders to listen.

"I'm just going to be a little creative. Don't worry, love." He patted my knee, and I was positive I needed to switch my drink to something stronger.

"I think I'll have a glass of wine," I said, standing. "Would anyone else like one?"

"Wine!" Aunt Itty sat bolt upright, and attack cat skirted off her lap. "Oh, horsefeathers!" she said, fingering her key under her sweater. "I'm supposed to be at the royal wine tasting tonight. I've got to get home and whip up a bottle of my famous Fairy Godmother Sparkling Pinot Noir."

Ace and I looked at each other as if doing a mental coin flip on who was going to see if she might need some assistance transporting home.

"What's the matter?" Aunt Itty asked, because everyone was staring at her.

"Well, Aunt Itty," Ace began. "Do you need me to ride home with you?"

"Of course not. I am perfectly capable of getting home by myself." She stood and smoothed down her top. I handed her the trench coat she had worn, and we followed her outside.

"Tootles, Jen," she said as she climbed into her vessel. She put her truck in reverse, slowly backed it out of the carport, and cranked down the window. "Nice to meet you, Gertie, dear." She motioned Ace toward her truck, and he moved to stand by her window. "Ace, let me know when you're ready to go snatch that blond god. Bye-bye, kids."

A loud backfire and enough smoke to make an elephant disappear erupted from the tailpipe of the truck, and she was gone.

"Holy smoke," I said, coughing and fanning the smoke away from me. "Do you think anyone saw that?"

When the smoke cleared, I could see that Ace got the brunt of that backfire. He had soot on his face and splotched randomly on his favorite jeans. The skull on his shirt looked like Kanye West. "I think she did that on purpose."

"What did she mean by 'snatch the blond god'?" I asked, hands on hips.

"Just a figure of speech, love." Ace called his vessel and headed home. Gertie and I went back in the house, and I passed on the wine for another cup of cocoa laced with two shots of Irish whiskey.

Gertie did the same, and we sat in the comfy chairs in the den, surfing the Internet for information on 1985.

Chapter 13

The next two days flew by as I struggled through learning about 1985. Jake was e-mailing me tons of information. I was preparing for my first solo trip back in time. Well, sort of solo. Gertie would be with me and Marco. At least I hoped Marco would be joining me. I felt confident that Gertie and I could find Caiyan, but I would feel better if we had Marco. Every time I texted Ace to see if he had convinced Marco to travel, he replied, "It's all in the bag, love, no worries."

I didn't have time to dwell on the problem. I was going with or without Marco's help. Jake's voice echoed in my head, reminding me I was not going without Marco. We would see about that.

I went into work on Monday morning to work half the day and then start my massage interviews. At least that's what Jake thought. It didn't matter because the two I had interviewed early were duds. I had one interview today that I hoped would work out because I would be out of town *so to speak* for the next three days. If everything worked out, I should return from my travel only a few hours after I left, and then I would take a day to recover, be back at work on Wednesday, and no one would be the wiser.

Mr. Crane had made another appearance at the clinic to see if the acupuncturist had returned. When Mary told him Su Le was still overseas, he pounded his giant fist on the counter and demanded his money back. Mary tried to refer him to another acupuncturist, but he refused. She was in the process of explaining that he had already received the treatments and she couldn't give a refund when I entered the front office. He looked up at me with those beady eyes and immediately left the clinic.

Mary turned and looked at me. "If I'd known your presence would get him out of here, I would have you working the front desk."

"I don't know why he gets so grumpy when I'm around," I replied.

I helped Eli with patients, and by noon I was jumping around like a jackrabbit. I was nervous about the upcoming travel. I could barely get in the car and drive to my massage. I told Eli I had three scheduled for Tuesday. It was just a little white lie. Mamma Bea says sometimes you have to tell a little white lie to keep things right in the family. I guess not telling Eli I was time traveling in Aint Elma's outhouse was keeping things right, because he would probably have me committed. Truthfully, I just wanted to get the massage over and get ready for my trip.

I left the office and drove a mile up the road to a business center. The center consisted of four groups of buildings clustered together in a square. I drove around back to the address Eli had given me. Apparently, Mary's cousin's friend had a massage here last week, and the girl was really good. I didn't know the friend, but I was beginning to wonder about her standards because the address was a tattoo shop called the Snooty Parrot. As I entered the shop, the smoke was so thick I thought I might need to pull out my GPS tracker to navigate my way through. As I moved farther into the shop, pictures of body parts with tattoos materialized on the walls in front of me. The woman at the desk was heavyset with red hair and very large breasts. She was wearing a purple V-neck top that clashed with her hair. A large tattoo of the Rolling Stones tongue logo was stretched across her ample bosom. I couldn't take my eyes off it. "You wanna get some ink?" she asked.

"Uhm, no," I answered, tearing my eyes away from her chest. "I'm here to see Helga."

"She's in the back." She pointed at a door behind her. I thanked her and entered the back office. There was more smoke, and a group of tattoo artists sat at a table smoking and playing cards. I guess the tattoo business was slow on Monday afternoon. They turned to look at me as I entered. "You want ink?" one of them asked me.

"No, no," I stuttered. "I'm just looking for Helga." My inner voice was telling me to get the hell out of there before I ended up with arms like Kat Von D.

"I Helga," said the woman who had her back to me. She unfolded from the chair and stood to over six feet tall. "You get good massage wit' Helga."

The other two people at the table snickered. I followed Helga down a hall into a room at the back. My inner voice was whispering, *Keep your undergarments on, and make sure she's a woman.* Good grief, how was I supposed to do that?

I was used to the protocol by now. I undressed and got comfortable under the sheets. Surprisingly, the room smelled of lavender. There was an air purifier in the corner, and the soft hum of the hot rock machine took away the concerns my inner voice was having. Helga reentered the room, punched a few buttons on her radio, and the entire room filled with the sound of ocean waves. She began massaging my back with firm strokes from my shoulders, down the muscles that surround my spine, and to the base of my back. I relaxed a little more, and Helga added some hot rocks. She laid them down my back and covered me with a warm towel while she worked all the kinks out of my neck and my arms. She followed the procedure with my legs and ended with a light mist of lavender to the air above me that fell in tiny droplets on to my neck and face. The entire massage was heaven, and I couldn't believe my good luck. Now I could concentrate on my travel. My inner voice sighed and said she knew this was going to be a good massage. I rolled my eyes at her as I got dressed. After paying Helga, I let her know we would be in touch. She smiled and thanked me, telling me she really vanted to get away from de smoke.

As soon as I got into the car, I pulled out my cell phone and let Eli know we had a possible candidate. I reminded him I still had a few more massages (white lies), but I would have a definite candidate when I returned to work on Wednesday. I put my car in gear and headed home. On the way I made a detour through Starbucks because if I got stuck in 1985, I wouldn't be getting my skinny vanilla bean Frappuccino with caramel drizzle for a long, long time.

I was hanging up my coat when Gertie came bursting through the front door, struggling to carry a large cardboard box. "JEN! JEN!" she hollered as she came into the den and set the obviously heavy box down on the floor with a loud bang.

"What's going on?" I asked, heading to the kitchen for a drink.

"Come here quickly," she said. "I know where Caiyan is."

I grabbed a bottle of water and went back into the den.

"He's stuck in 1985," I said.

"No, I mean, I know that, but I know who he's with." She threw her coat onto the couch, covering attack cat, and started rummaging through the big box. I set my water bottle down on the side table.

Gertie pulled a magazine from the box. Then she hesitated. "Promise not to get mad, OK?"

I frowned. "Why would I get mad?"

"I'm sure he's doing it for the good of time travel." She bit her bottom lip, as if in afterthought this wasn't such a great idea.

"Gertie, let me see," I demanded.

"Look," she said proudly as she handed me a copy of *Tiger beat* magazine. The teen magazine from 1985 had pictures of celebrities and the gossip about them. On the cover was a picture of a gorgeous blonde, wearing a black leather bustier and leopard hot pants. Around her neck was Caiyan's key.

"What the hell, Gertie?" I asked as I sat down haphazardly on the sofa, making sure my butt hit cushion and I didn't land on the floor.

"Yep, check out page six. I dog-eared it for you." She came and sat beside me.

I fumbled to page six, and there was the blonde. She was getting into a limousine, and helping her into the vehicle was Caiyan. He had that mad look on his face he gets when he is on protection mode, and it looked like he was shouting at one of the photographers who were crowded around the limo. The caption under the black-and-white photo read, "Who is Rocksanna's mystery man?" The little blub stated she had been seen out and about with this hunky dark-haired man, but they didn't have any information on the stud. There was a rumor this eye candy could be husband number three, as they were seen canoodling at Spago on Thursday.

Rocksanna was a rock legend, and she was also killed in a car accident. It happened before I was born, but people still listen to her music and talk about her sex appeal.

I felt my face drain of all color, and my palms became sweaty. I focused on the reality of the situation. She had his key. He couldn't return if he wasn't wearing his key, and he couldn't summon me for help.

"Gertie, this is bad." Gertie bobbed her head in agreement. "This is the only article I found so far, but I brought the rest of the magazines home from that month that I didn't have time to read."

"I need to call Jake," I said. My hands trembled as I made the call. Was this what everyone had warned me about? Caiyan the bad boy. Caiyan sleeps around. Caiyan the playboy. My inner voice sat shaking her head sadly, bidding farewell to the great sex Caiyan dished out. I disregarded her for the moment and focused on my call to Jake. I explained what Gertie had found. He exhaled slowly, and I knew he was trying not to say I told you so.

"I'll do some research on the situation," he said, and I could tell he was running his fingers through his hair. Then he dropped his voice low. He used this comforting tone when he knew I was upset. "You don't know what's going on, so don't make any assumptions."

I nodded my head, holding back tears.

"Jen, are you still there?" he asked.

"Yes," I said, regrouping. This was my job. If I wanted to be good at it, I needed to put all my emotions on hold and focus on getting Caiyan home and identifying Traveler X. Besides, he couldn't stay in 1985, so he must have a plan.

"I don't think you should go," Jake said. "Things may not turn out exactly like you want them to."

"Jake, I'm fine," I replied confidently. "I work for the WTF, and I will not allow my personal feelings to get in the way of doing my job."

Silence on the other end of the line followed by a sigh. "If I tell you not to go, you'll go anyway, and then you'll be in trouble with the WTF. Make sure you and Gertie are at the rendezvous at midnight."

"We'll be there," I said firmly. I agreed to send Jake a photo of the article and ended the call.

Gertie and I ordered pizza and went through the rest of the magazines. Rocksanna was in every magazine, but there were no more pictures or any mention of Caiyan.

I managed to eat one small piece of the veggie pizza Gertie had ordered. She showed me an article that Rocksanna was performing for three nights at Universal. Monday night, which would be tonight in 1985, would be her second night on tour with the Beasts as her opening act. They were an up-and-coming boy band. There was a picture next to the article, and a few of the members looked familiar, but I didn't know their music. Gertie was scanning another magazine when her eyes got really wide. "Jen, isn't this that Mafuso kid?" she asked, holding the magazine out so I could take a look.

Sure enough, the Beasts were pictured in front of the Christmas tree in Times Square. Arms all wrapped around one another's necks, and in the center was Caiyan's nephew. Another boy who looked vaguely familiar was standing off to the right. I squinted at the picture. It could be Mitchell, but the photo was blurred at the edges.

"Gertie, I think this might be Traveler X." She leaned in to look at the picture. "Caiyan's nephew might just have been going back to join a boy band." I laughed at the thought of Caiyan chasing this kid around LA because he wanted to be in a band. The article welcomed the new member of the band after the extrication of former group members. The November article featured a tree-lighting festival in New York City. It stated the band was off for warmer weather in California to complete their tour. I continued looking at the back issues of magazines, and Gertie booted up her laptop and Googled Rocksanna. There was a close-up of Campy playing his guitar. He was shirtless, and his teenage muscles were just beginning to appear on his gangly frame. The key around his neck was the same key I saw on Mrs. Oglivy's neck when I traveled last month. The crest of a wave with the tiny diamonds. Caiyan had been wrong. He told me that key was safe. It was not in a safe place because a fifteen-year-old boy found it and used it to travel. Did this mean Aunt Itty was a descendant of Mrs. Ogilvy? The memory of our trip to Scotland last month left a searing pain of anguish in my gut. How could Caiyan make me feel like he only had affection for me and then be canoodling with Rocksanna? The only way to solve this mystery was to go back to 1985 and find him.

Gertie nudged me out of my daydream of strangling Caiyan to show me a website she pulled up on her laptop. The website had grainy pictures of the auto accident. The car was a mangled mess.

Gertie read the media clip out loud: "Queen of pop Rocksanna was killed in an auto accident while being chased by paparazzi. Both of her bodyguards were severely injured."

Gertie sucked in air.

"What is it?" I asked. "Does it say anything about Caiyan?"

"It says the accident happened Tuesday night after her last concert in LA."

I dropped the magazine I was reading in my lap and scooted closer to Gertie. We both reread the article. No mention of Caiyan. "Look at the date." I pointed to the computer screen. "That's this Tuesday, tomorrow night." All the magazines had been published before our travel date in 1985.

"It hasn't happened yet, at least the way it reads in this article," said Gertie.

I swallowed the lump of fear that had begun to choke me. "If Caiyan gets in that car with her, history will change. There might be two people killed instead of one. Especially if he isn't wearing his key." My heart started to pound, and I felt light-headed. It was more important now for me to go back. We had to find him in time.

"Should we call Jake?" Gertie asked.

"No," I said, shaking my head. "We still need to go back and convince Traveler X to come home." *And possibly save Caiyan from dying before he was even born.*

Chapter 14

*G*ertie and I landed, as instructed, at straight-up midnight in the vacant lot by the Brooklyn Bridge. Ace still hadn't confirmed if Marco had agreed to travel. My stomach was in knots as we waited. Gertie had a nervous but goofy smile on her face like a child who was getting away with a good prank. We huddled together as the cold air had us pulling the hoods of our coats up for warmth. The sound of a few cars crossing the bridge broke the silence as the wind stirred. Gertie and I backed to the edge of the lot, knowing that when the wind started to swirl, a vessel was about to make an appearance. Sure enough, Ace's vessel came to a screeching halt about ten yards from us. Ace and Jake exited the photo booth.

"Jake?" I asked but gave him a hug.

"I wanted to see you off." He hugged me back. "Are you ready?"

"Yes, Dad," I joked, but my knees were knocking together.

"I'm ready, too," Gertie said, just a little too peppy.

Jake rolled his eyes at her. "Gertie, you are going as intel only. Please stay out of trouble."

"Aye, aye, Captain," she said as she saluted.

Ace sauntered over to where we were standing.

"Where's Marco?" I asked.

Jake and Ace looked at each other. Jake responded, "We have someone picking up Marco."

Warning bells went off inside my head. *Why wasn't Marco transporting here himself?* Before I could get too caught up in the whys, Jake started handing out orders.

"You will go now and take Gertie, then come back to get Marco."

"You're going to leave me alone in 1985?" Gertie asked, taking a step away from the group.

Ace put an arm around Gertie's shoulders. "It's OK, love. We can transport back and forth as long as the moon is full. Jennifer can drop you off, and then she can return at the exact location in a matter of minutes."

"What if she misses and goes back to 1984?" Gertie's lip started to quiver.

"Impossible," Jake said. "As long as Jennifer stays focused, her vessel will follow the emission trail it released in the first trip to 1985. It's like following a trail map, so to speak."

Gertie seemed content with the explanation, and I hoped they were right. Ace had more experience traveling than I, and so far, it worked the way they explained it. I just hoped I didn't encounter some kind of glitch in the system. Jake was telling Gertie to be patient while I came back for Marco.

"Why isn't Marco transporting himself?" I asked.

"I'll explain after you take Gertie." Jake pulled out a map of the Hollywood Hills from his jacket pocket. He motioned for Gertie and me to gather around. Ace just stood in the background, hands on hips, that cocky smile spread casually across his face. What was his problem? We had become very close in the past two months. He was my confidant, my bud, my stylist. Tonight he had a secret he wasn't sharing with me, and I was mad at the deception. I gathered around the map Jake held.

"You will land here in this clearing behind the Hollywood sign," he said, pointing at the map.

"Is that a clear space?" I asked. "I thought the sign was on a hill." Landing on a slope wasn't easy. We always tried to imagine a wide, clear area when we traveled or find a picture of where we were going so we could form the picture in our minds, and the vessel did its best to choose that spot or somewhere in the vicinity.

Jake pulled a picture from his other pocket. It was a satellite map of the landing location. "Here." He pointed at the map, showing Gertie and me the prime landing location.

"Oh, I see it," said Gertie. "There's a small flat area right here." She put her finger on the map. "The last time I was in Hollywood, I went on one of those tour buses, and we couldn't go to the sign. Our bus driver told us it was restricted and had a security fence around it."

"In 1985 it's not as secure, but it's the perfect place to land without detection," Jake explained.

"Why can't we land in a park that's not on a mountain? I mean, how are we supposed to get down to the city?"

"Jen, this is LA. People are everywhere and at all hours of the night. We thought this was the safest place."

"What is Gertie supposed to do while I come back for Marco?"

"It will only be a matter of minutes," Jake explained, and pausing, he looked at Gertie. "Just get clear of the area, Gertie. Marco and Jen will return in a few minutes."

He said the last part with some trepidation, as if he wasn't totally convinced Marco would be going along for the ride.

He folded the maps and put them in his pocket. "When you get there, try to get into the city quickly. I need you to make contact with Pickles."

"Pickles?" I asked.

"Yes, he worked in security in 1985. He was the bodyguard for the pop star, Rocksanna."

"Rocksanna?" Gertie asked, trying to tame the excitement in her voice. I gave her an evil eye, and she clamped her mouth shut.

"Remember, he hasn't met you yet, so he won't know you, but if you show him your key, he will help you."

"OK, how do I know where he is or how to find Caiyan?"

"Pickles said Rocksanna was performing at the Hollywood Bowl that year for the Christmas tour." Jake had small beads of perspiration forming at his hairline, even though it was a brisk thirty-four degrees outside. I tried to pay attention to what he was saying, but my inner voice kept reminding me I had never seen Jake act like this before. "They are staying at the Beverly Hills Hotel. That's where I would start."

I knew that was a five-star hotel, and if Pickles let us stay there, it would be a step up from the barns, country inns, and, God forbid, camping that I had experienced during my travels.

"Here, put these in your cheek, and keep your mouths closed when you transport." He handed Gertie and me two one-hundred-dollar bills folded in thirds and wrapped in plastic. "I made sure they were printed before 1985."

We walked over to my outhouse. Gertie eyed it nervously. "Don't worry. I'm a much better driver now that I've had some practice." That was the truth. Ace had taken me for "driving lessons," and I pretty much could control the vessel with relaxation techniques. If I was nervous, the vessel didn't travel as smoothly.

"See you in a few minutes," Jake said, and over his shoulder I saw Ace glance at his phone, then look anxiously at me. He gave me a small wave.

Gertie and I entered my vessel and put the folded money between our cheeks and gums. I took a few deep breaths. Gertie had her eyes closed, and she was holding on to the handles with a death grip. I made sure the money was tucked tight against my cheek. I focused on the spot in Hollywood and spoke the word given to me by the ancient gods to make my vessel travel: "*Hanhepi.*"

We rocked a bit, and then it stopped. We were both still sitting in the outhouse, in the pitch dark. A small amount of light filtered in through the slats in the outhouse.

Gertie turned toward me and pulled the money out of her mouth. "That was real good, Jen. I hardly felt it at all."

I removed my money and agreed. It was easier. Maybe it had something to do with how far back in the past we travel. We stepped out and surveyed our location. I'd hit right on the mark. We'd landed in the small flat area Jake had indicated on the map. The Hollywood sign was below us, and the light was coming from the illuminated sign. The

147

sign was much bigger standing next to it than I imagined. We were even with the top of the sign, and the view of the city lights was like tiny diamonds that had been poured over a black velvet cloth. The weather was cool but much warmer than the freezing temperatures of New York City or the current chill of Texas.

Gertie was wearing a red dress, channeling Stevie Nicks, chosen for her compliments of my vessel. The dress was flattering on her. It clung to all the right places and had a killer headband and lace-up boots. Gertie looked down at her clothes.

"Cool, I got the sexy outfit this time." She spun around. The handkerchief hem of the dress and butterfly sleeves floated parachute fashion around her.

"If you start singing 'Leather and Lace,' I'm taking you back," I said.

Gertie stuck her tongue out at me and then looked me up and down. I had on a skintight denim miniskirt, a blouse that had ruffles up the front, and a pair of clear plastic heels.

Gertie inspected my outfit. "Ooh, that doesn't look very comfortable to chase bad guys in." I agreed but had to return and get Marco.

I found a tree that looked to be a safe distance from our landing pad. I gave Gertie my cash, and she agreed to stay put by the tree. I entered my vessel for the return home.

Smooth sailing and I was back in my normal clothes at the vacant lot. Jake and Ace were waiting for me.

"It's all good. I landed exactly where you showed me on the map," I told them as I exited my vessel.

"That's great, Jen. You're really getting the hang of traveling." Jake put an arm around my back and squeezed my shoulders.

"Where's Marco?" I asked, looking around.

"He should be along any minute now," Jake said, but Ace pulled his phone out of his pocket, checked the time, and stared into outer space.

"What's going on?" I asked.

"It's all good, love," Ace said, as if he was trying to convince himself more than me.

As he said the words, a flash of lightning crossed the sky and a Chinese sedan chair sat before us in the center of the lot. It was magnificent. Red tapestry formed the background and covered the rectangular box. Gold adorned almost every spare surface. Trellis-like borders and intricate miniature oil paintings framed with gold covered the walls. The roof winged out in the traditional Chinese architectural style I had seen in photographs. The top plateaued outward, forming little balconies for gold figurines as if they were gathering to enjoy a concert. It was as if a treasure from the Ming Dynasty had plopped down right in the middle of Brooklyn. It lacked only two eunuchs to cart the thing around. I started toward it, and Jake tightened his grip on me.

"Hold on one second," he said.

A cyclone of wind and a loud bang had me ducking as a confessional set down next to the sedan chair. I was in awe. I had never seen a confessional like this one. It was definitely old Roman Catholic. A purple curtain hid the priest's centered compartment. Instead of another room for the confessor, it had side kneelers. The mahogany wood formed an intricate cross at the arch, and small engravings carved into the wood followed the arch to the floor. Jake and I both stood in awe, making the sign of the cross.

"Some of us have really cool sleds," Ace said, looking a bit sullen.

The dwarf pushed back the purple curtain and popped out of the priest's lair. He went over to the sedan chair and pulled the door open. He reached inside and dragged out a man with the help of Tina, who was pushing the man from behind, and then exited the vessel herself. Tina and Gerald supported him on each side as they draped him over their shoulders.

The man was obviously unconscious because he was unable to walk on his own. He had a pillowcase over his head, and because of their height, they dragged his legs behind them.

"A little help here," Gerald said.

Ace went to help carry the man. Jake lowered his arm, and we walked closer. The man's jeans were unintentionally ripped at the leg. His white T-shirt had a smidge of what looked like blood on it, and his head hung down on his chest. I could tell from his build that it was Marco.

"Let's get him in the outhouse." Jake directed them to my vessel, and they carefully lowered Marco on the bench inside.

"What is the meaning of this?" I asked, placing my hands on my hips and taking a wide stance.

"It's the only way we could get him to go," Ace replied.

"What did you do to him?" I asked, worried. "I can't take him like this. He's too heavy for me to lug around."

The dwarf spoke up. "I had to spike his drink, but the sleeping pill should wear off in about twenty minutes, I think."

"What kind of sleeping pill?" I asked the dwarf.

"I'm not sure." He shrugged. "It was something Aunt Itty made."

"Oh jeez," I said. "There's no telling when that will wear off, and I've left Gertie stranded in 1985."

"Don't panic," Jake said. But the calm CIA agent had worry lines running across his forehead.

The thought of what Marco would do when he woke up was frightening. I didn't want to be the one explaining things.

"He's going to call his vessel and return the moment he wakes up." I flapped my hands against the sides of my legs in frustration.

"No can do," Ace said, pulling the pillowcase up around his neck and exposing the lack of his key.

"Where is his key?" Jake asked.

"He only wears it when he's racing." Ace grinned like a two-year-old who had just had a good poopy.

Tina stepped forward to explain. "We found him at Ibiza, you know the dance club, and Gerry spiked his drink. When he started getting woozy, we nabbed him."

"What's the blood from?" I asked, indicating the smear on his shirt.

"He fought us a little when we tried to put him in the vessel," Gerry explained.

"Yes, he cut his leg on the gold lion's head." Tina gestured toward the bottom of her vessel. "But then the drug kicked in and it was easy peasy from there on out."

"Are you people done with us?" Gerry asked.

"Yes, thank you for your help," Jake said.

"No problem. Ace owes me," Gerry said with a nasty smile at Ace.

I didn't have time to worry about what Ace was up to or be concerned with our departing travelers. Marco was starting to make groaning noises, and to be honest, I needed him back in 1985 with me.

"C'mon, Jennifer," Jake commanded. "We're wasting valuable time."

"How am I supposed to transport all these people home?" I asked, uncertain of the circumstances I was now involved in. "Now I have Gertie, Traveler X, and a keyless Marco."

"I'm sure Marco will help you find Caiyan once he regains consciousness," Ace said. "Use your female ingenuity to persuade him."

"You'll figure it out." Jake smiled a dimple-free, concerned, but *let's get the job done* smile at me. "Remember, in order to transport back and forth, you'll need to get out before the moon cycle starts to close."

I nodded, and Ace added, "Yep, when the moon starts to wane, you only have a one-way ticket until it's completely closed. Caiyan and Traveler X should be able to transport themselves, and you can bring Gertie and Marco back in one trip, unless you don't get Caiyan's key back, and then you'll have to decide which stud you really want to shag."

"General Potts doesn't know about kidnapping Marco, does he?" I asked. "That's why we're not meeting at Gitmo."

"The general gave orders to clean up this mess with no problems to the present day." Jake looked worried. "I'm counting on you, Jen."

Ace was standing behind Jake, nodding in agreement. The backstabber. Poor Marco. How was I going to deal with him? I didn't have any cupcakes, and my ability to convince men to do my bidding was waning like the moon would be if we didn't get a move on.

"Just remember, Jennifer. Do NOT do anything that will change the present. No matter what the consequences." Jake gave me his most serious face.

I nodded. What was the matter with him? Of course I would protect our world. I took an oath, I signed a contract, and I made a promise to myself to be the best transporter I could be. How would I change the present, anyhow?

"Geesh," was all I could think to say about my situation.

"Off you go now, darling." Ace gestured toward the vessel.

⟶

I climbed in, frowned at the two men standing in front of me, and prepared for takeoff. I reached over, pulled the pillowcase off Marco's head, and tossed it at Jake. I thought it would be scary if he came to while he was in the middle of a travel. He groaned slightly and leaned against the wall. Jake grimaced and closed the door.

I really didn't like the clothing my vessel had selected for me when I dropped Gertie off earlier. I recalled a picture I had seen in the *Tiger beat* magazine. I focused on the location by the Hollywood sign and firmly grabbed one of the handles for support. I put my arm across Marco's chest like my mom used to do when I was a child riding shotgun in her car. I said the magic word and tried to think relaxed and smooth thoughts. We started off well. Gently swaying back and forth. Marco made a few moans as I felt the vessel touch down in 1985. The problem was it didn't stop moving. We were jostled around, and I felt it skid across the grassy embankment. Something sharp smacked against the front of the outhouse, and I heard a noise like a thousand prisoners banging their tin cups against the prison fence. I felt the vessel teeter, and then it fell backward, landing with a hard thud, knocking me against the back wall and throwing Marco on top of me. I opened one eye, and we were face-to-face. He was so heavy, and I was wedged in under him. I couldn't free my arms to push him off. His eyes fluttered open, and the grogginess of the drug created a haze over his blue-diamond eyes. I knew those beautiful baby blues were going to turn to ice when he figured out what had happened.

"Marco," I said.

"Mmmm, Jen," he replied and moved his left hand to cop a feel over my left breast. He brought his mouth to mine and exploded in a deep, passionate kiss. I couldn't help but respond to that one. It sent fire shooting straight to my groin and emanating outward. I knew any second my outhouse would catch fire and we would burn alive. It might have even been worth it, but my minute of passion was broken by the sound of Gertie's voice as she wrenched open the door and stood staring down at us.

"Are you OK?" she asked. Then she saw Marco's hand groping my boob, and she smirked.

He had dropped his head down on my shoulder, and I couldn't move. "I can't move—can you help?"

She reached down and pulled him up a little so I could get my arm free.

"What's wrong with Marco?" she asked.

"He's been drugged," I said. "Help me get him out of here."

We managed a push-pull maneuver until we had him off me. As I stood up, the outhouse was on its back, and we were balancing on the edge of a steep hill. We had taken out the chain-link fence that kept the trespassers from going down to the sign. The vessel had ripped up the posts, and the fence was holding us hammock-style, keeping us from going over the drop-off. Gertie and I managed to drag Marco out of the vessel, and we stood holding him up at the edge of the large hill. At least he was weight bearing and holding his head up now. Gertie and I looked at each other, wondering what the hell we were supposed to do now.

"Let's take him over there," I said, tipping my head in the direction of a flat area about three feet away. As we started to drag him, he opened his eyes and halted our progress. The drug was wearing off, and he had regained his balance. He stood looking at me. He was groggy and ran a hand through his sexy, mussed blond hair.

"Jen?" he asked in surprise. "Where am I?" Gertie and I loosened our grip on him, and he made a quick turn, toppled backward, and rolled like a link of sausage down the steep hill, coming to a stop against the giant L in the Hollywood sign.

"Shit, I probably killed him!" I carefully slid down the hill after him so I wouldn't go ass over elbows and take a chunk out of the Y. "GERTIE!" I shouted for help.

"I'm coming," she said, making her way down behind me.

Marco was lying at the bottom, face to the sky. His eyes were open, and he had a scrape along his right arm that was starting to ooze blood. It didn't look like he broke anything on the way down.

Gertie met me at the bottom of the hill. "Wow, I had no idea these letters were so large."

I was squatted down next to Marco, checking out his parts for injury.

"Is he going to be all right?" she asked.

"I think so. Aunt Itty made him a special potion that Gerry, one of the other defenders, put in his drink."

Marco blinked a few times, and I leaned over him. "Are you OK?"

He sat up, slowly rubbing his head. "Yeah, but I've got a whale of a headache, and my arm hurts." He looked down at his arm in awe. Wiping the blood off with a corner of his shirt, he seemed satisfied he was in one piece.

I helped him to his feet, and he swayed a little. Glancing around, he saw the sign, and a frown formed between his brows.

"Jen, please tell me that you kidnapped me for a sex-filled, all-night party in LA."

I bit my lower lip and peered at him out of the top of my eyes. "Uhm, no."

Gertie was standing next to me, looking confused. "You kidnapped Marco?"

"No, of course I didn't kidnap Marco." I scuffed my shoe in the dirt.

Marco looked at Gertie. "What year are we in?"

"It's 1985."

He flung his arms in the air. "Jesus, Jennifer. I told you I didn't want to travel." He stomped around a bit and then stopped dead in his tracks, reached for his neck, and froze.

I sucked in some air. "Jake thought it was for the best," I said.

"You kidnapped me when I wasn't wearing my key?" he shouted more than asked.

He stomped around a bit more, and then his voice crescendoed up the scale. "I'm stuck in 1985 WITHOUT MY KEY!" He looked like he might strangle me, so I took a few steps back. Gertie was still watching in amazement. He marched up to me and grabbed my arm. "Call your vessel and take me back."

I looked up at the top of the hill, and my vessel was gone. Lucky for me, it knew when to get the hell out of here. "Marco, I need you here."

"I don't want to be here."

Gertie piped in. "We're going to meet Rocksanna, the diva, singer, and movie star. Aren't you interested?"

"No."

"Please help, Marco." I was begging, but I felt safer with him here. I didn't know if Gertie and I could move around Los Angeles alone. I knew Marco came here frequently and his family owned a winery in Napa. "We can't let an unidentified traveler run around causing problems. What if Mitchell gets him to mess up one of our lives?"

"I CAN'T HELP YOU WITHOUT MY KEY!" he shouted.

"IF YOU HAD AGREED TO HELP IN THE FIRST PLACE, YOU WOULD HAVE YOUR KEY!" I yelled back.

Marco reached out as if he was going to put the Vulcan death grip on me, then balled up his fists and rubbed them on either side of his head.

My eyes started to cloud, and I could feel my bottom lip tremble. What kind of agent am I? Crying at the first roadblock. As I mentally recited my mantra, Marco calmed down.

"Pretty please?" I asked again.

"With sugar on top," came Gertie's voice from behind me.

Marco crossed his arms and was silent in thought for a few seconds. "Here's the deal. I want payment."

"I'm sure the WTF will pay you whatever you want," I told him, hoping there wasn't a limit to my bribery.

"No," he said, picking up a strand of my hair and sliding it through his fingers. "From you."

Somewhere deep down my inner voice was jumping up and down with joy.

"What is it that you want from me?" I asked.

He raised a dark eyebrow.

"Marco, I can't make promises like that."

"No sex, no deal. I have needs, you know."

Then the picture of Caiyan canoodling with Rocksanna flashed in front of my eyes, and I agreed. "Deal."

Chapter 15

It was after midnight, and we were stuck at the top of the Hollywood Hills with the lights of Los Angeles spread out before us like a field of diamonds reflecting off the stars twinkling in the night sky. It was beautiful, and if I weren't on a mission that made my stomach queasy, I would have enjoyed being here with Marco. We climbed back up the hill and surveyed our surroundings. The fence was mangled, and I'm sure the park rangers would have a field day trying to figure that one out. Jake told me in a few years the security up here would be beefed up with satellite dishes, razor wire, and security cameras to keep trespassers from destroying the sign. A noise caught our attention, and we ducked behind a bush. Three teenage kids came down the small access road toward the sign. They were drinking cans of beer and acted like they might have started the night with more than just the cans in their hand.

"Whoa, look at that," one of them said, pointing to the mangled mess of chain-link fence. They ran over to look.

Marco whispered, "Let's go see how they got here."

We circled to the top of the hill, keeping the kids in our sight, but staying out of theirs. Parked on the side of the small road that led down out of the hills was a red Chevy Camaro. The windows were down, and the seats were leather. Gertie and I snuck around to the passenger side and slowly opened the door. Marco slid into the driver's seat.

"Are you sure you're OK to drive?" I asked. "You fell pretty hard."

"And you were drugged," Gertie added.

Yeah, there was that. My inner voice cleared her throat and gave me a look of dissatisfaction.

"I'm fine. I have a fast recovery against drugs and falls." He looked at me and smiled. "All my parts are working A-OK."

I bit my bottom lip to stop it from quivering with fear. I wasn't sure how or when Marco would want payment, but it made my knees shake. My inner voice, however, was scheduling an appointment to get a Brazilian wax.

The car reeked of weed and beer. There weren't any keys in the ignition, and I frowned at Marco. "We don't have the keys."

Marco reached down to the left and released the hatch. He helped himself to a screwdriver he found in the back of the car. He used it to break the console on the steering wheel, and in three magic minutes, the car roared to life.

"Let's go," he ordered.

Gertie, who had been squatting next to me, pushed my seat forward and climbed in the backseat. We pulled away, spitting gravel from under the tires. It dawned on me that in my time I could have used my cell and phoned for help, but those kids would have to walk all the way down the mountain to get help.

We left the park, and Marco pulled over at a gas station. "Where should we go at almost one o'clock in the morning?"

I wasn't sure. "Where would you go if you were a celebrity?"

"I would go to a party," Gertie said, leaning in from the backseat.

"I need some water. That drug made my mouth dry," Marco said.

I retrieved my money from Gertie and held up one of the one-hundred-dollar bills. "I'll get this one."

He raised an eyebrow at me as if to say, *That's not even close to the payment I have in mind.*

I got out of the car before any more innuendos could begin. Gertie stuck her head out the window. "Get some gum, too, please."

The gas station looked old to me. The pumps were devoid of the electronic readouts I was used to in my time. The flashy screens displaying ads were missing, and the price of gas was ninety-five cents. I entered the store, and the clerk peered at me over his newspaper. There was a glass refrigeration case in the back of the store, and as I approached the case, I caught a look at my own hair in the reflection off the glass. Gads. My bangs were sticking straight up, then made a sharp left turn over my forehead. A purple gauze headband peeked out through my massive hair and was knotted into a giant bow on the top of my head. I remembered asking the vessel to make some changes to my wardrobe. I guess that's how Ace keeps his vessel from changing his clothes when he travels. I was wearing an outfit very similar to the one I had pictured in my mind. Black fishnet hose covered by a purple mini dress belted with two slim studded belts wrapped around my middle. The dress had a button-up lace panel across the front, which I hadn't planned on, revealing a black bra. A stack of necklaces and a fishnet scarf hung around my neck, disguising my key. Both arms had bracelets from wrist to midforearm that clinked when I moved my arms. My hands had fingerless fishnet gloves that matched the lace on my top. The only part of the outfit I truly liked was the lace-up leather combat boots. I opened the door and searched for the bottled water. Rows and rows of canned soft drinks and juice glistened back at me. No Ozarka, no Dasani, and definitely no Voss. Along the bottom, I saw green glass bottles of Perrier. That would have to do. Two women about my age were checking out in front of me. One girl had bleached-blond hair that stood a mile high off her head. The other was a brunette with stick-straight hair pulled back in a headband. I reached up and adjusted the giant bow on my head.

"That was such an awesome concert," one of them said, pulling me away from my narcissism.

"Totally," the girl with bottle-blond hair responded. "Rocksanna was radical."

My ears perked up at the performer's name.

"Did you go to the Rocksanna concert tonight?" I asked.

"Yes, did you?" the girl with brown hair turned around and asked me.

"No, I didn't."

"You missed a great concert," said the bottle blonde, and then she turned to pay for her items.

"We're going again tomorrow night," said the brunette, looking me up and down. Maybe my outfit wasn't in style. I didn't have a clue. Gertie and I had read a few fashion magazines in our fast-paced research, but what if I'd overvogued it?

"Your dress is totally rad," said the bottle blonde.

"Yeah, totally," said the brunette.

The bottle blonde added, "We heard Rocksanna and her band are partying at the Choke Club tonight. The drummer is a dreamboat."

Her friend nudged her. "Don't tell everyone. We won't be able to get in if the crowd is too big."

They argued for a brief second, and I butted in. "One of my friends actually works for Rocksanna. Maybe he can help get us in."

They stood, mouths open, staring at me. "Really?" they said in unison, as if this was the greatest day of their lives.

I paid for the waters and a pack of gum, and they followed me outside to the Camaro.

Marco saw us approaching and got out of the car.

They stopped dead in their tracks. One of them gasped, "Is that the dude who was on *Highway to Heaven* the other night?"

The other girl replied in a shrill giggle, "Oh, fer sure, I think his name was Paul Walker. He's such a stud."

There was a small tug on my heart because I was a big fan of the movie star, and Marco did resemble him a little. Paul Walker had died in a car accident, and millions of girls across the nation cried themselves to sleep at night.

"No, that's my friend, Marco," I told them as I waved off the air of melancholy.

Gertie had also gotten out of the car by the time we arrived. Introductions were made, and I passed out the water.

The girls were both named Christie, one with a K and one with a CH. Christie and Kristy. I could remember that, but I also stored them as the blonde and the brunette. We agreed to follow them to the club.

Everyone got in their cars, and we tailed the girls' Honda Prelude into the City of Angels.

⌒

he girls took a right on Sunset Boulevard, and we followed closely behind them. The traffic was heavy for this time of night.

"According to my research," Gertie said, unwrapping the gum I had purchased and popping it into her mouth, "the after party will start at some highfalutin' club and then probably go back to the hotel for an after-after party."

I felt heat rise to the surface. I hoped Caiyan wasn't going to the after-after party with Rocksanna. I took in a slow, deep breath and casually pointed out the window as we passed by the Viper Room. There were so many things I would love to see while I was here. I had never been shopping on Rodeo Drive, I had never see the stars' handprints outside Grauman's Chinese Theatre, and I would love to see all the famous homes of the movie stars, but I had a job to do, and being a tourist wasn't part of it.

The smell of Gertie's grape gum engulfed the small car.

"What kind of gum did you buy her?" Marco asked, cracking the window.

"It was called Bubble Yum." I turned and looked at Gertie. She blew a huge purple bubble. Even in the shadows of the car, I could see her lips had turned a bright purple color. She winked at me, and I couldn't help but be happy she was here. Gertie was a walking, talking Google with a side order of Calamity Jane. Hopefully, the latter part would stay under control this trip.

The girls pulled into a parking lot, and we forked over another ten bucks of our precious money for parking. If Pickles wasn't at this club, we were going to be in trouble when it came to hotel money. I didn't think we could get a decent hotel in Hollywood for under $100, even in 1985. Everyone got out of his or her car, and Marco made small talk with the girls as we approached the Choke Club. I knew from research it was the hottest nightclub in this time. Unfortunately, it burned down in 2006. Twenty people perished in the fire when the multilevel dance floor came crashing down. Tonight, there was a long line around the building with hopefuls waiting to enter the club.

"Now what do we do?" Gertie asked.

The two girls were busy drooling over Marco, and we were at a standstill. Marco surveyed the scene. The Christies were dressed like mini-Madonnas. Black leggings and skintight corsets that their small boobs hung on to for dear life. Marco looked at me and frowned.

"I need to make an alteration to your clothing," he said, moving closer to me and unbuttoning the top four buttons on the lace panel of my minidress. The girls gathered around to see what Marco was up to. His hot fingertips ran down the swell of my breasts as he opened the buttons, and a small smile threatened at the corners of his mouth. He knew exactly what he was doing to me, and I stiffened in retaliation. He pulled the lace open until the black lace bra I was wearing peeked out the top. Reaching inside my sleeves, he peeled the shoulder pads away from the Velcro that kept them secure and handed them to me.

"Stuff these in your bra." I frowned but did as I was told, thankful he didn't take that task on himself. My boobs were already a C cup. I didn't think I needed any help in that department, but when I stuffed the shoulder pads in the bottom of my bra, my dress could barely contain them. Both of our new friends squealed with glee.

"What a totally tubular idea," one of them said. I knew if they had been wearing shoulder pads we would have all been stacked like Dolly Parton. I adjusted the lacy black scarf I had around my neck that hid my key to cover some of my cleavage. Gertie and the girls began walking toward the club entrance.

"Give me the fifty you've got in your pocket." Marco held out a hand and turned his back on the others.

Pressing my lips together, I held out the money I had left after I purchased the waters. He took the one hundred and the fifty, leaving me with the pocket change.

"Hey," I started to complain.

"I have to buy you girls a drink, right?"

I grimaced, and he grabbed my shoulders and turned me toward the club. Marco led our little group past all the people standing in line and walked up to the bouncer who was checking IDs at the door. This man could give the Hulk a run for his money. He was very large and didn't have much of a neck. Marco pushed me forward so I bumped into him. The two people in line started to complain when Marco interrupted.

"Hey, my man, haven't seen you in a while," Marco said, holding out his hand. The big man looked at me, leaned over, and shook Marco's outstretched hand, never taking his eyes off my chest. I saw the money pass between the men in the handshake. He raised his eyes to meet Marco and unhooked the black velvet cording that separated us from the entrance to the club. The people in line started to raise a fuss, but one grunt from the bouncer and they silenced.

"That was a nice con," I said to Marco.

"He probably gets so drunk after work he doesn't remember who he's met. Some things never change."

We trooped in, and Marco paid for everyone's cover. Damn, now we were really low on money. I hoped Gertie didn't tell him about her stash. They stamped our hands, and Marco explained to his new groupies that we would need to go in search of our friend.

The place was packed. We were body to body, and the shoulder pads under my boobs were making them sweat. The multilevel dance floor was centered in the large room. A semicircular bar hugged the back of the dance floor, and U-shaped booths stretched across the wall behind the bar and to our right. There was another bar across the far end of the room with girls dancing on each end. Smoke from a hidden fog machine snaked around the dance floor, making it difficult to see across to the other side. A stage was to our left, and roadies were setting up equipment. Gertie pointed up to a loft area at the far end of the club. A DJ was playing music from a booth in the center of the loft, and on either side of the booth was a spiral staircase that was policed by more very large bouncers.

"Where's your friend?" asked the brunette.

"I need to find him," Marco replied, scanning the room.

"We can dance while you look for him, OK?" the blonde said, pulling Gertie toward the dance floor. She shrugged reluctantly and followed them. Marco and I made our way to the back bar, where we could get a good view of the room. I was keeping a lookout for Caiyan and Mitchell. I didn't want either of them to see me first. Marco ordered two beers, and he tapped the neck of my bottle with his.

"Happy hunting," he said, taking a long pull on his bottle.

I watched Gertie dance and drank my beer slowly. At the end of the next song, the music stopped and a spotlight illuminated the stage. The DJ announced they had a special performance tonight from a new band that was opening for Rocksanna tomorrow night, the Beasts.

Three boys dressed in baggy blue jeans, faded concert T-shirts, and baseball hats took the stage. They started what I would call a rap but my research on the band revealed it was called hip-hop. The crowd gathered around as the boys jumped and chanted into the microphone. This was all wrong. Where was Traveler X? I'd seen his photo in the magazines Gertie had brought home from the library. After the first song, one of the boys said, "Most of you know our lead guitarist left to go solo." The crowd booed ferociously. "But," he said as he held up a finger, and the crowd grew quiet. "We have a new man on the axe. Please welcome the Camp man."

The spotlight angled over to the corner, and playing his heart out was Campy. His dark hair glistened in the stage lights, and he played like a born rock star. The crowd went wild. Various undergarments began flying up on the stage. Campy ignored the crowd and focused on his guitar.

Marco bent close and spoke in my ear. "He's pretty good, but his key is visible, and that could get him in a lot of trouble."

Sure enough, Campy had on a white T-shirt and jeans. The medallion around his neck looked like a key, and all eyes could see it. The eyes I saw looking at it were Mitchell's. He was positioned at the base of the steps leading up to the stage. He was wearing a badge, indicating he worked with the band. He had on a black button-down, black jeans, and a leather choke collar that conveniently hid his key. He was practically drooling. I assumed the Mafusos had threatened Mitchell about obtaining a new key before Mortas got out of jail. I was going to make it my personal mission to make sure that did not happen. I nudged Marco and pointed in Mitchell's direction. We immediately turned our backs to the concert to avoid recognition by the little prick.

"Do you think it's Liam's key?" I asked Marco.

"Most likely, but hard to tell from this distance."

I surveyed the room. No sign of Caiyan or Rocksanna. Surely the crowd would be going crazy if she were here. I looked up and saw a balcony that ran above the back half of the club. A few people were leaning over the railing to get a better view of the band. I squinted through the smoky haze, but I didn't recognize anyone.

The band played a few songs and then invited the crowd to see them tomorrow night at the concert. Afterward they called it a night, and I saw them escorted out of the building. I couldn't get close enough to Campy without Mitchell identifying me. Damn.

"Should we go after them?" I asked.

"Let's try to find your boyfriend first and see what he knows," Marco said.

"He's not my boyfriend," I stammered.

Marco stared into my eyes for a long minute. The heat between us sizzled, and my inner voice was putting an ice pack between her legs. "Right," he said, cutting his eyes away and turning back around toward the stage. The DJ had resumed playing Def Leppard's *Pyromania*, and I saw Gertie and her groupies bebop back onto the dance floor.

"I think we should check out up there," I said to Marco, pointing to the balcony. He followed my gaze and agreed, motioning toward a set of stairs near the back of the club. One very large man was standing at the base of the staircase. A bouncer, no doubt. I assumed the balcony was VIP. If that was the case, then maybe Rocksanna was up there.

I grabbed Marco's hand, making him jump at the spark of the connection. Holding hands was definitely out of the question. As we got closer to the bouncer and away from the smoke on the dance floor, I could see he was very clean cut with skin the color of my favorite mocha latte. We made eye contact, and a look of frustration crossed his face.

"You can't go up dere, dat is VIP only," he said. When he spoke, I recognized the voice immediately.

"You've got legs," I shouted before I could stop myself.

He eyed me warily. "Vat did you say?"

I realized he didn't know me. It was eerie, my friend Pickles, an agent from the WTF had no idea who I was, and he wasn't in a wheelchair. He was also about six foot five, dressed in head to toe black leather, and built like the Rock.

I said, "You have really nice legs."

He smiled, his white teeth gleaming in the dark club. "Why tank you, but you are still not getting in dare."

Marco moved in and pulled the scarf loose from around my neck. My key glowed in the fluorescent lights.

Pickles eyes widened. "Vere did you get dat?"

"We are with the WTF, and we need your help," I explained.

The music increased to higher decibels, and I couldn't make out what Pickles was saying. Gertie appeared minus the girls and smiled at Pickles.

He nodded and pointed a questioning finger at Gertie. I shook my head no. I pointed at Marco and bobbed my head. He smiled and they shook hands.

"We need to get upstairs. We're looking for Caiyan," I shouted as Pickles bent down to hear me.

Pickles said, "I will take you up to an empty booth, but do not approach him. Rocksanna has his key and won't give it back. She tinks it's some kind of lucky charm. If she knows you want her new boy toy or de key, he is doomed."

Just as we were about to head upstairs, Marco's groupies appeared, patting me on the back for finding my friend and jumping up and down that they were going to meet Rocksanna. He looked at Pickles and shrugged. Pickles led us up the spiral staircase and to a semicircular booth to the right of the DJ. We piled in, and I glanced around at the other tables. In the corner was a booth triple the size of the one

166

we occupied. Almost a dozen people were crammed into it, and sitting center was Rocksanna. She was sipping something out of a fluted glass, and Caiyan was sitting next to her with his arms across the back of the seat. He was engaged in conversation with a guy on his right. I pressed my lips together and tried to fight the urge to walk across the tables until I was standing on his.

A server appeared, and Marco ordered our drinks. Gertie was trying to discourage our two guests from going over to Rocksanna's table.

"I can't see her from here," the blonde complained. I realized there was a supporting column that blocked half the view from their table. Caiyan had the perfect view of Marco and me, but the rest of our table remained hidden. I scooted over a little so she could see Rocksanna. This put me up close and personal with Marco, who stopped ordering in midsentence to squeeze my knee.

The blonde sucked in a breath. "OH MY GOD, there is her new man. Isn't he cute?" She turned to me.

"Oh yeah, real cute," I said.

The brunette, who had obviously had a few cocktails, chimed in. "When she's done with him, I'm going to fuck him."

Marco chuckled.

Was Caiyan really sleeping with this woman? My inner voice was holding up her hand, ticking off all the people who had warned me he was a man whore. Was I jealous? I didn't know the roller coaster of emotions that were swimming around in my head.

"Let's go over and get an autograph," the blonde insisted.

"You don't want to make a big deal about it," Gertie was saying when I came back to reality and joined in the conversation. "Rocksanna hates when people ask for her autograph."

"But the *National Enquirer* said she loves her fans," the blond girl said with her eyes welling up as if she might cry if she didn't get to meet her idol.

"Yep, we shoub devinitly go ober," the brunette slurred, and I gave Marco a *should we really get her another drink* glare.

The server brought our drinks. Thankfully, Marco chose a pitcher of beer instead of mixed drinks that probably cost a bundle.

I sipped my beer and watched their table. Rocksanna, catching us staring at them, reached up and turned Caiyan's face away from the man he was talking to and kissed him full on the mouth. Apparently this caught him by surprise, because his eyes were open and he looked my way. When he saw me, he jumped away from Rocksanna, spilling her tall cocktail on the table. She thought this was incredibly funny, and she bubbled with laughter. His eyes darkened, and I could feel the anger resonate from where I sat in my comfy booth. I could see him making excuses as the gaggle of people began sopping up the drink with napkins before it could run over on the precious Rocksanna. I was certain spilling the drink was intentional so he could leave his booth and come strangle me.

The people to his right cleared out of the way for him, and he stalked off in the direction of the men's room. Marco looked at me and raised an eyebrow. "He's seen you now. I should probably collect my payment before he comes to kill you."

"Do you think he might?"

"I would if I were him, and I will if you don't get me home in the next two days."

Gertie was checking out one of the men at Rocksanna's table, and then all three of them scooted out of our booth.

"We're going to get an autograph," Gertie stated matter-of-factly.

"I thought Rocksanna hated that?" I asked.

"That's all bull dookie. You can't believe what you read in the *National* whatever," said the drunk girl. Then she linked arms with Gertie, and they went over to say hi to my newest archenemy.

"I'd better go catch Caiyan as he leaves the men's room." I took a long drink of my beer. "Better to get this part over and find out how we can help."

"That's the spirit." Marco raised his glass in a toast as I scooted out of the booth.

The men's room was downstairs in the back of the club. At least it was away from all the noise and smoke. I loitered outside the men's room, but after getting a few offers from the men leaving the restroom, I moved back into an alcove under the stairs. A hand clamped around my mouth and muffled my scream. I used the elbow-jab-twist maneuver that Jake had taught me and almost brought my captor to his knees.

"Bloody hell, stop it," Caiyan said.

"Damn, why did you grab me?" I asked. "Why can't you just tap me on the shoulder like a normal person?"

The music was loud, and he pulled me back into the alcove so we could speak without shouting.

"Why are ye here?" he demanded.

"I'm here to help you."

"I dinnae need any help."

"I could see that from where I was sitting."

Caiyan tensed. "It's just a job."

"She has your key," I said, tapping his naked throat.

"I know," he said, but his eyes clouded as if there had been a mishap.

"Jake told me about Traveler X—it's Campbell, isn't it?"

"Aye, it is Campy, and I'm trying to get him to come home."

"I gather it's not working."

"Not so far." He ran a hand through his hair, and I noticed his eyes were bloodshot, and he seemed tired. This was new to me because even during our past travels Caiyan never acted or looked tired. He was always ready to go and dragging me along behind him.

"Why is Marco here?"

"Jake didn't want me to come by myself. He was worried I didn't have enough training to capture a fifteen-year-old." I rolled my eyes. "Why did he choose this time anyway?"

"He's rebelling. He joined a band, the Beasts." Caiyan sighed. "He's mad at my sister for leaving him with Aunt Itty. The problem is Mitchell is here, and he's dangerous."

"I'm sure he's out for blood after last month when we tied him up and put him behind bars." We had custody of Mitchell after the October travel. The unadulterated praise from his family made him cocky. Fortunately for us, he wasn't the sharpest tool in the shed, so he was easily captured. Hopefully, we could complete our mission without having to deal with the little twerp.

"Why can't you just knock Rocksanna out, take your key, grab Campy, and we can all go home?" I thought it was the perfect plan.

"It's not that simple." Caiyan ran a hand down my arm, making it tingle. He looked deep into my eyes, and I thought he was going to lean in and kiss me.

Before Caiyan could relieve me of my fears that he might actually be taking this "job" to a level I wasn't comfortable with, we were interrupted.

"Caiyan, darling, what are you doing down here?" Rocksanna had found her lost boy toy. Her two bodyguards flanked her on each side. Pickles had his arms crossed over his chest.

Caiyan was caught with me in the alcove. "This is an old family friend of mine, Jennifer." He motioned toward the rock goddess. "Rocksy."

Damn, he had a pet name for her. This was not going well. Up close, she was even more stunning than in photos. Her blond hair cascaded down her back and framed her beautiful face. Her skin was flawless, and her low-cut shirt showed off a pair of perky breasts that stood up to perfection in lieu of not wearing a bra. I always thought my boobs were one of my best assets, but after seeing her rack, I felt like I had rocks in tube socks.

"Hello," I greeted her, staring into her big brown eyes with perfectly curled eyelashes.

"Yes, hello," she said. "I met more of your family friends upstairs. I think one was called Gertie."

Caiyan frowned and gave me an evil eye.

"Good to meet you, Jennifer," Rocksanna said, interlacing her fingers through Caiyan's fingers and pulling him along. "Come along now, darling. I need my rest. Hope you can make it to the show tomorrow night," she said over her shoulder to me as they walked away.

"Bye," I said to myself as one of the most glamorous women in the world pulled my defender toward the door. For the first time I saw Caiyan look helpless. She had his key, and he had to keep her close to get it back.

Before Pickles followed after them, he handed me a card. "Get in touch with de man at dis hotel. He will give you a place ta stay tonight. It's de same hotel dat Campy is staying. I will be in contact wit' you tomorrow." He caught up with Rocksanna's entourage and did booty patrol on the way out the door.

Chapter 16

I returned to Marco, and he was sitting alone in the booth. He moved over, and I sat down next to him. "No luck?" he asked.

"He didn't kill me, if that's what you mean. I didn't get much info on Campy."

"He doesn't know where Campy is?"

"I don't know. We were interrupted by Miss Fuck Me 'Cuz I'm So Glamorous."

"You were told he's a player, right?" Marco asked, and my inner voice held up another finger indicating an entire hand had warned me to keep away from Caiyan.

I rolled my eyes at him and changed the subject. "Pickles gave me a card for a hotel we can stay in tonight." Marco took the card.

I took a sip of my beer and asked, "Where's Gertie?"

"Dancing with her new friends." He motioned toward the dance floor. I stood and leaned over the railing. The dance floor was divided into three levels. The girls were on the middle level. Gertie was dirty dancing with a guy who resembled Vanilla Ice. Our two friends were dancing together, and I thought this might be a great time to ditch them.

"Let's get out of here," I told Marco.

"OK, but let me get the phone numbers of our friends." I glared at him.

He laughed. "Not for that reason. Whenever you travel, if you meet someone, it's always good to have a way to get in touch with the person. If you end up in jail, you would need to get bailed out, or if you need money, they might be able to help you faster than the WTF."

"I thought the WTF was our go-to?"

"They are still a government organization, and that means red tape." He shrugged. "Besides, you never know when you might be in a time before the WTF was around."

I thought of my most recent travel with Caiyan to 1602. "The WTF was organized during the Johnson administration. Not long ago when you're talking time travel." I nodded. I remembered Jake telling me about "making friends" in a training session, but my anger at Caiyan had clouded my brain. *Get a grip, Jen. You are a professional transporter for the WTF, and you have a job to do.*

I stood on the edge of the dance floor, trying to get Gertie's attention. The smoke from the fog machine combined with all the cigarette smoke was so thick I could barely see her.

Marco smiled at me. "C'mon, let's go." He grabbed my hand, and we made our way out to get Gertie. In the process we danced, and it was liberating. The DJ had a Prince song blaring, and everyone was bouncing up and down in time with the beat. I shouted over to Gertie that it was time to go.

She held up a finger and mouthed, "One more."

The music slowed, and one of Madonna's songs, "Crazy for You," played over the speakers. It was the song Jake and I had danced to at our senior prom. The first time he kissed me. The nostalgia was a bit overwhelming for me, so I exited the dance floor. Marco grabbed my hand and reeled me into him. "I like this song," he said. We danced, but our contact had us hot and bothered before the song ended, and he broke his hold on me. I thought, *If Marco and I have sex, we're going to self-combust.*

We gathered the telephone numbers from the girls, and Gertie got Vanilla Ice's number. As we cleared the club and inhaled fresh air, she said, "He was such a STUD!"

Marco and I both stared at her.

"What?" she asked. "I'm just working the lingo."

We caught a cab outside the club, choosing to leave our stolen Camaro in the parking lot. Marco gave the driver the name of our hotel. The streets were still alive at two in morning, and I sat back against the vinyl seats of the cab and wondered if Caiyan was at the after-after party with the rock star, or did they slink off to a five-star hotel and get busy.

⌒

Our hotel was the Chateau Marmont. I knew this hotel because it was written up in the gossip columns when famous celebrities either trashed the place or died in one of the cabanas. As we pulled up to the hotel, it had that funky castle feel, and I could understand why a young band of boys would want to stay here. According to Gertie, they were an up-and-coming band in 1985 but only lasted a few years and then disbanded for solo careers. They had dance routines that made tween girls swoon and MILFs throw their underwear up on the stage. I laughed to myself, knowing these terms hadn't been invented yet. I wondered what they called a MILF in the eighties.

The lobby was quaint with huge potted palms and funky mismatched seating. I could picture Greta Garbo leaning against the baby grand piano we passed as we made our way to the check-in counter. The man on the card Pickles had given us greeted us before we could get to the concierge. His name was Georgish, and he explained he was the hotel manager.

He certainly dressed the part in his dark suit and tie. I was amazed the manager would be here at two in the morning, but he didn't seem alarmed by the early hour. Based on his accent, dark hair, and skin, I pegged him to be part Jamaican. My linguistics training was paying off. He didn't question the fact that we didn't have any luggage, and we didn't sign any paperwork. The three of us followed him into the nearest elevator. His athletic build added to his smug demeanor as he held the elevator door open without a care about our identities. He led us down a corridor and up a short flight of stairs.

"This is the only room we have available tonight," he said as he slipped the key into the lock and opened the door. "I hope you can make it work for you."

We entered the small living room with a puce-colored sofa and matching chair facing an enormous console television. A kitchenette was located to the left with a half bath next to it. A bedroom opened up off the living room. A queen-size bed was centered in the room, and a bathroom was to the left. A large papasan chair stood in the corner of the room. "The hotel was built to withstand earthquakes, so the walls are soundproof, and the grounds are very secure."

"Thank you, Georgish," I said, remembering my training to repeat names often to help with recall.

"I have left some necessities in the kitchen and bathrooms for you. Please feel free to contact me if you need anything else."

He handed me a brass key with an ornate head and long shaft—very antique looking. I couldn't remember the last time I had actually used a real key at a hotel. I dug in my pocket for tip money and came up with a five. Georgish waved away my offering.

"Not necessary. Andre is my cousin." He left us standing in the center of the living room as he closed the door behind him.

"Andre?" I looked at Marco.

"I think he means Pickles," Marco said. I never knew Pickles's real name was Andre. I would have to razz him about that when we returned. If we returned. The doubt made my stomach queasy.

"Do you think Georgish is one of you?" Gertie asked Marco.

"Why don't you ask Miss Touchy Feely over there," he said, pointing to me.

"I didn't get that feeling, but I didn't touch him either."

Marco told us he would take the couch as he headed into the bathroom to shower. Gertie and I surveyed the contents of the kitchen. We had a two-burner stove, a microwave, and a full-size refrigerator. The fridge was stocked with everything from eggs to cold cuts. I grabbed a jug of milk and poured a glass as Gertie was going through the contents of the cabinet above the stove. She pulled out a package of Oreos, and we smiled at each other. We stacked the pillows against the headboard and took turns dipping the Oreos in the glass of milk.

"You know Marco is in there naked right now?" Gertie asked.

"Yep, I would assume he usually showers without clothes."

"You could go in there and find out what he's like in the sack."

"I'm on an assignment, Gert." I licked the cookie off my fingers and stood to pull off my clothes, opting to sleep in the pink lace bra and underwear.

"Party pooper. I bet he's great, and I bet he's got a nice package."

I threw a pillow at Gertie, and she giggled.

"I could turn up the TV really loud. I wouldn't hear a thing."

We were both in the bed with the covers pulled up to our necks when Marco came out with a towel wrapped around his waist. His abs were cut in a way no man should be able to accomplish. The shower made his blond hair curl around his face. He looked like an Abercrombie model, and Gertie's mouth was hanging open. She looked over at me in complete disgust at the missed opportunity.

He threw a wad of clothes at us. "Looks like Georgish left you some complimentary T-shirts." I shook out one of the shirts and saw that it had the hotel logo across the front. Good enough for me. I pulled it on over my head, and I realized Marco was watching me. A small smile crept across his face as he grabbed his towel and ripped it off, throwing it at Gertie and me. We both let out a shriek, but we didn't cover our eyes, and this made Marco laugh as he turned and left the room wearing silk boxers with "Chateau Marmont" emblazoned across the butt.

"Made you look," he said, still laughing as he shut the door between our rooms. Gertie and I brushed our teeth with the complimentary toothbrushes from the hotel and turned out the lights. The energy Marco emitted from the next room made my toes tingle, and I knew getting a good night's sleep was going to be a tough one.

Chapter 17

A loud buzzing noise had me jumping out of bed in attack mode. Marco came barreling into our room with fists up, as if an intruder was coming in the window. We stood facing off until Gertie sleepily reached over and answered the telephone. Marco and I sighed with relief.

"It was Pickles," Gertie said. "He's sending over tickets to the concert tonight, and he said to let you know he notified the WTF."

When we go back in time, the WTF of that time is supposed to monitor and help out but not interfere with our mission. They are busy running their own travels and don't want to mess up our plans. We are not allowed to communicate any knowledge of the future to them. Thankfully, they had also wired cash to the hotel.

We dressed in the clothes from last night and made plans to shop after grabbing a bite to eat at the IHOP a few blocks from the hotel. As we waited for the elevator, I kept an eye out for Mitchell. If he saw Gertie and me, he might warn Campy. I assumed they would still be asleep, considering they were teenage boys. The doors opened, and Campy stood in the center of the elevator. Alone. He was wearing a swimsuit and a white tank top. His dark wavy hair was sticking up in all directions as if he had just rolled out of bed. Liam's key gleamed around his neck, available for anyone to see.

We all stood staring at him.

"Uhm, are you going down?" he asked, his accent a blend of Scottish and Cockney.

I nodded my head, and we entered. We could just grab him right now, and we would be done. Marco had the same idea. Gertie was shaking her head no. "It would just be futile," she said. "You know, like *Groundhog Day.*"

Campy looked confused at her words, but I got them. *Groundhog Day* was a movie where the main character kept repeating the same day over and over. If we took Campy against his will, he would just return at the next moon cycle. We needed to make him want to come home. Besides, I still needed to help Caiyan get his key.

"Are you going for a swim?" I asked him.

"Yeah," he said, speaking directly at my chest. He was definitely Caiyan's blood relative.

"That sounds like fun," Gertie chipped in. "Going swimming in December."

"The pool's heated," he told Gertie. "Are you from Texas?" He looked her up and down, as if she should be wearing cowboy boots with spurs.

"I sure am," she replied, adding the extra twang for good measure.

"I thought so. I'm pretty good at picking up accents."

"I detect a slight English accent. You're not from LA, are you?" she asked.

"English!" he muttered, as if Gertie had said a bad word. "No, I'm from Scotland, but I lived in England for a short time. I'm here with my band, the Beasts."

Gertie turned on her Texas charm. "The Beasts—I'm such a huge fan. We're going to the concert tonight."

"Awesome," Campy said, again to my boobs. "Maybe I can get you backstage."

"That would be totally tubular," Gertie said, making introductions to Campy. He offered his hand to me, and when I reached out to shake it, Marco cut me off. He pulled me to him and kissed me hard with lots of tongue.

I pulled away from him as Gertie and Campy stood with mouths hanging open.

"She just has that effect on me," Marco explained to Campy. Campy nodded as the elevator pinged at the lobby level.

As the elevator doors opened, I saw Mitchell with his back to us yelling at the concierge. I grabbed Gertie's arm, and we skedaddled out the front door, leaving our mark standing in the foyer, waving bye.

⟶

"*W*hy did you do that in the elevator?" I asked Marco. "Are you kidding?" He grinned. "That kid's hormones are going ninety to nothing. If you have the same effect on him as you do on me, when you touched his hand, we might have exploded."

"Not everyone I touch turns to brimstone like you do."

We headed over to IHOP, and after a satisfying Rooty Tooty Fresh 'N Fruity breakfast, we walked to the shops along Santa Monica Boulevard. Michael Jackson zippered parachute pants and Madonna regalia adorned most of the store windows. Gertie spotted a zebra shirt with shoulder pads that looked like they were stolen from Mean Joe Greene. We followed her into the store and combed through the racks of clothes to find an outfit to wear to the concert. Here I was in one of the famous shopping meccas of the world, and I was at a Mervyn's. There was a reason this store went out of business. Rodeo Drive was a few blocks away but not in our budget. The shopping gods were not on my side this trip. I held up a sweater that had a green fuzzy picture of Marilyn Monroe and frowned. Marco came up behind me and massaged my shoulders. His touch shot fire down my arms and out my elbows.

"I know you're salivating to shop at the other end of town, but I promise, if you get me home before the moon cycle closes, I will personally take you there."

I shrugged off his divine massage.

"I know you want to go home, but I don't feel like we have accomplished anything," I said. "It's been almost twelve hours, and we have let Caiyan disappear to who knows where, and Campy slipped right between our fingertips."

"It's all about timing," Marco replied. "Gertie was right. If we had taken Campy against his will, he would have retaliated. He might even be tempted to join up with the Mafusos. It's easier if he decides to be a brigand on his own, but if he joins their little cult, we'll have a much harder time getting him to convert."

"This comes from the man who is Switzerland," I said.

"I don't believe what the brigands do is right, and if I go to work for the WTF, it could affect more than just my life." He shrugged and walked over to where Gertie was trying on jean jackets.

I recalled the time I met Marco's family at his teammate Enzio's wedding. I thought maybe I was supposed to be his transporter instead of Caiyan's, but he told me there was someone else. I wondered if that someone else was his sister, Evangeline. There was warmth when I touched her hands, and maybe Marco was protecting her from her gift. My inner voice was clicking her tongue at me as if to say, *Quit making up stories.* Holding up a bustier, Gertie pulled me out of my inner battle.

"What do ya think?"

The thing was tiny, black leather, and had little pointed spikes all over it.

"I think you would look like Zelda, the Amazon warrior."

Gertie frowned. "You gotta dress to impress. How are we gonna get backstage if we look like we shopped at Kmart?"

"Uhm, we have backstage passes that Pickles left us this morning."

"True, but we still want to stand out. Did you see the drummer in the Beasts?" She licked her lips. "I'd rather watch him than eat fried chicken."

"Whoa, that sounds serious," Marco said.

"Gertie, he's in a boy band. He's probably a lot younger than you."

"Actually, he's about ten years older than me when we get home. That should be about perfect." She flipped her hair over her shoulder. I wonder if he's on Sweetie Swipe."

"He's probably fat, bald, and has three kids," I said. "The Beasts didn't last long, remember?"

Gertie huffed, put down the bustier, and purchased a black lace bodice, black tutu, fishnet stockings, and a cute gray minijacket with leopard trim instead. Marco bought an Ozzy Osbourne T-shirt to wear with the jeans he was transported in. I went for a red sparkly off-the-shoulder shirt and black parachute pants. I felt like all those zippers could hold a lot of secrets. I was debating the purchase of a jean jacket. It was cute with rhinestones on the collar, but it was a little pricey. The store clerk told me I would need that because of the winter winds. She explained they were called Santa Ana winds, and they happened in the late fall and winter.

As we left the store, the sky was overcast, and the temperature was brisk, but a warm wind kicked up and almost blew me sideways. I was glad I purchased the jean jacket. We were set for tonight. All we needed now was a plan. Marco went to find a cab because we had bags to take back to the hotel. Gertie and I bought an ice cream from a corner vendor and waited for Marco. People around us were dressed like the cast of *Growing Pains* with big-necked sweaters and skinny ties. A few men wore dark sunglasses like Tom Cruise in *Risky Business*. As we waited for a cab, I felt the hairs on the back of my neck raise up. I turned to see a man staring at me. He had long black stringy hair, and he wore faded blue jeans and a gray Members Only jacket zipped up over his gut. He looked vaguely familiar. My mind raced. Who would I have known in Hollywood in 1985? Marco returned, wearing a pair of the Tom Cruise glasses, and pulled me in close.

"I think you have an admirer," he said, jerking a thumb toward the man. His warmth didn't faze the chill down my spine.

"I know. He reminds me of someone," I said.

"Do you think he's a brigand?" Marco asked.

"No, I don't think so." As I was racking my brain, trying to place the guy, our cab came screeching to halt in front of us. We climbed in, and I looked back to see Mr. Creepy staring us down as we sped away.

*G*eorgish was behind the desk when we entered the hotel, and he nodded in our direction. We scoped the lobby for Mitchell and discovered it was all clear. I stopped by the desk and asked Georgish if the Beasts were still here. He eyed me curiously and told me they had gone to the concert hall for rehearsal. I returned to the room with Marco and Gertie.

"We need a plan," I said as I flopped down on the couch.

"I say we go and enjoy the concert, and then we go backstage and convince Campy he needs to go home," Gertie said as she pulled the cold cuts out of the fridge to make sandwiches.

"How are we going to convince him?" I asked.

Marco was lifting up the cushions on the couch and looking under the chair.

"What on earth are you doing?" I asked.

"I'm looking for the remote. I can't turn on the TV," he said, sticking his hand under the sofa cushion.

"Oh, for heaven's sake," said Gertie as she marched over to the big console TV and pulled a knob. "Am I the only one here who watched reruns of *Family Ties* and *I Love Lucy*?"

Gertie returned to the kitchen while Marco messed with the dial on the TV. He stopped at a news program, and a newscaster with hair shaped like a helmet reported the most recent news on the Bus Stop Killer. Apparently, the murderer had killed several women between the ages of eighteen and thirty, up and down the California coast. He would pick up an unsuspecting woman at a bus stop, strangle her, and leave her body at the bus stop with the word *slut* carved across her dead forehead. His last kill was in November, and they were issuing a warning for all women to be careful while waiting for a bus.

"That's awful," Gertie said, handing us a plate with a sandwich and potato chips. She sat down next to me on the sofa. "I read about this guy at school. They never caught him, and every year for the last thirty years they find one girl."

"He has been killing women for thirty years and they still haven't caught him?" Marco asked.

"Yes, it's amazing someone can commit crimes for that long and not get caught." Gertie took a bite out of her sandwich. "He started out killing one girl a month, and then he almost got caught. He was finishing up his artwork on the victim's forehead, and the bus pulled up. The police almost nabbed him. Now he just kills one a year. I think he's trying to make his way through all fifty states."

"That's terrible," I said.

"No, what's terrible is he hasn't made it to Texas yet."

"Are you sure?"

"Yep, his last kill before he started his yearly killing spree was right here in LA." Gertie rolled her eyes upward as if she was checking her data log. "He hasn't killed anyone in Texas, Louisiana, or Alabama. Then of course, the noncontinental states Hawaii and Alaska." Gertie stopped chewing for a second. "No, I take that back. They did find one in Hawaii last year."

"Gertie, are you sure?" I asked. "How do you remember all that?"

She shrugged. "I remembered it because it was the same day as Rocksanna's terrible car crash, which is…tonight."

The three of us were silent for a few minutes. I asked myself, if we knew where a murder was going to happen, should we report it? We finished our lunch in silence, watching the TV.

"Gertie, do you know which bus stop?" Marco broke the silence.

"It was somewhere on Vine, like in the song 'Love Potion Number Nine.'"

Marco raised an unbelievable eyebrow at Gertie.

"It's how I remember things." Gertie gave him a palms-up. "I know she was wearing a red raincoat because the lead story in the paper was 'Red Riding Hood Gets the Ax by the Bus Stop Killer.'"

"That's morbid," I said.

"I'm going to call Pickles and ask him what he thinks we should do," Marco said.

The news had changed from the Bus Stop Killer to the traffic report. A shot of the bumper-to-bumper traffic flashed across the screen, and I was amazed at the number of station wagons on the road. I hadn't seen one in a long time.

"It's hard to believe those will be replaced by SUVs," Marco said.

"Thank God. Jennifer, do you remember riding backward in Uncle Durr's old wagon?" Gertie asked.

I did remember. We were young and visiting Mama Bea in Dallas. Uncle Durr needed to go to the store to buy his Copenhagen, and Mama Bea sent Gertie, Eli, and me along for the ride. The station wagon had a third row of seats that faced the back of the car. Uncle Durr would roll down the window so we could hang our feet out. Eli spent the entire ride squatted down in the floorboard only poking his head up to shoot spit wads at the car behind us. Eventually we pulled into the store parking lot, and so did the car behind us. Tiny wads of paper covered the windshield. The offended driver was from Minnesota and talked as if his lips could only make the O sound. They just wouldn't open far enough to get out the entire word. Uncle Durr got an earful about his bad-mannered nieces as Eli hid in the car. Chickenshit. The only thing Uncle Durr had to say to Eli was, "Nice shootin', Tex." Jeez.

⌣⌢

The concert was at the Hollywood Bowl. It was adjacent to the Rock City Hotel, an old hotel that had been converted into the dressing rooms, preperformance lounging areas, and prop storage for the performers and staff members. The stage was under a grouping of arches that formed a dome. The arena was across the back of the hotel with seating nestled into the side of the Hollywood Hills. We took a cab to the entrance and made our way to the backstage area. A large man was checking backstage passes. We presented him with the passes Pickles had left us at the hotel. We were granted permission to enter and proceeded down a long hall into a large open room with a bar and lounging area. Rocksanna was in the corner snuggled up to Caiyan, who looked miserable. She still sported his key around her lovely neck, and I had a vision of the chokehold maneuver that Jake taught me. My inner voice looked at me in disgrace. The woman was about to be involved in a deadly car crash. I took a deep breath and gave Caiyan a finger wave. He removed her arm from around his neck and stalked over to where I was standing with Marco and Gertie.

"Ferrari." Caiyan gave Marco a head nod.

"McGregor," Marco replied and excused himself to get drinks.

"Now what are ye three stooges up ta?" Caiyan asked.

"Oh, just convincing Campy to come home, helping you get your key back, and hoping Mitchell will lose his."

"Aye, the boys just left to get ready. Mitchell hasn't spotted ye, then?"

"No, he's so preoccupied with Campy's key, he's not paying attention," I said. "Why, isn't he giving you any trouble?"

"Oh, he's giving me plenty. Ye see, it was he who told Rocksanna my key was an old Irish good luck charm."

I snickered. "So that's why she wanted it."

"Aye, Irish—can ye believe it? He's aff his heid."

"Can't you just take it off her?" Gertie asked.

"That's jest it, ye see. I tried, but the damn thing won't budge. It means she has some of the bloodline."

"Is she a transporter?" I swallowed hard at the thought this woman may mean more to Caiyan than even he realized.

"Pickles told me she doesn't know. Sometimes that happens. People without family to guide them get lost. I asked her if she had ever seen anything like my key before, and she said no."

"It could have saved her from her car accident," I said. "Caiyan, if she doesn't give you the key back tonight, she might live through the accident."

He ran a hand through his hair and looked away.

"You care about her," I said. He avoided eye contact with me.

I nudged Gertie for help.

"If she doesn't perish in that wreck, a ton of things could change in the music industry," Gertie said.

Marco returned and handed Gertie and me a blue concoction.

"Is that so bad?" Caiyan asked.

"Her death inspired a whole culture of music," Gertie added.

"Maybe her life would be as inspiring."

"You're off your game, man," Marco said. Caiyan's head snapped up at his words.

"And what's yer game, aye?" He looked at the two of us.

"Whoa, I'm just trying to get back home. I need you to get that key and get that kid so I can have my life back."

Just as the tension was mounting, Rocksanna strolled over to our group.

"We meet again," she purred. "It's time for me to get ready, sugar. Let's go to my dressing room."

Caiyan followed obediently. He had never been so submissive in the short amount of time I had known him.

"What's his problem?" Gertie asked. "He's usually so bossy."

Pickles entered the room and gave us a nod. After he spoke with a few of the other security people, he made his way over to us.

"Caiyan told us about the situation with his key," I said.

"I'm surprised he stayed, considering de amount of pain it caused 'im. Three days in de hospital. We told de doctors it was food poisoning. I guess he must really love her. He almost didn't return de last time he was here."

"The last time?" I questioned.

"Yeah, he was here last May," Pickles said. "He tried to convince her not to go on tour."

"How long have they known each other?" Marco asked.

"Oh, I tink dey met a few years ago. He was sent back to catch a brigand that was after Ronald Reagan right before his second term, I believe. Dey met at de White House. Now dat was a good party."

The room suddenly started spinning, and I felt like I was in a tunnel. I heard Gertie's voice. "Jen, are you OK?"

When I came to, I was reclined on one of the lounge chairs with a cold rag pressed to my forehead.

"What happened?" I asked.

"You found out your Scottish Romeo has been having a time-traveling affair for the last two years and hit the floor," Marco said.

"That's not possible. He knows it can't go anywhere, right?"

Gertie nodded her head.

"He's not even born yet, for crying out loud," I stammered.

"I vote we get the kid and get out of here." Marco stood and offered me a hand. "Caiyan got himself into this mess; he can get himself out."

"I'm OK," I said, removing the rag and standing on wobbly legs.

"Let's roll," Marco said as he led the way into the heartbreak hotel.

Chapter 18

We arrived at our fourth-row seats as the Beasts took the stage. The three front boys did all the harmonizing along with a synchronized dance routine, while Campy and the drummer played the music. Occasionally one of the band members would go over and peck out a few notes on a keyboard. The teenage girls who surrounded us screamed, and one on the front row fainted. The crowd passed her body over them as if we were in a mosh pit. I guess if you need emergency medical attention, that's the fastest way to get it. Gertie was hooting and hollering for the drummer, and I swear he winked at her. Fans were dancing in the aisles, and it was difficult to keep from joining them. I turned to see a voluptuous blonde grind up against Marco. He shrugged as a redhead came up behind him, and they made a Marco sandwich. I rolled my eyes as my inner voice reminded me that I brought him here. A doobie was passed to me from the guy on my right, who couldn't have been more than fifteen. I tried to wave it off, but the redhead relinquished her booty shake against Marco to take it from the boy. She took a long drag and then blew the smoke into Marco's mouth. The blonde decided she wanted a hit and took the joint from Marco. The blonde and redhead repeated the drill with each other as Marco stood by, relishing in his good fortune. I reached up and yanked him down to my level.

"What are you doing?" I asked. "We're on a mission."

"No, *you* are on a mission." He smiled all glassy-eyed at me. "I was abducted, and now I'm having fun."

I frowned, and my inner voice screamed, *You are losing them both!*

I reminded her I never really had either one of these men to begin with, and maybe I didn't really want them at all. Gertie had made her way to the front row and was hoisted up on some large man's shoulders. She was steadily working her bra off to throw up on the stage like the fifty that had preceded it. I think the entire inventory from Victoria's Secret was covering the stage floor. The band gave their final song and left the stage. I pried Marco away from his entourage.

"We should go backstage," I shouted over the crowd noise.

"Wait for the encore," Gertie yelled as she joined us back at ground level.

Most of the audience was holding up small lighters and chanting, "BEASTS, BEASTS, BEASTS!"

The band returned and played one final song. Then the lights came up, and the crowd was given a thirty-minute intermission.

Gertie was holding on to the back of my jacket as we made our way through the crowd. We presented our special passes and were allowed backstage. Once we were in the backstage hallway, the crowd noise dissipated, and we could speak without shouting. Marco took us back to the lounge area, where the Beasts were celebrating an after-performance success.

There was already a ton of people in the lounge. One or two adoring fans draped each band member. Campy was sitting on one of the lounge chairs, alone.

"This is my opportunity," I said. "I'm going over to talk to him."

The blonde from the concert appeared and attached herself to Marco. Gertie mouthed, "Good luck!" and made a beeline for the drummer boy.

I walked over to Campy and asked, "Mind if I sit?"

He looked up at me and then at my chest. A sign of recognition crossed his face. "I met you at the hotel this morning, right?"

"Yes, how was your swim?" I asked as he scooted over so I could sit.

"Good. It was the first time I've been alone in a long time."

Just as I was about to inquire about his key, I heard, "Well, well, well. Who do we have here?" Mitchell, the little rat, was standing in front of us.

"This is Jennifer. I met her at the hotel," Campy said.

"Bullshit. She's come to get you," Mitchell said and reached toward me, ripping my scarf from my neck.

"Hey, I liked that scarf!" I said.

Campy looked startled and then saw my key. "More people are coming after me?"

"Well, you have a special gift, and we would like to teach you how to use it," I explained, glaring at Mitchell and snatching my scarf back from him.

"Don't listen to her," Mitchell spat. "He's doing fine on his own."

Campy scratched at the side of his leather pants. I looked him right in the eyes. Eyes the same color as the ones that belonged to the man I thought I loved. "I want to take you home, if you want to go. You see, you can only stay here until you're born. Then you'll die."

"Die?" Campy's voice sounded a little shaky.

"Yep. I guess you didn't tell him that, did you, Mitchell?"

"He's with me, bitch, so get your ass out of here," Mitchell said, lunging at me.

Marco grabbed him by the scruff of his collar and held him a few inches off the floor.

Pickles came over, and together they escorted Mitchell, screaming obscenities, outside.

"That's why Caiyan came back for you. But he can't stay because if he doesn't leave this moon cycle, he'll be born in January."

"He told me he came back for Rocksanna," Campy said.

"That would be impossible. He can't take her into the future, and he can't stay," I explained.

Campy shrugged. "I don't know. Maybe I could stay for a little while. I like playing the guitar and some of the guys in the band."

"But you being here might change the way things are in our time."

Campy frowned. "Some things need to be changed."

"Your mom is really worried about you."

"She is?"

"Yes, and Aunt Itty." I reached over and placed my hand over his. A smooth warm feeling encircled our hands like a winter muffler. Apparently this young man had his hormones in check, unlike Marco and Caiyan.

"You know, they don't have iPhones, Xbox, or *Call of Duty*. And they only have five TV channels that you can watch."

"It's going to be a while before those things are invented."

"I'm getting tired of Mitchell telling me what to do all the time. He's worse than Mom." Campy made a face. "Every night the guys have hooch, girls, and blow. Caiyan said if I touched the blow, he would tell my mom." His shoulders sagged as he relayed the rest of his story. "I liked the girls at first, but they all smell like cigarettes and hairspray." He looked up at me and sat up straight. "Not like you. You're pretty, and you smell nice."

"Thanks, Campy," I said. "I work for an agency that could train you to be a secret time travel agent."

"For real?"

"Yep, your uncle Caiyan works for them, and I'm sure in time you would be really good at it. You might even be able to come back and visit your friends."

Campy looked in awe, like maybe a secret agent was equally as cool as a lead guitarist. "I think I'm ready to go home."

"Go back to the hotel with your band. I need to have a chat with your uncle."

"OK. I guess I need to break it to the guys that I won't be playing with them anymore."

"Do you think they're going to be upset?"

"No, they're talking about splitting up. They keep trying to get me to choose sides and go with them, but I can't decide which one to go with. They're all stellar."

My inner voice was pointing to the tall one with curly hair, and I agreed that his solo career took off, while the other band members stayed unknown. I decided to keep this to myself. I saw Marco making his way back into the lounge.

I turned to Campy and said, "Stay at the hotel, and I'll come get you. If you see Mitchell, do not take off your key for any reason. He can't take it off you, and he can't kill you."

Campy nodded as I stood to meet Marco. A petite girl dressed in, well, not much, came over and squeezed in next to Campy. He rolled his eyes, but I saw him place his hand nonchalantly on her knee. I hoped he would be waiting for us when we returned with or without Caiyan. Our time was running out, and I hated to take him by force. Gertie was right. If we took him against his will, he would probably just return to 1985, but at least the WTF would have a crack at him first. Based on all those black pins on Al's map, we could use the help. As I watched Marco make his way through the crowd, I wished there was a way to convince him to join as well. My inner voice put that on her to-do list right under rescuing Caiyan from the rock slut.

*M*arco finally reached me, after avoiding the blonde he'd been wearing earlier. He told me Pickles had Mitchell tied up and secured for now. I related the info on Campy, and we both agreed to find Gertie, get Caiyan, and get the hell back home. Caiyan might have to sacrifice his key, but hey, that's the choice he made when he took the damned thing off. I was not feeling any sorrow for the two-timing Don Juan, even if the other woman was in the past.

My inner voice pulled out her notepad and showed me the facts. Caiyan had not been back to see Rocksanna since he had met me in October. Caiyan only went back at Jake's request and to help his nephew. Caiyan never actually said he loved me or that we were exclusive. Man, I wanted to wad up that paper and shove it up Caiyan's behind.

Gertie was sitting on the drummer boy's lap and sticking her tongue in his ear. *Groady* as they say in 1985.

"Gertie, let's go."

"Aw, Jen, right now?"

"Right now!"

The drummer boy squeezed Gertie's butt as she got up, and with a very charming English accent, he said, "Catch you later, alligator."

"Remember what I told ya," Gertie replied. "I'm coming to get you in the year 2013."

"Radical, babe."

"Gertie!" I shoved her toward the door. "You can't tell him that."

"Oh, what's the difference?" She pouted. "He doesn't know what I meant anyhow."

Marco, Gertie, and I made our way back to our seats. We were not going to miss Rocksanna's final concert. Marco's groupies had found other attachments, and we stood as the lights were lowered. Rocksanna came up through a lift in the center of the stage. Two men were strapped to poles on either side of her, and she began singing her number one hit, "S&M Is What I Like." Her fans went wild, and my inner voice was wondering if Caiyan was into S&M. He never mentioned it to me, but with Rocksanna parading around in a black leather bustier and fishnets, whipping the crap out of the men she had tethered to poles, it was difficult to believe she preferred the missionary position.

The rest of the concert was exhilarating. I will give her credit; she put on an amazing show. At one point, she flew over the audience with the help of a safety harness. Rocksanna's concert was coming to a close. This was it. The final performance. After she got into her limo, that was the end of her life. Her finale.

The band returned, and we listened to another song as the crowd went crazy and glitter shot out of air canons and doused us all with a stream of gold glitz. I looked over at Marco, and he seemed to be untouched by the glitter. Gertie and I were in the running for Christmas tree toppers.

"How come you don't have any glitter?" I asked loudly.

"I have an internal sparkle. Let's go." He grabbed my hand and zap! His internal sparkle shot straight to my doodah.

Pickles told us earlier that after she performed, Rocksanna would be escorted down the hall to her dressing room. She would not go to the lounge, but she would make an exciting exit for her fans who were lucky enough to figure out which exit she would use. She would go to an after-concert publicity party at a club, where the manager paid her a ton of money for an appearance, and then on to the after-after party, usually at her hotel.

We waited patiently in the long hallway of the Rock City Hotel that led to the outside exit. The security team started to pass us, making a cluster around Rocksanna. Caiyan was right there holding her hand. I shouted for him, but he couldn't hear me. They made a pit stop in her dressing room for a quick change. The fans were chanting her name, and the security people were barking orders like the Third Reich. I followed the remaining entourage out to a secure area where the performers' limousines waited to take then back to the safety of their hotel. A small crowd of VIP fans and paparazzi gathered for the exit. The Beasts entered their limousine, and I gave Campy a wave as they dove inside.

Next a woman who looked like Rocksanna, but I was pretty sure wasn't, waved to the crowd and got in the next limo, and it drove away. The crowd cheered, and a million flash bulbs went off, making me feel slightly dizzy. I scanned the building. Where were Caiyan and the real Rocksanna? Then I saw Pickles standing next to a black BMW.

I walked over to Pickles. "What's going on?" I asked.

"Dat was de decoy car," he said. One of the security team came out of a side door and nodded at Pickles.

He looked at me. "Time to go." He got into the BMW.

Before he could close the door I said, "Don't forget to buckle up. Better safe than sorry, I always say." He nodded and put on his seat belt. I backed out of the way so he could shut the door and start the engine.

He rolled down the window. "I hope to meet you again real soon."

"Thanks for all your help." I said a little prayer as he rolled up the window.

A light mist of rain had begun to sprinkle on us, and the cool wind had me pulling my jean jacket tighter and putting my hands in my pockets. Marco and Gertie were standing back under the cover of the building, motioning for me to come over.

I started toward them but was stopped by a couple leaving out of the side door. The woman had a shawl draped over her head and Caiyan on her arm. One of her large bodyguards was helping her into the BMW. I made a mad dash around the car.

"Caiyan!" I yelled. "Do not get in that car!"

He stopped and looked at me. I grabbed his arm. "You know—" was all I said, when he pulled me to him and kissed me with such passion all ten of my toes curled.

He broke the kiss, and his green eyes were soft as they stared deep into my soul. "I love you, Jennifer Cloud," he said. Then he turned, climbed into the car, and it sped away.

Chapter 19

I stood staring at the taillights of the BMW as it disappeared into the night. Gertie came over and put a hand on my shoulder. "You tried to stop him."

"Stop him?" I asked, reeling from what just happened. "Yes, we have to stop him." I looked frantically around for a car. I reached for my key. I was going to call my vessel and cut him off at the pass. Marco grabbed me bear hug-style from behind, pinning my arms to my sides.

"Not here," he said.

"Let me go!" I screamed, drawing the attention of a few people standing near us.

"Jennifer," he said with his mouth pressed against my ear. "Look around. If you call your vessel here, the paparazzi will get it on film. You might not EVER be able to leave this time."

My eyes cleared, and I could see he was right. The street was crowded with photographers, crazed fans, and people leaving the concert. I stopped struggling and just began to cry. Marco held me, and the electric shock that usually sends us into a fit of ecstasy wrapped me in a warm blanket of comfort.

After I calmed down, I heard Marco's name being shouted from the street. I turned and saw the two Christies from last night. They were driving by in their Honda Prelude. Marco grabbed my hand, and Gertie followed us over to the car.

"Hello, Christies," Marco said, leaning against the car door. "Would you two lovely ladies assist us in locating another one of our friends?"

"Sure, that would be rad," said the blonde.

"Anything for you, stud," the brunette replied.

We piled into the backseat as Marco gave the blonde directions to the way the BMW headed. "The Heat Is On" was blaring over the radio as we made our way south on Highland Avenue and took a left on Hollywood Boulevard.

I was sitting on the edge of my seat, keeping a lookout for the BMW. I caught sight of the car as we made the turn. "There's Rocksanna's car!" I shouted over the music

The blonde shouted back, "They're going to the Avalon for the after party." I guess as groupies, they knew the rock star's every move. She floored the Honda, but we lost them in traffic. When we didn't make the stoplight, my inner voice started biting her fingernails. We sat idle, waiting for the light to turn green. My heart was thumping hard in my chest. How were we going to save them? Gertie couldn't remember what time or where the accident took place. She thought it might be after they stopped at the publicity party. I was mentally running scenarios through my mind, when Gertie said, "Oh my God."

Marco and I both looked at her. She was pointing to the opposite corner with her hand covering her mouth. "It's her."

"Her who?" I asked.

"Red Riding Hood," she said. "You know, the next victim of the Bus Stop Killer."

Everyone looked out through rain-covered windows and saw the girl standing at the bus stop, wearing the red raincoat. Then we looked up at the street sign. "Hollywood and Vine."

Gertie looked over at me. "We have to help her."

"What about Caiyan?" I asked.

"We can't catch them, Jen." Marco stroked my cheek with the back of his hand. "We have a moment in time to prevent something bad."

"What if it messes up the future?" I asked.

"Then so be it," he said, pointing his finger to the stereo speaker as Duran Duran's "A View to a Kill" began playing on the radio. It was kismet. I had to help this girl. Maybe we could help her and still get to Caiyan.

"Hey, I think that's one of our friends over there at the bus stop." Marco pointed, and the blonde made a turn and pulled into a convenience store on the corner. The three of us got out of the car and told the girls to go on to the after party that Rocksanna would never attend.

⌒

The rain was coming down harder, and I took off my jacket and held it over my head.

"Now what, Magnum PI?" Gertie asked.

"I don't see any sign of the killer," I said. "Let's go have a chat with Red Riding Hood."

We walked over to the bus stop and introduced ourselves as undercover agents who were investigating the Bus Stop Killer. We told her she was in danger, and she agreed to let me wear her red raincoat. We swapped jackets, and Gertie escorted her to a cluster of bushes where they could hide until the bus arrived. I sat on the bench, pretending to wait for the bus, mentally praying that the car accident happened after they made their stop at the after party, and Caiyan could get out safely.

Marco was hiding with Gertie in the group of bushes about thirty yards away. The rain had stopped, and I felt a cold shiver run down my spine. I reassured myself Marco was a short distance away. My inner voice crossed her arms over her chest and reminded me he didn't have his key. He'd saved us the last time we were in trouble by using his ability to slow down time for a few seconds. It was long enough for him to pull Gertie out of harm's way and take a bullet in the chest.

An old Cutlass slowed down and cruised past the bus stop. The windows were tinted, and I couldn't make out the driver. The car turned the corner, and I lost sight of it. The girl told us the bus ran every half hour, and it should be here fairly soon. The air felt creepy. A few people wandered the streets, but no one was close to the bus stop. It left an eerie feeling in the pit of my stomach. I started to recite my mantra: *I'm spunky and I'm fierce and I'm smarter than most men. Bad guys run and hide 'cuz here comes SuperJen.*

I felt better. The mantra my brother and I had created when we were kids made me feel brave. I sat praying for Caiyan and hoping the Bus Stop Killer decided tonight was not his night. After about twenty minutes, I was about to tell Marco this was a bust, when a hand clamped over my mouth and I felt a jab in my ribs.

"Don't move a muscle," came the voice from behind me.

Now how did this asshole sneak up on me? My inner voice drew a dream bubble with Caiyan inside. He had come around the bench and grabbed me as I was leaning forward to look down the street toward the Avalon Club.

"What do you want?" I asked into the hand.

"I'm going to cut you, cheating bitch." He slurred the words into my ear. He had been drinking. That was good. Slow reaction time. *Cheating bitch?* Now that set my blood to boiling. If anything, I was the faithful one. Wait a minute. I grasped reality. I don't think he was referring to me specifically. I think his crazy was for women. All women. I moved cautiously into the object that was jabbing my side. It sent a sharp pain into my skin. Not a gun, maybe a knife. Most likely a knife because that's how he created his forehead masterpieces.

"You're going to come with me." He gripped my arm and stood, pulling me to my feet. There was something oddly familiar about him. I couldn't put my finger on it, but I was sure I knew this person.

"I think I know you," I said as I caught a look at his face. He had a black knit cap on his head and wore a gray Members Only jacket. I realized it was the guy from the shopping mall. But there was something more familiar about him. Like someone from church you only run into at the grocery store, and you can't figure out how you know him.

He stopped, grabbed me around the neck, and threw me over the bench. I landed on my back in the shadows of the bus stop. He straddled me as I tried to recover from the sudden attack. I could feel his hard penis rub against my stomach as he held me down. Ewww. My arm flung out and knocked the knife out of his hand. His beady eyes stared down at me in the darkness as his hands closed around my throat. I was bucking and fighting, but his grip was cutting off my air. I felt like all the training Jake had put me through was for nothing. I couldn't move. Arms came around his neck, and he released his grip on me. Marco had him in a chokehold, and he reared back, ready to fight. I gasped for air as I watched Marco throw a right hook into the man's gut. The man reared back in pain, knocking Marco's grip loose. Marco stumbled back a few steps, and the man swung one of his bear-size paws at him. He caught Marco on the left cheek and knocked him to the ground. I saw Gertie and Red Riding Hood come running down the block behind him. I stood up, finally breathing again, and we squared off. He lunged for me just as Gertie jumped on his back and bit his ear. He yelped in pain, swatting at Gertie. I gave the guy a good hard kick in the balls. He grabbed his crotch and doubled over. Marco gave him a few hard punches until the man lost consciousness. I pulled Marco off him and hugged him.

The bus had arrived just as the action was going down, and a bus full of people had their noses pressed to the windows.

"Are y'all OK?" Gertie asked as we pulled her into our adrenaline-filled huddle. Red Riding Hood stood off to the left in the shadows of the night.

"Now what do we do?" I asked Marco.

The people on the bus saw me, but they didn't get a look at everyone else. In the darkness of the street, I gave Red Riding Hood back her raincoat, and Marco asked her to tell the police she was the one who was attacked. He explained Gertie and I were deep under cover. The witnesses wouldn't be able to tell the difference between us. She saw the whole thing go down and agreed, thanking us for saving her life.

The driver radioed for the police, and they arrived in minutes with sirens blaring. They cuffed the man who had finally regained consciousness. The stare he gave me as they put him in the patrol car was pure evil. The police took our statements and started interviewing the twenty witnesses on the bus. I wasn't sure our statements would hold up in court because we would not be found after tonight, but with all those witnesses, he would definitely get jail time. At least we'd saved Red Riding Hood.

⟜⟶

*G*ertie and I snuck off into the shadows, leaving Marco to handle the police. We walked down the street to the Avalon Club. "He got out, Jen," Gertie said, as if she was reading my thoughts.

I nodded and prayed Caiyan was safe. As we got closer, Gertie tugged on my sleeve and pointed to a man sitting curbside in front of the club. It was Caiyan. His head was bent down, resting on his knees. My heart skipped a beat as I ran across the street to him.

"Caiyan," I said.

He raised his eyes to mine. "She had the driver pull over and kicked me oot of the car." He opened his hands, and in his palm was his key. The blazing sun filled his hand, and the tiny blue diamonds that formed the rays of the sun blinked back at me. "She made me get out and threw my key at me. She told me if I was in love with ye, then I could just get the hell oot of her car and her life."

"You didn't have a choice," I said.

"Aye, I did. I thought maybe I had changed fate." He ran a hand through his hair, and I sat down beside him. "I thought maybe the accident wouldn't happen. Ye see? That they would come into the club, and I could convince her to let me drive her home." He shrugged. "As I got oot, the paparazzi saw me and started shouting and taking pictures. She told Pickles to get her the hell oot of there. They took off, with the paparazzi chasing them."

I knew at that moment her car had met the bridge wall on the Hollywood Freeway, just as the tabloids had reported before we made our journey to 1985.

I put my hand on his shoulder, and a warm trickle of heat melted down my arm. He reached up and placed a hand over mine. "Ye really can't change the past. No matter how hard ye try."

I thought about the Bus Stop Killer and wondered if we'd made a difference. What about the lives of all those women he had killed for the last twenty-eight years? Surely their lives would be changed. Jake was going to have plenty of recon to do on this mission.

I stood and held out my hand. "Let's go home. Campy is waiting for us back at the hotel."

Caiyan rose and pulled me into his arms. "I'm sorry," he said. "I should have told ye aboot her before I left to help Campy."

"It's all in the past," I said, but I felt my heart take a step backward. I should be overjoyed. Caiyan was safe and he had said the three magic words, but all I felt was confusion. He loved me, but he was willing to die for her. The proof was in the pudding, as Mamma Bea always used to say. I needed to have some pudding.

I took his key from his hands and secured it around his neck. The key gave off a swift blue glow, as they all do when they are connected to their owner. He ran a soft caress down my arm and interlocked my fingers with his. We walked hand in hand down the street to meet up with Gertie and Marco.

⟜

It was after two in the morning when we made it back to the hotel, and I was exhausted. I filled Caiyan in on the way about Campy's decision to return home with us. Marco was unusually silent, and I felt a pang of guilt toward him.

"Ye did good," Caiyan said, raising my hand to his lips and kissing the tops of my fingers. We greeted Georgish as we entered the hotel and asked him for Campy's room number. He gave it reluctantly. The penthouse. I should have known that's where a boy band would stay. We took the elevator to the top and knocked on the door. Campy flung it open, saw Caiyan, and threw his arms around him.

"I thought you were with Rocksanna. It's all over the news," he said. A streak of tears stained his face.

"No, I'm here to take ye home." He hugged the boy tight, and I couldn't help it; my eyes pricked with tears.

Everyone agreed our work here was done, and we were ready to go home. There was a small park behind the hotel. We made sure it was clear, and I called my vessel. Campy was a little put back that we wouldn't let him travel alone, but because he wasn't familiar with Gitmo, Caiyan thought I should transport him there. When my outhouse made an appearance, Campy burst into a fit of laughter.

"Well what have you got, Mr. Fancy Pants?" I asked him.

"That's for me to know and you to find out." Smart aleck. Caiyan's training had already begun. First rule, never let anyone outside the WTF know your vessel. I broke that rule by accident, of course.

Gertie, Campy, and I got in my vessel. Caiyan agreed to wait with a brooding Marco until I returned for him. I said, "*Hanhepi*," and we were bounced along until I felt the outhouse land with a thunk. I opened the door, and Jake was standing in front of the transporter pad.

"Great work, Jen," he said as he saw Campy climb down. Aunt Itty was behind Jake and gave Campy a big hug followed by a stern lecture.

"Caiyan is waiting for me to come back for Marco," I said to Jake.

He frowned and then nodded. "If you must."

Did he want me to leave them in the past? Men, geesh.

I returned to my outhouse, and Gertie gave me a high five on the way. When I arrived back in 1985, I pushed out of the vessel and watched as Caiyan and Marco were swapping punches.

"Ye no good Italian asshole," Caiyan yelled as Marco threw a right hook into his ribs.

"Scottish bastard, you don't know a good thing when you've got one." Caiyan threw a punch, and Marco dodged it and grabbed Caiyan around the waist. Both men went head over ass down a small hill.

I used what Mamma Bea called the pig whistle. I put two fingers in my mouth and let out a loud screeching whistle. Normally, it would be followed by, "Here pig!" but I refrained. Both men stopped fighting and stood looking up the hill at me.

"I'm going home—anyone want a ride?" I asked.

Caiyan marched off, mumbling something about how he would find his own space. "Fucking dick." There was no good-bye kiss or "see ye back at the base." He just huffed off into the darkness.

"What happened?" I asked Marco as he ascended the grassy hill toward me.

"The asshole actually thought I might have made a play for you."

"You did make a play for me," I said. *And made me promise sex in exchange for helping me,* I thought to myself as my inner voice started stretching her hamstrings in anticipation.

Marco grinned.

"What did you tell him?" I asked.

"It was none of his damn business." He smiled down at me. The dimple in his chin intensified. It was the first genuine smile I had seen since I kidnapped him two days ago. "I don't want you to take me to Gitmo. I want to go home."

"But Jake said—"

Marco cut me off. "I don't give a fuck. I'm not WTF, and I want to go home."

It was the least I could do because I'd brought him against his will. "OK, to the rooftop?" I asked, indicating Marco's rooftop landing pad in his SoHo apartment building.

"That'll do."

We entered the vessel, and he said, "OK, Dorothy, click your heels and take me back to Kansas."

I said the magic word, and we were whisked away into the night.

Chapter 20

My vessel came to a halt. The cold air met us as we exited my vessel. It was snowing in New York, and tiny snowflakes fluttered down around us. Marco's race car sat glowing against the fresh snow that covered the ground.

I ran my hand across the tail fin, raking away a fresh pile of snow. "She's really pretty," I said.

"Yep, my first love and hopefully not my last." He looked deep into my eyes. The ice blue that made women flock to him like bees to honey melted the chill from the snow. I turned toward my vessel, but he grabbed my hand and pulled me in tight.

"What are you doing?" I asked.

"Just so you have something to think about."

He brought his lips down to meet mine, and fire rushed through my blood. We kissed until neither of us could stand the heat any longer.

"What about our little agreement?" I asked when we broke apart.

"Oh, I'll collect when I'm ready," he said with a smirk and released me to return to Gitmo.

As I climbed out of my vessel, I noticed several other vessels were on the landing pads. It was the close of the moon cycle. Jake had other travelers besides me to worry about. He stood front and center waiting for me.

"You have snow in your hair," he said, pointing to my head.

"Yep, I took Marco home."

"Damn it, Jen. This was our opportunity to talk him into joining the WTF." Jake grimaced.

"He wanted to go home, and I don't think he has any plans on becoming a defender," I said. "We're lucky he doesn't sue us for kidnapping him."

"Who is he going to sue?" Jake put his hands on his hips. "We don't exist in the eyes of the government."

"Where is Caiyan?"

"He is down in debriefing and getting his ass chewed out by General Potts for having a relationship with that rock star."

I raised an eyebrow in question.

"Oh yeah, don't think your playboy's actions went unnoticed. He is in all the newspapers from 1985."

"He's not my playboy," I said, brushing the snow from my hair.

"Let's go. It's your turn to add to the story."

I walked into the conference room. Gertie, Caiyan, Campy, Aunt Itty, and Pickles were seated around the table. A wave of relief washed over me as I saw Pickles. He'd survived the wreck as before. I smiled at Pickles. He smiled back, but something was different.

"Jesus H. Christ, Miss Cloud!" General Potts bellowed. I jumped at his booming voice.

What was he so upset about? We'd rescued Campy and Caiyan. We'd saved the life of an innocent girl. I also brought back, safely to be exact, everyone I was responsible for.

The room went silent, and Pickles stood up. My eyes grew big. He was standing. There wasn't a wheelchair in sight. That was it. He could walk. Then it hit me. He'd met his wife in rehab, and they had a child together. Did I ruin his life?

"You can walk," I said.

"Yes, Miss Cloud," General Potts boomed. "Do you realize all the problems you have caused this travel?"

My head started to spin, and I felt the room go black. When I came to, Pickles and Jake were hovering over me. I was stretched out on the pleather sofa in the break room. "You fainted," Jake said.

I looked at Pickles. "Did I ruin your life?"

"Nah, ya saved it," he said, tapping his leg. It gave a metallic clank. "Instead of breaking me back, I lost a leg. I still went to rehab and met my wife."

"Thank goodness!" I said, sitting up.

Jake clapped a hand on my shoulder. "I don't know how you do it."

"Do what?" I asked.

"Go back in time. Mess things up and come out smelling like a rose."

Pickles smiled. "I can still play de futball with ma kid."

"Let's go, Nancy Drew." Jake pulled me to my feet. "General Potts still wants to speak to you. He promised not to yell."

After a few hours of debriefing, I was released. My ears hurt from the lecture we received for aiding in the capture of the Bus Stop Killer. Jake was going to be very busy the next few weeks researching the past victims and the chaos that might have surfaced from the butterfly effect of our choices.

Caiyan and Campy were at the medical facility getting checked out because they had stayed through a time travel. Jake gave us the all clear to return home, but I was dragging my feet, hoping Caiyan would be released soon. Gertie and I had said our good-byes to just about everyone, and we were walking down the long hall to the hangar to go home.

"What do you think they check when you stay overtime?" Gertie asked.

"I don't know, and I hope I never find out." I cringed at the thought of having to stay in the past for more than three days. "I heard it's pretty painful."

"Maybe Caiyan will need an anal probe." Gertie giggled.

"He would deserve one," I said, still upset at his double standard. How could he possibly be angry with me for traveling with Marco, when he was doing who knows what with Rocksanna? We didn't talk about the details of their little tryst, and I think it was better to keep it that way.

"Since we have only been gone three hours our time," Gertie asked, "what's keeping him from going back now and rescuing the fair Rocksanna?"

"It doesn't work like that. The time portal opens when the moon is full, and when we travel, we only have until the moon begins to wane, about three days. Then we have to return, and the portal closes."

"I know all that, but now that we have returned, isn't it like déjà vu?" As she was talking, her hands were emphasizing every word. "Isn't the moon cycle still open?"

"If we tried to go back now, we would end up at the same time we left," I explained. "We would miss the accident. Technically, we lived those three days in the past, so we would have to wait until the next moon cycle to go back to that exact time. The WTF doesn't allow us to travel unless they order it. I can't see them allowing Caiyan to save her. They don't like us screwing with the past, no matter what lives may be lost."

"I guess that's why the general was so mad at us for stopping the Bus Stop Killer."

"Yes, they will have a lot of research to figure that one out. He killed so many women. Now they all have lives and probably families."

Gertie yawned. "This time travel stuff is so confusing."

I agreed. It didn't make sense, but I didn't make the rules. I was happy we returned as we did. I didn't want to lose any of my present lifetime.

We entered the hangar where the vessels were docked. Ace was sitting on my landing pad.

"Ace!" Gertie skipped over to him. "Did you arrange for our double date?" she asked him. That girl never forgets a thing.

"Don't get your knickers in a wad. He should be here any second."

Jake entered the hangar. "I thought you left," he said.

"We were about to leave, but we decided to hang around and see how Brodie and Ace did on their travel." OK, it was a little lie. I was waiting for Caiyan, but Jake didn't need to know my lingering details.

"Yeah, right," he said, then looked at Ace. "What are you smiling about?"

Ace looked very smug with himself, and a crack and a gurgle later Brodie's bathtub appeared on the landing pad next to Ace's photo booth.

He leaped out of his vessel and grinned his megawatt smile.

"Did you show them?" he asked Ace.

Ace smiled. "I was waiting on you, love."

Ace pulled a key from his pocket. It was beautiful. A Celtic pattern formed the chain, a thundercloud was on the medallion, and tiny blue diamonds fell from the cloud representing rain.

"Where did that come from?" I asked.

"I talked it off a wee Irish lass who was admired by a young but foolish future brigand," Brodie bragged.

"How did you get it back here?" asked Gertie.

"A key is different," Jake said. "It travels across the time barrier."

"Remember when Malia Mafuso abducted you and Jennifer's ancestor's key the last time you traveled?" Brodie asked.

"Oh, that's right," Gertie said, batting her eyelashes at Brodie. Jeez.

"Go ahead, touch it." Ace held out the key, and I reached up and placed my hand over the stone. A small sound of thunder rang out.

"It talks," I said.

"Yeah, it's grand, right?" Brodie stated more than asked.

"It's only grand until the real owner comes looking for it," Caiyan said as he joined our group.

"Aw, laddie, don't ruin our fun," said Ace.

"Yeah, I broke me nose protecting it from the Cracky clan." Brodie massaged the bridge of his nose.

"Both of you into debriefing," Jake ordered. "The rest of you go home and get some rest."

Brodie gave Caiyan a man hug. "Glad ta have you home, mate."

"Good to be back," Caiyan said, cutting his eyes to me.

"Did you get the wee lad?" Ace asked.

"Aye, Jen got him to return," Caiyan said. "WTF wants to keep him for a week, get him acquainted with the program. Apparently someone told him he could be a secret agent."

All eyes turned toward me. I kicked at some imaginary dirt and shrugged.

"Later, mates," Brodie said and started to walk toward the exit.

Gertie stood, looking rejected. Ace cleared his throat, and Brodie did an about-face, marched up to Gertie, and said, "How would you like to accompany me to grab a bite on Friday night?"

Gertie's mouth opened, but no sound came out. A silent Gertie—there's a first time for everything.

"She would love to," I answered for her. "Well, got to go."

We said good-bye to Ace and Brodie. I stole a glance at Caiyan. He looked mad, and I felt mad. The dishonesty was left in the past, but the present still held a lot of resentment.

Brodie and Ace left the hangar, patting each other on their backs as they went.

Gertie did a little happy dance, and we headed toward my vessel.

As I was about to climb aboard, Caiyan caught up with me. "After Campy's week is done, I'm taking him back to my sister." I nodded. "I'm going to stay with them awhile and help her get him settled in a new school. Aye? Make sure he adjusts and teach him aboot traveling."

"I think that would be the best thing for Campy."

"Aye, but what aboot us?" he asked, raking his hand through his thick hair, leaving it disheveled.

"I don't know," I said, and my inner voice pulled out a tissue. "I still have training, and General Potts doesn't want me to travel again until Jake thinks I'm officially ready. It may take months."

"Jennifer Cloud, ye are an amazing woman. Don't underestimate yer power."

"Aye," I said, and he laughed.

He reached over and tucked a stray hair behind my ear. "Until next time." He bent down and brushed a kiss across my lips.

"Later, Gert," he said to Gertie, who had already climbed aboard and was holding on for dear life.

"See ya, Romeo," she said, blowing him a kiss. He rolled his eyes and took a step back. I entered my vessel and returned home.

Chapter 21

*B*y the time Gertie and I returned home, it was almost 5:00 a.m. Tuesday morning. The travel makes me so tired I have to sleep at least a day to recover. I knew Eli thought I was out doing massage research, so I planned to return to the clinic on Wednesday.

I woke Wednesday morning before my alarm went off to the smell of coffee and bacon frying. Thank the Lord, Gertie was throwing her shake diet to the wind and cooking breakfast. I pulled on a robe and opened my bedroom door to follow the smell downstairs. Gertie stepped out of her room at the same time, yawning.

"Are you making breakfast, Jen?" she asked, stretching her arms above her head and yawning again.

"No, I thought you were."

We both looked at each other. "Wait here," I told her. I went back into my room and pulled the 9 mm handgun that Jake had given me during my training sessions out of my travel case. I had practiced at the gun range and with Jake, but so far it had spent the rest of its life hidden under my maxipads for safekeeping.

I met Gertie back in the hallway, and her eyes grew wide at the sight of my gun. "Do you think the bad guy is going to poison us with a home-cooked breakfast?" she asked.

True, I agreed. But a girl can't be too careful. I pressed a finger to my lips, and we crept down the stairs.

My foot had just hit the bottom step when a familiar voice sang out, "If you're going to be sneaking about, dear, try not to step on that creaky stair."

Aunt Itty. I sighed and pocketed the gun. Aunt Itty was at the stove, scooting the bacon around in my cast-iron skillet. She was wearing blue polyester pants and a flowing flowered tunic. Chunky jewelry was adorning her neck, camouflaging her key. A plate of freshly scrambled eggs steamed from a bowl on the kitchen table, and fluffy biscuits looked promising through the window on the oven.

"Aunt Itty, what are you doing?" I asked.

"I'm cooking breakfast. What does it look like?" she scoffed at me.

"No, I mean, what are you doing here?" I waved a hand out in front of me, indicating my kitchen.

"I don't care what she's doing. I'm eating," Gertie said, grabbing a plate and giving Aunt Itty a peck on the cheek.

"Why thank you, sweetness, and help yourself." Aunt Itty turned and removed the biscuits from the oven. My stomach grumbled loudly. She looked at me over the top of her cheaters. I grabbed a cup of coffee and sat down at the table. Aunt Itty placed a heaping plate of food in front of me. "Eat. Travel makes you hungry."

"Thank you," I said, taking a bite of the eggs. It was the truth. I was starving.

Gertie was spreading jelly on her biscuits, and Aunt Itty sat down with a cup of tea. "Are these magic eggs?" Gertie asked Aunt Itty. "Because they taste delicious."

"It's the travel, dear, makes you want to eat a buffalo." She sipped her tea, and I waited patiently for her to tell me the reason for her visit.

"These are really good, but I have to get ready for work," I said, hoping to get a response from her.

"Oh, of course, dear. You go right ahead. Gertie and I can clean up." Multiple bracelets that ringed up her arms clanged together as she raised the teacup to drink.

I sighed, finished my plate, and stood to go upstairs and get ready for work.

"Your gun's going to rip a hole in that skimpy robe." Aunt Itty pointed to my pocket, which was weighted down by the 9 mm. "You should really get a holster. I prefer the leg holster myself—back holsters are so bulky." She pulled up her pant leg to reveal a small handgun tucked neatly into a holster on her inner calf.

"Wow, that's pretty cool," said Gertie. Jeez, at least one of us was brave enough to carry concealed.

"I'll be ready when you are, dear," Aunt Itty said to my back as I was leaving the kitchen.

I spun around. "Wait, are you going to work with me?"

She nodded. I folded my arms across my chest. "Spill it, or I'm calling Jake."

"No need; he's the one who sent me."

"Why would he do that?"

"That Mitchell character fled 1985, and Agent Yummy seems to think you might be in some danger." Aunt Itty took a biscuit and lathered it with butter.

Good grief, Jake sent Aunt Itty to babysit me. That was a slap in the face. How was this little old lady going to protect me from Mitchell? I huffed in irritation as I headed upstairs to get ready. I liked Aunt Itty, but I couldn't take her to work with me.

I grabbed my cell from the charger and pressed my speed dial for Jake. He answered on the first ring. "I was expecting your call."

"What's up with you putting Aunt Itty on security detail?" I paced around the room, my huffy disposition increasing.

"Now, don't get huffy," he said.

"I'm not huffy," I said, making a trail from my bed to my closet.

"I know you, Jen. You are huffy, and you're pacing."

"Fine, explain and I'll curtail my huff." I sat down on the side of the bed, waiting for an answer.

"Al tracked Mitchell's return, and he didn't go back home to New York. The embarrassment of letting Campy's key get away from him was probably too much for him."

"Where did he go?" I asked.

"Texas."

"But he's not supposed to do anything in the present. We have an agreement with the Mafusos."

"That pretty much went south when we invaded them to save Gertie last October."

"So you sent Aunt Itty?" I asked.

"All you need is someone to watch your back. She's pretty safe. Every time I send one of the guys, I get more trouble than I bargained for." I heard the tension in his voice. I knew all the other travelers had just returned from the last moon cycle. They would be tired. Some had jobs to return to like myself, and Aunt Itty was the best choice. She was semiretired, available, and enough of a busybody that she probably wouldn't let a brigand sneak up on me.

"Does Caiyan know about Mitchell's travel plans?"

"No, I wanted him to stay with Campy. We're training him with Liam's vessel, and there's a special bond that must be created. Caiyan is helping with that."

I remembered the first time I sat in my vessel. Gertie and I were nine and hiding from her twin brothers. The outhouse regurgitated both of us out on our asses. I guess it wasn't love at first sight, but after a few travels, I felt the connection.

"Fine, but what am I supposed to do with her while I'm at work?" I asked.

"You'll think of something, and don't worry. I have Ace working on finding Mitchell."

"Great," I said and disconnected. I put my gun in my handbag. I had a license to carry concealed, even though it wouldn't do any good against Mitchell. I couldn't kill him, or I would die as well.

"Stupid rules!" I shouted as I washed my hair in the shower. Was I really willing to kill the little shit? I wouldn't mind cutting off a testicle or two. *Now where did that come from?* I asked myself. My inner voice pulled out a biker jacket, indicating I was joining the club. I cursed the ancient god who put all these rules in place. In retaliation, the hot water turned cold, and my teeth chattered as I exited the shower. That would be the last time I questioned a higher power.

⟨⟩

I dressed in my Wednesday scrubs, which had little pink whales floating in a blue background. I added some Kendra Scott earrings and a pink scarf. Sprayed on Luck and Love, just for good measure, and I was ready to start the day. Gertie and Aunt Itty were still sitting at the table. Their heads were bent together, looking at Gertie's cell phone.

"What are y'all doing?" I asked them.

"Gertie has a Sweetie Swipe," Aunt Itty said. "And he's real bonnie, too."

Gertie turned the cell so I could get a look at her latest conquest. He was very cute. He looked a little like the movie star Charlie Hunnam. All long blond locks and a small goatee-type beard. He had on board shorts and nothing else. His torso was definitely worth a second look.

"I thought you were happy to go out with Brodie on Friday night," I said.

"A girl's got to keep her options open," she said, nibbling at the corner of her fingernail.

"She swiped right, so now he has to send a message to set up the date," Aunt Itty said, as if she were a Sweetie Swipe pro.

Gertie's phone pinged, and she giggled with glee. "All done. We're meeting tonight at the Muddled Duck."

The Muddled Duck was a bar in the not-so-good part of town. The only time I had been there was with Jake when he was on an assignment. The place was loaded with thugs.

"Why can't you meet at Starbucks like all the normal people do?" I asked.

"He wants to buy me his special drink, the Strangler." She put her phone away and looked all dreamy eyed. "Doesn't he sound like fun?"

"Do you think you should go so soon after a travel?" I asked Gertie.

"Sure, I'm fine. The medical staff at WTF told me I was healthy as a horse."

"OK. But be careful. Jake said Mitchell might be running loose in Texas."

"I think they figured out I'm not the one with all the special effects." Gertie waved her fingers in the air.

"Be careful anyway, and leave Mr. Board Shorts's info on the fridge. I have to get to work." I looked over at Aunt Itty, who was tying a scarf over her hair.

"Are we taking the vessel?" Aunt Itty asked.

"No, we're taking the Mustang," I said as we walked to my car.

"Oh, good. Can we put the top down?" She smiled.

"Itty, its December." My inner self zipped up her parka.

"You have to live a little." Aunt Itty elbowed me. I sighed, put the top down, and turned up the heater. It was a mild December day, and if we kept the windows up, we might make it to Coffee Creek without frostbite.

Aunt Itty cranked Nicki Minaj on the radio, and we drove down the highway rapping to "Super Bass."

She knew every word. *Go figure.*

⟶

*W*e pulled into the parking lot at my job. I cut the engine and looked over at Aunt Itty. "Don't worry, dear. I brought my crossword puzzle book to keep my occupied. Give me the keys to your car, and I can just sit here and do a stakeout."

I handed over my keys. "I need to work about three hours, and then I can go to lunch. There's a great barbecue place on the square I can take you to if you're interested."

"Oh my, yes. I love barbeque. It has been ages since I've had any. Did I tell you about the time I ate barbeque with John Wayne?"

My mouth dropped open, and then I realized the many stories my fellow travelers must have tucked away. Maybe I should take Aunt Itty to the Muddled Duck tonight. She could tell me about her travels, and

I could keep an eye on Gertie. My inner voice pocketed her mace and nodded.

"No, but I would love to hear about it after work," I said, tipping my head toward the office.

"Oh, horsefeathers! I forgot the time. You scoot along, or you'll be late."

I instructed Aunt Itty on how to put the top up if she got cold and gave her a wave as I climbed out of the car.

The staff greeted me as I entered the clinic. I stopped and talked with Eli about Helga, the massage therapist who had given me a massage before I left for Gitmo. He agreed to give her a shot at the position. I spent the morning reminding myself it was only Wednesday. I agreed with Gertie; time travel was complicated. I wasn't sure how long I could go without my family figuring out something in my life was different.

Elvira, our insurance CA, was running late. Her son was getting his ankle bracelet removed, and she wanted to be there for the special occasion. I guess being free from house arrest was a big deal. She came barreling through the back door around noon. I was in the front office doing follow-up on some insurance for her.

"Hi, Jennifer," she said, hanging up her leather coat. "Thanks for helping me out this morning."

"No problem," I said, scooting from her chair and trading places with her. "How did it go?"

"Great," she said, smiling. "Mikey is now free to get a job and start acting like a human instead of the like the animal that gang he joined created."

"That's good. I heard the Ice Cream Factory was looking for someone to clean the machines at night."

"I'll tell him. That would keep him busy in the hours when trouble-making seems to prosper." She pulled her hair back into a banana clip. "By the way, who is that old lady sitting in your car?"

I had been so focused on work, I had forgotten about Aunt Itty. "That's Aunt Itty. She was bored, so I let her ride to work with me today."

"That's so kind of you," Elvira said.

The voice behind me made me cringe. "Jen, did we uncover an old aunt I don't know about?"

Eli was standing behind me, arms crossed over his chest, eyebrow raised in question.

"Uhm, she's actually the aunt of a guy I'm dating," I stammered out. I was still sort of dating Caiyan. Right?

"You're twisting your hair." He pointed to my fingers, which were somehow wrapped through a strand of my hair. Damn, I was going to have to get a new nervous habit. When everyone knows your tell, what's the point in lying?

Eli pressed his lips together. His starched blue scrubs made his eyes look three shades darker than a finely cut sapphire. "Why don't you go get this aunt and bring her in. She can wait in the reception area until your lunch break."

Jeez. Eli was going to want details about Caiyan. Why are big brothers always so overprotective? I barely had a date in high school, thanks to his interrogating ways.

I went outside to get Aunt Itty. The top on the Mustang was still down, and she had the motor running. I could hear the blast of Janis Joplin coming from the car stereo from the back door of the clinic. Aunt Itty needed to go home. After lunch for sure. When I reached the car, I saw Aunt Itty was fast asleep. Her spectacles were balancing on the end of her nose, and her head was dropped to one side. This was my lookout? I opened the car door and sat down in the driver's seat, turning off the radio. Aunt Itty jumped alive, almost whacking me in the head with her crossword puzzle book.

"Sorry, dear, I must have grabbed a quick catnap." She put the book into her coat pocket.

"Why don't you come in until lunch?" I asked turning the car off. " I'm easier to protect inside anyway."

"That's true, dear, and these seats are giving me a chafe." She started to gather her things, and I put a hand on her arm.

"Aunt Itty, I told my brother I was dating your nephew. He might ask you a few questions."

"I see. How long have you and my Caiyan been, uhm, dating?"

The way she said it made my heart sink. Even Aunt Itty knew about Caiyan's playboy lifestyle. Had Caiyan and I ever been on a real date? He had picked me up, whisked me away to a few romantic locations, and then we went at it like horny monkeys. We never actually got all dressed up and went out on a real date.

Aunt Itty patted my hand. "I feel there is a change in the air where that boy is concerned. He's Scottish, you know, and a true Scot does everything with passion. When the time is right, he will change his wily ways."

I smiled and decided to put that on the back burner. "OK, let's keep the information about Caiyan on the down low."

"Sure thing, dear. I like the candlesticks you have on the floorboard there." She pointed to the candlesticks I had purchased for my mother. Aunt Itty had unwrapped one from the bubble wrap. It was heavy silver and would look good on my mother's breakfront.

"Thanks, I bought them for my mom, a housewarming gift, but I keep forgetting to give them to her."

"Good quality. Where did you get them?"

"A small store on the square here. I can take you there after lunch if you like."

We entered the clinic through the back door. Eli was standing in the hallway, giving Aunt Itty the once-over.

I made the introductions.

Eli smiled down at her. "It's a pleasure to meet a family member of someone Jen is dating." His voice was laced with a hint of sarcasm.

"My, my," said Aunt Itty. "Aren't you the handsome one."

Genius. Nothing wins over my ex-jock brother like a little flattery. I didn't know Aunt Itty was so full of guile.

He escorted Aunt Itty to the waiting room and set her up with a back issue of *Good Housekeeping*.

"OK, I'm ready for those patients," I said, waiting for him in the hallway.

"They're still in therapy. Let's go into my office for a second." He put an arm on my elbow and led me into his office. "Have a seat." He pointed to one of the leather chairs in front of his desk. I sighed. Here it came, the interrogation.

"Soooo, who is this new guy you've been dating?" he asked, clicking his pen a few times. His blue eyes stared at me as if he had a window to my mind.

"He's just a guy I met on Sweetie Swipe."

"Sweetie Swipe." Eli slammed his pen down on the desk. "Do you know how dangerous those app dating sites can be?"

"Gertie uses it all the time." I shrugged. "He's from Scotland but lives here now. And by the way, I'm too old for my big brother to be giving me the third degree about the men I choose to date."

"Jen, you're caring for his elderly aunt. I'm concerned."

If Eli only knew the truth. That elderly aunt was my bodyguard. Jake had really put me in a tight spot. "She just wanted a day away from where she lives."

"And where is that?" Eli asked.

I felt my hand grab a strand of hair, and I immediately dropped it. I wasn't going to give in to my tell. As I was trying to think of something to say to Eli other than Wonderland, Paulina poked her head in to let Eli know the next patient was ready. I smiled at her, and Eli frowned at me.

"This isn't over." He stood. "I want to meet this new guy who lets you watch his aunt. Right now you can come help me with the last few patients."

Chapter 22

I escaped from Eli before he could ask any more questions. I collected Aunt Itty, and we walked around the square to the restaurant. The smell of barbeque hung in the air, making my mouth water. The sign outside the door said it was the best in Texas, and I had to agree. Aunt Itty and I went through the line and chose chopped beef sandwiches, potato salad, a side of fried okra, and banana pudding. I was still starving from the travel. My stomach grumbled loudly as we found a table in the corner covered in a red-and-white checkered tablecloth. Aunt Itty admired the posters of the local high school teams and told me she needed a new pair of shitkicking boots.

Pictures of old Western movies hung on the walls, and between each booth was a set of hooks to hang coats. Aunt Itty and I took off our jackets and hung them on the hooks closest to our table. A drink station sat at the wall to my right. Aunt Itty pulled a packet of tea from her pocket, and I went to the drink station to fill a cup of hot water for her. As I was retrieving my sweet tea, I felt the hair on the back of my neck stand up. I looked around, and in the opposite corner of the room, stuffed into a booth, was Mr. Crane. His beady eyes were tracking me as I returned to my table. I gave him a finger wave because I thought it was polite to at least acknowledge the man. I mean he was a patient, after all. He frowned and continued to wolf down his lunch.

"Who is that extra-large man, dear?" Aunt Itty asked.

"He's a patient at the clinic," I said. Aunt Itty and I ate our lunch, and she agreed it was the best barbecue she had eaten. Although I doubt she had eaten much barbecue in her life. I pictured her more as a tea sandwich sort of gal. The restaurant was starting to fill up with lunch customers. The chatter of people at nearby tables and the country music piped into the room made me calm down. I couldn't figure out why Mr. Crane made me feel so at odds, other than the fact that he was smelly and creepy. I was halfway through my meal when I saw him stand and reach for his jacket, which hung on the hook next to his table.

I almost choked on my sandwich as I watched Mr. Crane pull on his gray Members Only jacket. My heart started to race, and I realized Mr. Crane looked a lot like the Bus Stop Killer. Was that even possible? Surely the Bus Stop Killer was still in prison. I mean, he should be in for life, right?

I reached in my bag for my cell. My hands were shaking as I pulled out the phone.

"What is the matter, dear?" Aunt Itty asked, pausing the forkful of potato salad halfway to her mouth.

"I'm not sure. I need to call Jake." As I fumbled with the buttons on my phone, Aunt Itty looked around the room in bodyguard mode.

Jake answered on the first ring. "What's wrong?"

"How do you know something is wrong?" I asked, a little apprehensive.

"You're with Aunt Itty. The possibilities are endless."

"Well, that was your decision, right?" I was starting to get a little mad at his thinking Aunt Itty and I were troublemakers. Then again, we could probably give Lucille Ball and Ethel Mertz a run for their money.

"Jen." He stopped me midcomplaint. "Why did you call?"

"Is the Bus Stop Killer still in prison?" I asked.

"I'm not sure. He got a reduced sentence because they couldn't pin any of the other killings on him. And without the testimony of the male witness who captured him, he almost got off. Why?"

"I just saw a man who reminded me of the Bus Stop Killer."

"In Texas?" Jake asked.

"In Coffee Creek. I have seen him for the past two months at the clinic. He is very creepy, and he was wearing the same jacket as the Bus Stop Killer."

"Jen, maybe you're having posttraumatic stress travel syndrome."

"Jake. It was a gray Members Only jacket."

"Yeah, and David Hasselhoff was wearing one in *People* magazine last week. Is he the Bus Stop Killer, too?

"OK. I get it. Maybe I'm a little paranoid, but this guy just gives me the creeps."

"I'll check it out and get back with you." Jake sighed. "You and Aunt Itty stay away from him."

"Thanks, Jake." I ended the call and dropped the phone into my bag. I knew he was busy with all the research from the victims we saved when we had the Bus Stop Killer arrested. Lord knows what all the other travelers stirred up on their missions. Poor Jake. I don't think this was what he had in mind when he joined the CIA. I think he was hoping for more *Mission Impossible* instead of Inspector Jacques Clouseau.

Itty was sipping her tea, looking at me suspiciously.

"It's fine. That patient gives me the creeps, and I might have him mixed up with someone else." I took a sip of my tea.

Itty looked at me over the top of her cheaters. "Never underestimate the power of a woman's intuition."

Great.

We finished our lunch, and the funky feeling I had washed away with my last sip of sweet tea. I had about thirty minutes before I had to be back at work, so I took Aunt Itty to Baubles and Beads, where I'd purchased the candlesticks for my mother. I found a cute pair of earrings that she insisted on buying for me. She chose a hand-painted china tea set that would look pretty sitting on her coffee table. Aunt Itty paid the cashier, and we headed to my car to store our items. I was trying to figure out a nice way to tell Aunt Itty she could go home. There was no reason for her to stay, and Eli was getting suspicious.

We made our way around the square. The traffic flow was light in the middle of the day. Eli's side was mostly commercial businesses. There was a taxidermist and the new plastic surgery center scheduled to open next week. Aunt Itty and I were the lone souls walking down the sidewalk. Planters of flowers flanked iron park benches for the shoppers who would come on the weekends. During the week, this side of the square was barren of other people. Occasionally someone would back a truck up to the taxidermist and then return a few days later to pick up a mount. I never saw anyone except Mr. Crane go in or out of the new surgery center. I knew his line of work was something in construction. Maybe he was helping with the renovation. Eli had us return from lunch thirty minutes before patients came in for their afternoon appointments. I looked at my watch. Damn, I was late. Oh well. I was sure Eli would understand because I had an aunt I was looking after. As we passed the new plastic surgery center, Aunt Itty stopped and looked in the window.

"I wouldn't mind making a few wrinkles disappear." She grabbed the back of her neck and pulled her skin taut. The wrinkles from chin to collarbone tightened, giving her turkey neck a more youthful appearance. "What do you think?" she asked me.

"I think you're perfect as is," I responded, peering into the window. My gut clenched, and my hands started to sweat. Mr. Crane was inside, staring out at us. Instant recognition crossed his face. Was it from his experience with me as a patient or as the girl who captured the Bus Stop Killer and then vanished? Jake was wrong. My gut told me this was the same man Marco and I had taken down in Hollywood. I grabbed Aunt Itty's arm. "Let's go."

We rounded the corner to the quaint courtyard that cut through to the parking lot. More planters and benches were lined up on either side of the cobblestone walkway. We almost made it to the car when Mitchell Mafuso jumped out from the shadows.

"Hold it right there, ladies," he said, pointing a gun at both of us.

"What are you going to do?" I asked Mitchell. "You can't kill us."

"I can make you wish you were dead," he said. "You screwed up my plans. That was my key. I did the time. I stayed in the past. Do you have any idea how bad it hurts to stay through a moon cycle?" He waved the gun around, and I was afraid it might fire and kill one of us by accident. Mitchell wasn't the smartest tool in the shed.

"Since I didn't get that kid's key, I'll be taking yours in its place," he said to me, and then he pointed the gun at Aunt Itty. "Hand it over, or I'll put a bullet in the old lady's knee. She'll never walk again."

"Old lady!" Aunt Itty harrumphed. "Well I never—"

"Shut up!" Mitchell yelled, grabbing Aunt Itty and leveling the gun at her knee. Aunt Itty dropped her package, and I could hear the china tea set shatter.

"You just broke my china!" Aunt Itty yelled.

Mitchell cocked the pistol.

"OK, OK!" I said, holding a hand out to halt Mitchell. "Just let me set my bag down, and I'll give you my key." Mitchell was obviously suffering from some kind of posttraumatic travel stress. Sweat was pouring down the sides of his face, and he had an odd green tint to his skin. I turned and set my package down on the ground, trying to figure out some way to get the gun from him. When I turned around, I saw one of my heavy silver candlesticks dancing above Mitchell's head. I cut my eyes toward Aunt Itty. She had one hand on her key, and the other hand was directing the candlestick like a conductor directing the symphony orchestra. Mitchell still had a hold of Aunt Itty, gun pointing at her kneecap, but he was watching me.

Aunt Itty threw her head back and shouted, "Hibbidi bibbity boo!" The candlestick fell, clocking Mitchell on the head and sending him down for the count.

I was about to run and hug Aunt Itty when I felt a sharp pain in my head, and then my world went black.

⌒⟶

*W*hen I woke, I was lying spread-eagle in a hospital bed, wearing nothing except my red Victoria's Secret bra and matching lacy racer panties. My hands and feet were tied to the bed with surgical restraints, and my mouth was taped shut with duct tape. The room was dark, but I could make out the contents of the shelves in front of me. My head was thumping, and I tried to recall what had happened. There was no sign of Aunt Itty. My eyes focused on the boxes in front of me. One read "Surgical Tape" on the side. If I guessed right, I was probably in the surgery center. My blue scrubs lay in a heap on the floor with my shoes. My key was still secured around my neck. Thank God. If Mitchell snagged my key, Jake would never let me hear the end of it, and my days of being Caiyan's transporter would possibly be over.

I heard a noise, and the light was flipped on in the room. Mr. Crane walked in and glared at me.

"You!" He pointed a stubby finger at me. "I was in jail for twenty-five years because of you, bitch."

He came closer, his stench creeping around the room in an invisible fog. He picked up a knife off the stainless steel tray at my bedside table. "I'm going to show you what should have happened that night in LA." He ran the knife down the side of my temple, and I squirmed, pulling my head away from him. "You look exactly the same as you did before. Just as slutty as when you had on the red raincoat." He eyed my red panties, and my heart was beating wildly in my chest.

"I don't know how you were able to switch places with that other slut back in 1985," he said. "I figured you must have had some outstanding warrants for prostitution." He sneered and ran the knife around the leg of my panties.

Prostitution? You dumb jerk. I shuddered, and he moved his girth closer to me on the table.

"Last night it finally hit me where I had seen you before. I remembered, it was you at the bus stop in L.A. Now, I am going I was going to make you and your little friends pay for what you did to me."

I watched him leer at my breasts, and I cursed myself for wearing the bra with the super-push-up enhancement. I tried to talk, but the tape prevented my words from forming.

"Don't worry. I have that old lady and the kid in safekeeping." His watch let out a ding. He smiled his evil Grinch smile. "You will have to wait until later. I have a date with a redhead."

A date with a redhead? Gertie. He had set up the Sweetie Swipe and posted a fake picture to get to Gertie. How was I going to get out of here? He pulled a small bottle off the shelf and inserted a syringe into it, filling the syringe with the liquid. He moved toward me.

"Just a little something to keep you still while I'm gone." He jabbed the needle into my thigh, and I screeched out in pain. He leaned in and whispered into my ear: "And when I'm done with all of you, I'm going to track down that blond asshole and gut him." He turned and shut the light out as he went out the door. My head started to swim, and I felt fuzzy all over. I prayed Aunt Itty and Mitchell were not hurt. Maybe Gertie wouldn't show for her date. Who was I kidding? She would be there to meet board shorts boy only to be abducted by creepy Mr. Crane. I needed help. He was going to kill us and then go after Marco. I started to drift off into the land of make-believe, dreaming of Marco getting a knife in the back by Crane. Then my dream changed to Caiyan's strong arms wrapping around me and his three magic words echoing in the caverns of my heart.

Chapter 23

I felt a light shine into my eyes, and I blinked them open. My head and body felt heavy, like the morning after a really good frat party. I felt a release on my limbs, and I was being lifted off my bed. I raised my head and looked up at Caiyan.

"Are ye all right, lass?"

"How did you find me?" I slurred out.

"Ye summoned me," he said.

"I did?" I asked in surprise. Normally the defender is the one who can summon the transporter, not the other way around.

"Aye." He placed me gently on the side of the bed.

"We have to find Aunt Itty and help Gertie." As I said the words, Ace came from down a hallway with Aunt Itty. Aunt Itty was rubbing her head. No doubt she had been treated to the same cocktail as me.

"Oh good, love. So glad you're OK," Ace said to me. "Nice VS. Is that the new line?"

I looked down and realized I was only wearing my bra and panties. I covered myself with my arms.

A small smile threatened at the corners of Caiyan's mouth. "When I first arrived, I thought ye were giving me some kind of present."

I scowled at him.

"Then I realized ye were unconscious," Caiyan said.

"Where's Mitchell?" I asked, rolling my eyes at Caiyan's idea of a present.

"He's still tied up in the storage room, snoozing like a baby," Ace said.

"That knot I gave him combined with that sedative the fat man gave us will probably keep him out for a good while," Aunt Itty said.

"We have to help Gertie," I said, and then I explained to Caiyan about Mr. Crane, aka the Bus Stop Killer, and how he was going to get Gertie at the Muddled Duck.

"He's going to be returning here?" Caiyan asked.

I nodded. "To finish with me."

Caiyan thought about this for a moment. "Well, let's get you tied back up, then."

"What?" I asked, my voice escalating.

"We wouldn't want to disappoint our mark, now would we?" Caiyan asked.

Ace smiled, as if they had some secret mind connection. Aunt Itty and I just looked at each other in confusion.

"Ace, go follow him from the meeting place with Gertie. Make sure he grabs her and brings her back here."

"Sure thing." Ace left out the back door, and a few seconds later there was a flash of lightning through the plate glass windows.

"I bet my brother was concerned I didn't come back from lunch," I told Caiyan.

"When ye summoned me, I landed in the parking lot." He ran a hand through his hair, and I felt a tingle between my legs. "It's a wonder no one saw me. But I put two and two together that this was big brother's office."

"You did?" I asked.

"Aye, and when I went inside to inquire aboot ye, he told me ye had left him a note on his car that ye were taking Aunt Itty home after lunch."

"I didn't write a note."

"I figured as much, but I told him we must have had a miscommunication because I thought I was supposed to pick her up."

229

"That was good thinking."

"Then he had a few words to say to me aboot the way I should be treating my girlfriend."

Jeez, Eli ever protecting his baby sister. "Sorry, he's my brother."

"I told him he was right, and we're meeting for a brew next week."

"You did?"

"Aye, and now I'll be needin' ye to get oot of those panties."

Oh my gosh!

⟶

We waited in the shadows for Mr. Creepy. Ace returned and let us know Mr. Crane had nabbed Gertie as planned, and she was out cold because he shot her up with the sedative. He was parking his car around back.

When Mr. Creepy brought Gertie in through the back door, I pressed tightly to the wall. I had returned to my blue scrubs, thankful I was no longer on display. His scent carried through the clinic, and I heard Ace groan from across the room in disgust. He laid Gertie on the floor, as if she was an afterthought to his murderous ways.

I heard him say out loud, "I'm going to kill the blond slut first and save the redhead for dessert."

My stomach churned, and Caiyan let out a low, deep growl next to me. We had Aunt Itty return to the storage room in case he checked in on his other two hostages before coming for the kill. Mr. Crane was humming as he waddled down the hall and opened the door to the room where he had previously held me captive. He flipped on the light switch and stepped forward as his eyes adjusted to the light.

"What the hell?" he shouted as Caiyan moved from the shadows, pointing a gun at Mr. Crane's head.

"I thought this might be more to yer taste." Caiyan cut his eyes toward an unconscious Mitchell, who was now strapped down to the table wearing my Victoria's Secret bra and panties. Mr. Crane's eyes narrowed, and his face turned as red as a vine-ripe tomato.

Ace moved in from behind and jabbed a syringe into his neck. "Sweet dreams, lover boy."

Mr. Crane swatted at the air in front of Caiyan before passing out face-first on the floor.

"He's a big, smelly one," Ace said.

Aunt Itty came in and gave Ace a peck on the cheek. "Such a good lad."

"Aw, thanks, Auntie." Ace put an arm around her.

Caiyan raised his palms up as if to say, *What about me?*

"You have caused much trouble this moon cycle," Aunt Itty said, crossing her arms over her chest. "You will have to do more than a simple rescue to earn your kisses."

"I've caused trouble? Bloody hell if that's not the pot calling the kettle black." Caiyan stood in his black leather jacket, white button-down, and jeans, hands on hips, staring at Aunt Itty.

"What now?" I asked, looking down at the enormous figure passed out on the floor.

"Let's help Jen get Gertie in her vessel," Caiyan said.

"Sure thing," Ace said, glancing down at Mr. Crane. "I gave him enough tranquilizer to sedate an elephant. He's going to be out for a while."

"That's good, considering what I have planned for him," Caiyan said, rubbing his palms together. "Aunt Itty, are you OK to travel alone?"

"I'm fine, dear. Nothing a spot of tea won't cure."

Caiyan carried Gertie outside and loaded her into my vessel. I raised an eyebrow, and he promised to stop by and check on me after he was done. Aunt Itty left with a backfire and a cloud of smoke. He leaned in and kissed me. "See ye in a bit."

⌣⁀

*G*ertie was almost awake by the time we landed at home. I helped her into the house and sat her at the table while I fixed us both a cup of tea. Aunt Itty suggested oolong was the best tea to detox the body. She was still groggy as I explained the events of the night.

"I can't believe I missed everything," Gertie said as she took a sip of her tea. "The only thing I can remember was the bartender giving me a note to meet my Sweetie Swipe in the parking lot."

I raised an eyebrow at her.

"I know that was stupid." Gertie made a gun with her fingers and put it to her head. "But he was super cute in the picture."

We drank our tea in silence as we thought about almost being killed twice by the Bus Stop Killer. My hands were still a little shaky when Caiyan arrived after midnight. Gertie had gone to bed, complaining about a putrid smell she couldn't get rid of, even after her shower. I agreed the stench of Mr. Crane would be around for quite some time.

I opened the sliding door for Caiyan. He handed me the keys to my car.

"I drove it back for you," he said, a small smile curling at the ends of his mouth. Dark circles shadowed his eyes, and his hair was unusually disheveled, even for him. He looked "worn ass out," as Mamma Bea would say.

"What did you do?" I asked Caiyan, handing him a beer from the fridge. He drank with gratitude and sat down on the couch. He smelled of leather and cinnamon. The urge to crawl into his lap was almost too difficult to resist. Instead, I sat down next to him and waited for him to tell me what happened to creepy Mr. Crane.

"Well, lassie, we guaranteed Mr. Crane would be back in jail for a very long time, and Mitchell Mafuso won't be bothering ye, either." He took a long pull on his beer, as if to wash down all the stress of the last two months. He retrieved his cell out of his jacket and showed me pictures he took of Mr. Crane in a few compromising positions with Mitchell.

"What does this mean?" I asked, scrolling through about twenty photos.

"It means," he said, taking his phone from me, "we made a deal. Mitchell is going to testify that the fat man was using him for child porn. I mean the kid's only sixteen, so the charges should stick. We placed a few more websites and pictures on the guy's home and office computers, ye know, just to make things look legit."

"You framed him?"

"Aye." He took another long drink of the beer.

"What does Mitchell get in return?" I asked cautiously.

Caiyan paused, and I could tell it was something important. "He gets a key."

"Which key? The thunder?" I thought of the key Brodie had brought back from his latest travel.

Caiyan shook his head and looked down at his beer bottle. "No, mine."

I reached over and pulled his shirt collar aside. His key was gone.

"You gave up your key for me?" My gut twisted into knots. I blinked back the tears that threatened to spill onto my cheeks. How was Caiyan going to travel? This life defined him. He was a defender, and a damn good one.

"Aye, the key now and my vessel after the bastard has been sentenced to life in prison."

"Your vessel?" I stood and slammed my hands down on the sides of my legs in anger and frustration.

He shrugged. "That was the deal. The key and the vessel were born together. The key will work with other vessels, but it's never the same as having the original." He came over to me and put his arms around me. "It was worth it. Besides, the little fucker will probably screw up, and I'll be takin' it back from him."

"Why can't we just give him the thunder key?"

"The WTF has secured it, and I doubt they would give it away, especially to such scoundrels as the Mafusos."

"How will you travel?" I asked, and a small tear slipped down my cheek for what he had given up for me.

"Well, I will probably be grounded for a while." He smiled, wiping away my tear with his thumb. "It should give me some time to get caught up with all my real jobs and help Campy get adjusted to his new school."

"You'll have to fly on an airplane to visit me."

"I will, aye, but well, ye will just have to come visit me. Ye ken?"

"I don't know where you live." The dam broke, and the tears flowed like a river to a spring.

"Maybe we can go on a date." He chuckled, and I wiped away my sadness with the palm of my hand.

I laughed through tears. "A real date?"

"Aye, it's time I turned over a new leaf," Caiyan said, raking a hand through his hair. "Maybe try taking ye out to a fancy restaurant instead of taking off yer clothes. I can dress to impress, ye know. I'm not just a piece of meat to be feasted on by all the lassies."

Here was my pudding. I wanted proof that he meant it when he said he loved me, and in the world of time travel, there was no greater sacrifice than giving up your key and your vessel. He wanted to go on a real date. I couldn't wait to find out what that was like. No hidden agendas, no brigands, no sex to complicate everything.

Let's not get crazy, my inner voice chided.

"It's too bad you're turning over a new leaf because I was hoping to show you the new Victoria's Secret line tonight."

He scooped me up and headed toward my vessel.

"Where are we going?" I asked, laughing and knowing full well I was about to slip on a pair of shoes that might leave a blister.

"Only time will tell."

—The End—

About the Author

Janet Leigh was born in Garland, Texas, and has remained a loyal Texas native her entire life. After practicing chiropractic for twenty years, she decided to write her own novel. She began taking writing classes at night and eventually published her literary debut, *The Shoes Come First*, a B.R.A.G. Medallion Honoree. Today, she is a full-time chiropractor and acupuncturist who splits her time between seeing patients and working on her next Jennifer Cloud novel.

Leigh lives in Dallas, Texas, with her husband, three children, one mean cat, and a dog with allergies. After working all day, chauffeuring kids around, and writing at every opportunity, she enjoys relaxing with a funny romance or mystery novel. Her favorite authors are Nora Roberts, Janet Evanovich, Leigh Michaels, Diana Gabaldon, John Grisham, and for those times when she needs a good cry, Nicholas Sparks.

Visit Janet Leigh at HYPERLINK "http://www.Janetleighbooks.com" www.Janetleighbooks.com or on Facebook at https://www.facebook.com/Janetleighbooks.

Made in the USA
Lexington, KY
07 August 2019